DISAPPEAR...

by the same author
Disappearer
Colin Cleveland and the End of the World
Girl's Rock
The Eternal Prisoner
Rogue Males

Mark Hunter series
Beautiful Chaos
Sixty-Six Curses
Trouble at School
Mysterious Girlfriend
The Beasts of Bellend
Countdown to Zero

Disappearer

Chris Johnson

**Samurai
West**

Published by Samurai West
disappearer007@gmail.com

Story and Art © Chris Johnson 2021
All rights reserved

This paperback edition published 2025
ISBN-13: 979-8340805263

Chapter One

'Chad…?'

'What the hell do you want, Martin? It's five o'clock!'

'I know what time it is, dude! But I'm in trouble! Big trouble!'

'You're in trouble? What sort of trouble? Where are you?'

'I'm at home. But I can't get out. *They're* here.'

'Who's here?'

'*Them.*'

'Oh, *them.* One of your *them.* What is it this time: Men in Black?'

'No, not Men in Black, dude. Men in Black hassle people who've seen UFOs and shit. These are Men in Overalls. These're *removal men.*'

'Removal men?'

'Yeah, but I'm not talking normal removal men. These removal men remove *people.* Get it? They've come to remove *me.*'

'Remove you? What are you on about? You're saying they're right there with you in your flat?'

''Course they're not! If they were here already, I couldn't be talking to you, could I? Wake up, man. They're outside, in the street—that's what I'm saying. I can see them through the window.'

'Look, it's too early in the morning for your conspiracy-theory bullshit. I'll see you later.'

'Don't hang up! I'm serious, for Christ's sake! They're outside now, with a van. The removal men. They're going to take me away. I'm *scared* here, Chad; I'm fucking scared.'

'Look, mate, you're paranoid. You've been taking something, haven't you? Even if there *are* some removal men outside your place, they'll just be ordinary removal men: furniture collectors; they're not coming to take you away.'

'But they are! Don't you get it? I've seen these guys before. I've been piling up evidence, dude—investigating. I know what they're doing, and now *they* know that I know. They're *on* to me. I dunno how they found out; I thought I'd been too smart for 'em, but I guess they were too smart for me. That's why they're going to make me disappear; just like Fiona and Frank.'

'Fiona and Frank? What are you on about? Frank moved to London and Fiona went back home to her parents.'

'That's just what they *didn't*. They've been disappeared.'

'They've *been* disappeared? That's from *Catch-22*, Martin.'

'I'm telling you; they were disappeared! Removed! I found out about it! I've got proof, man! That's why they're coming for me!'

'You've lost it, haven't you? Why would anyone want to make Fiona and Frank disappear? Why would they be after you? We're nothing. We're nobody. Just a bunch of aimless twenty-somethings. You, me, Frank, Fiona; all of us.'

'Yeah, we're nobodies. That may be just *why* they're after us. Listen, Chad, I haven't got long. You know my stash?'

'Yeah.'

'Well, I've—'

'You've what? Hello…? Hello…?'

Of course, I don't get back to sleep after that phone call.

I lie on my bed (my 'bed' being a mattress on the floor) and after twice trying to call Martin back (I get sent straight through to his message service) I think about what the hell I'm supposed to do now.

I always seem to wake-up around daybreak anyway, and at this time of year daybreak is pretty early…

Was he pulling my leg? Well, he's never done anything like that before; he's not a practical joker. In that case, if you ignore the ludicrous (i.e., that he was telling the truth), then you're left with the conclusion that old Martin has lost it completely; that he's finally lost his grip on reality and plunged into the deep, dark abyss of paranoia…

And I thought *I* had problems.

Martin is a conspiracy freak. He trawls the internet for all those tall stories and wild theories, and he just laps them up and accepts them all as fact. It's like his philosophy is: 'if someone put it up on-line then it must be true!' Everything from old chestnuts like the CIA orchestrating the 9/11 attacks, to people saying that cancer is contagious. He laps it all up. He's one of those people who always go on about 'Them' with a capital 't' when he's referring to those insidious powers-that-be he reckons are manipulating things from behind the scenes.

The left-wing conspiracy-theorists think it's some Old-Boys Network that secretly rules the world, the right-wing conspiracy-theorists think it's the Jews. *I* think it's all bullshit. These theories just get concocted out of thin-air; there's no substance to them. It's all imagination. If these people just wrote up their crazy theories as novels instead of trying to pass them off as fact, they'd make some very entertaining books out of them.

So, what do I do about Martin? Rush round to his flat, to see if those 'removal men' are staking-out the place? And if they're not, what'll he say when I knock on the door? S'pose he'll just say that they've gone…

Removal men. That's a new one on me.

And what was that about his stash? I know what his 'stash' is: it's a place underneath the sink in his bathroom where he hides his drugs whenever he's got any. Pretty pointless, really. If the cops raided his place looking for drugs, the sniffer dogs would still find his stuff easily enough. Maybe he's worried about burglars; he is in a ground-floor flat… Could drugs explain that phone-call? Was he on something? His usual snorts are cocaine or mephedrone… I wonder if he's been dropping acid this time? *That* stuff can make you paranoid as fuck. I know from bitter experience. Aldous Huxley was right when he said that if a fuck-up takes hallucinogenics it'll only make them even more fucked-up—I mean, Aldous didn't put it in exactly those words, but that was the gist of it…

I need a cigarette.

I live alone in a one-bedroom flat in Kings Hedges, a flashy name for part of the kebab van end of this fair city of Cambridge. I just turned twenty-eight last month, so I've now officially out-lived Kurt Cobain, Jimi Hendrix and the rest of Club-27.

My parents, for reasons best known to themselves, named me Charles; but everyone calls me Chad, unless they want a slap round the face. I don't have a job. I say this first, but I don't think it's the most important fact about me: it's just that the rest of the world thinks that. ('What do you do?' asks new acquaintance to new acquaintance.) Okay, some people are defined by their careers, especially the people who get paid for doing something they're interested in, or those go-getters who make it their life's work to climb the career ladder; but to those people who just have jobs to pay the bills, then it's what they do in their spare time, it's their hobbies that tell you more about them, right? That's assuming that their hobbies go further than just watching Netflix.

There's an episode of *Voyage to the Bottom of the Sea* (that 60s spy-fi series about the nuclear submarine) where they meet this guy from the far future, and in this future time they only have a four-hour working week, so they've got a 'hobbies act,' and it's people's hobbies that are the most important thing in their lives. (The future guy in the story had made collecting military figures from history his main hobby, and he wanted to add Richard Basehart to his collection.)

Like I said, I don't have a job right now, so my interests are me; they're who I am. I like alternative rock; I've liked it since I was in my teens. Mostly US and UK bands, but recently I've been discovering a lot of Japanese bands, thanks to this Japanese girl I've met. Until a couple of years ago I was playing guitar in a band myself, and yeah, I had the usual wild dreams of fame and fortune; people in every aspiring band have 'em. We played the local circuit and people seemed to like us, but we got no response from labels we sent our demo to and after a while we all just started to lose interest; our vocalist walked out and then the thing just fizzled out after that, and now my jaguar and amp sit gathering dust in a corner of my living room.

Music aside, I don't have any other creative interests; I don't paint pictures or write poetry or anything. I like reading when I'm in the mood; classic fiction, mostly. I like the grim stuff like Zola and Dostoevsky; you know, books with fucked up people and fucked up lives and unhappy endings. As for 'visual art' I've always been into 60s cult TV (as you might have worked out from the reference above), but recently I've been getting into Japanese animation, 'anime' for short, thanks also to the Japanese girl I mentioned. Her name's Yuri Yamanaka and she's an art student.

So, there you have it; this is me: a slacker who's trying to pretend he's not also a sad fanboy.

I throw on some clothes and I plod through the living room and into the kitchen, put the kettle on and take my morning anti-depressant pill.

Yes, I'm on the happy-pills. Except they don't really make me happy; they just make me feel better than I would be if I didn't take 'em. They say that unless depression is successfully treated in the early stages, you're pretty much stuck with it for life. I think my depression has pretty well reached that stage.

I said I didn't have a job right now, and yeah, I am technically on the sick-list, but I have done some part-time work. I'm attached to this place, this foundation that basically finds work placements for the terminally unemployable. My last placement was just in some council office, working as a drudge. It didn't last long. There was this one guy, the office junior; he was a few years younger than me, and the git obviously wanted to make the most of having someone lower down the ladder than he was, to boss around. So he was always telling me to do this and do that and making pointed comments to the rest of the office that I was too slow... I put up with it for so long, but then I sort of lost my rag. I started swearing, telling the douche what I thought of him, and I sort of chucked some stuff around the room and stormed out. The fact is, I have 'authority issues': I don't like being told what to do.

My flat's a small one: the typical one bedroom, bathroom, living room and kitchen place that they decant the losers into. Apart from the living room, all the rooms are poky, but that's fine: I live on my own and I've got no intention of changing that arrangement. You probably expect the whole place to be a tip, don't you? But no, I keep it pretty tidy.

I sit down on the sofa and drink my first cup of coffee of the day, and smoke my first cigarette. Caffeine and tobacco: the two habits pretty much sustain each other. Smoking ciggies makes me drowsy, so I drink more coffee to wake myself up...

I can't get that bloody telephone conversation out of my head: he'd sounded scared, had Martin. Drug-induced? Put on? And all that stuff about Frank and Fiona... Yeah, they *had* both moved away kind of suddenly, but even so, not completely unexpected in either case...

And if he really *was* in trouble, why the hell did he have to ring *me* of all people? There are some much more together people in our set than yours truly.

I don't know if it's Asperger's or something, but things get stuck in my head and go round and round like mad, and right now I've got all *this* shit spinning around in my noddle; removal men; Disappeared...

I know what I'm going to do of course. I'm going to go round Martin's and I'm going to find out if he was bullshitting me or if he's even still there because I'm not going to be able to do anything else until I know for sure…

Trainers. Jeans. T-shirt. Lumber-jack shirt, unbuttoned. Do I even have to tell you what I wear every day? I don't even think it's a conscious uniform, like Goth-Punks wearing black; no, people like me just naturally pick out that set of clothes; we just find them lying on our bedroom floors when we get up in the morning.

It's a warm morning, overcast. Martin's place is only about twenty minutes' walk from me. He's actually in the neighbouring district of Arbury, which is also in the working-class end of town; they all are: Kings Hedges, Arbury, Chesterton, Abbey. It's not nice, but it's not that bad, either; compared to the urban areas of some of those big cities (and Cambridge is a very *small* city), it's fairly quiet and rusticated. Five minutes out of town and you're into turnip country: farmland and fenny villages.

Thinking about urban areas reminds me of a Hardy Boys book I read when I was a kid. Frank and Joe were pursuing a gang of terrorists (who were supposed to have killed Joe's girlfriend Iola Morton, but she turns up alive again later in the series) and they went to Brixton in London, and the area was described like it was some Middle-East warzone. The book was written in the late 1980s and the American ghost-writer (there's no such person as Franklin W Dixon and there never was) had obviously heard about the Brixton riots from around that time and had built up a seriously exaggerated idea of what the area was like.

Walking down Mere Way, I bump into Errol. Now he *is* a fanboy who looks like a fanboy. A skinny geek with glasses and unmanageable hair.

I rustle up a smile, which the git doesn't bother to return.

''Morning, Errol. On your way to work?'

'No, I'm going to the park to pick daisies,' says Errol. (That's my Errol! Bastard can't open his mouth without being sarcastic.) 'What are you doing up this early? I thought you didn't surface till around lunchtime.'

'I'm going round Martin's.'

'Ooh, an early morning booty call, is it? Are you gunna do him, or is he gunna do you?'

'Christ you're funny, Errol.'

'Yeah, and you're not. Well, I can stand around chatting about you and your bum-chum; some of us have to work for a living.'

And with that, Errol drifts off, on his way to stack shelves in Budgens. (Do they actually still call them shelf-stackers? Or do they consider that that name has too many negative connotations? Maybe there's some official term for it, like 'Stock Administrator' or something…)

Errol is a shining example of why I don't like to be labelled a fanboy. I went to school with that fucker, and he hasn't changed a bit since he was thirteen. I mean, the guy's a walking stereotype! You'd think he'd realise that and try and do something to adjust his behaviour… But no, I guess it's only to everyone else that he's a walking stereotype; not to himself. I'm sure he thinks of himself as a totally unique human being. Well, we all do, don't we? I mean no-one thinks: 'Yeah, I'm exactly the same as so-and-so!' At least, I assume no-one does. But that's how it is: there's two of everyone, isn't there? There's the You that you perceive yourself to be, and the You that everyone else sees you as. And which of those is actually the real You? I guess you'd have to say that it's the external You, the You that the rest of the world sees. People can only assess you by what you say and do, the same way you can only assess other people that way.

I know it's just vanity, but I like to think I'm not as sad those real anal fanboys like Errol. So, what arguments do I put forward in my defence? Well, I'm not a virgin. (Although

I can't boast of that many notches in my belt, either.) But then, even sad geeks can sometimes have a sex life if there happens to be a willing girl-geek amongst their number... What else? Well, I like alternative rock. Fine and dandy, but the rock scene itself has its fair share of anoraks... Anything else? Well, I'm aware of the world around me. Not all fanboys can boast that. Yep, a lot of them just shut themselves off in their own comfy little worlds. Like the *Doctor Who* fan who lives, breathes, and eats *Doctor Who*. (I'm quite partial to *Doctor Who* myself, but I only like the classic series; I've given up on the new version.)

Yeah, so I like to think I'm better than most fanboys. Actually, never mind that; I like to think I'm better than most *people*. That old chestnut 'the ignorant masses'; that's how people like me like to think about everyone else... But I'm self-aware enough to know what's behind that feeling. The person who truly has a superiority complex (and I don't think there are actually that many of those) is someone who goes around acting like they're better than everyone else all the time. But the person who just privately thinks they're better than everyone else: that's actually a symptom of an *in*feriority complex.

I arrive at Martin's flats. There's a carpark in front of the buildings, and Martin's flat is one of the ground floor row facing the carpark, but his front door is round the other side; so I cross the carpark, pass a stairwell, and I'm in an alley with the front doors of the flats (painted a uniform green) facing a dead wall.

When I get to Martin's front door, I see that it's ajar.

'Martin?'

I push open the door, stick my head inside. Like my place, the door opens straight into the front room. It looks a tip, but this is normal: Martin's a lazy, untidy so-and-so. And he's not here. I call out again. No reply.

Okay, there *could* be a simple explanation: Martin might have just stepped out to get rid of some rubbish. The recycling bins on the other side of that wall facing the door. But I had that phone call, didn't I? That 'they're coming to get me!' phone call. And here I am in response to that call, and there's no Martin and an open front door. Door! That's a point. I check the door, the frame, the lock. Nope: there's no sign that the door has been forced. If Martin thought someone was coming to get him, he'd lock the door; he wouldn't let them in!

So is it all a mare's nest? I would have thought so except for this open door. Martin wouldn't have gone out and left his door open, even if he'd just gone down the road to the shops; no-one leaves their doors open on this estate; no-one even leaves them unlocked.

Okay, so he would only have left the door open if he's just gone out to do his recycling. But like I said, the recycling bins are just over that wall, and if someone was there, you'd hear the sound of those cans and bottles being dropped into the bins. I *don't* hear those sounds.

I go into the bathroom. Martin was saying something about his stash when the call ended; something he'd hidden there, I guess. Maybe that proof he was talking about. I squat down at the sink; his stash is a kind of shelf behind the pedestal where he keeps any stuff he's got in an old Strepsils tin. Yeah; the tin's there. I bring it out and shake it. There's something inside alright. I pull off the lid; inside the tin there's a roll of camera film.

Is this what he wanted me to find? What could be on the film that's so important? Pictures of those 'removal men' outside his flat? He did say 'I've got proof.' So, is this the proof?

This is crazy. This is turning into some spy thriller.

And now I hear someone coming into the flat. I closed the bathroom door to when I came in, because the bathroom's small and it's in the way. Something warns me not to be too hasty, that it might not be Martin who's just come in; so I don't open the door: I just look through the gap instead.

That's what I do, and I'm glad I did it. It isn't Martin. There are two men in overalls in the front room. Beige overalls and peaked caps like baseball caps. There's something not right about these men. They don't speak: they just start ransacking the room.

The removal men? Is this them?

Is it all true then?

This is where I start panicking. Most of the time in my day-to-day life I avoid anxiety by not having anything to feel anxious about: a steady routine, no surprises, no upheavals… But this… This is something that's right off the scale. Here I am, stuck in the bathroom, with two bad guys between me and the front door.

The window. Unless I want to try my luck running past those men in the next room and out through the front door, the only other way is the bathroom window. The trouble is, the bathroom only has one of those small frosted glass windows, and it's high up on the wall. Can I even squeeze out through that?

I tip-toe across the bathroom and stand on the bath. Slowly I push the window open as far as it will go. I can see it's going to be a tight squeeze, and I'm not a contortionist, so there's no way I can get a leg through there first. I'm gunna have to just slide through headfirst, caterpillar style.

The trick is not to break my neck while I'm doing this.

I squeeze through, and somehow manage to fall without killing myself; I land on my hands and then sort of do a forward roll, and I'm up on my feet. I don't stop to see if those men have heard me; I start running.

There's a furniture van. Parked at the inner end of the carpark, it's got its rear door open, the ramp down. It's a plain beige vehicle, no markings. And it definitely wasn't there when I arrived a few minutes ago. It's not something you'd miss. There's no-one near the van, so I stop and look in the back. The interior space is empty. Definitely here for furniture collection, not furniture delivery. I step back and look at the side-panel. It looks odd without any writing, and it's painted the same beige colour as those men's overalls. Not just anonymous, but like it self-consciously *wants* to look anonymous. (If that isn't a contradiction.)

That aside, could this be the reasonable explanation staring me in the face here? Could it be that they're going to take Martin's furniture away because he's just moving house, and *not* because they've taken him away as well? Did Martin just come up with that 'removal men' bullshit because he actually was having his furniture removed today?—and so that he knew that removal men would be what I would see if I came round to check on him…?

No. Nice try, Chad, but no, that doesn't hold water. If Martin was moving house, all his stuff would be packed up in boxes… And those two goons looked like they were ransacking the place…

And then I look round and I see them standing there, by the stairwell. The removal men. The same two, I'm guessing. Just standing there, about twenty metres from me, and looking right at me. I don't know what it is, but something about those blank stares makes me go cold. Not a trace of emotion on either of those faces… Just staring… I don't think I've ever felt fear of actual imminent physical danger that many times in my life, but I'm feeling it right now. In spades. It's like every alarm bell in my head is crying out; no, it's like those two zombies are actually *making* every alarm bell in my head start crying out. Even from that distance, it's like they're radiating bad vibes, directing them straight at me.

I back away from the men. They don't move; they just keep looking at me. I back away, and as soon as I've got the removal van between me and them, I start running.

Chapter Two

I dreamt about that building again.

A white oblong box with, standing forlorn in the middle of the flat fenland countryside. I say I dreamed about it, but this building actually exists; it's a scene from my past. Before my family moved to Cambridge, we used to live in a backside-of-nowhere village called Mepal; a village with about five streets, one shop, one pub, and one primary school that took in kids from all the surrounding area. The nearest big shopping-town from Mepal was Ely, and whenever we were travelling there by car, usually on Saturday, our family's big shopping day, I would see that building, standing there way out amongst the fields, on the road between Sutton and Witchford. To me as a kid, there was something creepy, unsettling about that lonely building; it was an enigma, a puzzle; a row of windows along one wall was all you could see from the road; apart from that it was featureless. To this day I don't know exactly what the building was; from its size and shape it could have been a power-station, or some other utilities building. (Now I think about it, it seems strange that I never asked my family what that building was when we were driving past it. Maybe I did, and I've forgotten it.)

But then, we moved out of Mepal just before I started secondary school and with everything new that was going on, I completely forgot about that building.

Until now.

I've been dreaming about it a lot recently; always seeing it from a distance, like I did when I was a kid sitting in the back seat of my family's car. In my dreams I feel like I have to get to this building; that there's something there waiting for me. But if I try walking towards the building, however much I walk, it never gets any nearer.

Don't ask me why I've started having this dream. It

probably means nothing; just a random image from my childhood. They say that most of the visual material in our dreams comes from our memories.

This dream stands out not just because it keeps reoccurring, but because compared to a lot of my dreams, it's a fairly lucid one. My average dream is a twisted, chaotic jumble, with no sense or perspective, where a building becomes kitchen cabinet and my duvet is made of orange-peel and full of insects... I remember reading in one of Vladimir Nabokov's novels (I *think* it was *Look at the Harlequins!* but don't quote me on that), where the narrator said that other people's dreams always sounded so normal compared to his own. If Nabokov was talking about himself there, I know how he feels.

Do dreams mean anything at all? I know some people say that they're just random images thrown up by a brain on standby, but I think there's got to be more to it than that. I mean, even if you don't agree with all of Freud's dream interpretations, you can still agree that dreams can reflect the mental state of the dreamer... Before Freud came along, I guess the main belief was that dreams predicted events in your future. Now, I'm not saying I believe that one, but I think most of us have had experiences where something we dreamed about *did* go and happen in reality... It's probably happened to most people at least once. One I always remember is from my secondary school days: I fancied this particular girl in my class, and over the summer holidays, I had a dream that she was going out with a particular boy. And lo and behold, when I got back to school the next term, the girl I fancied *was* going out with that particular boy! That may not sound so amazing, but it really struck me at the time. You see, this boy wasn't even in the same class as the girl I fancied, and I hadn't even been aware that they were even particularly good friends—so I'd had no reason at all to suspect that they were likely to end up being an item.

But yeah, that was a one-off, and it could be explained by

the law of averages. Now that I think about it, the old dreams-predicting-the-future thing is meant to be all symbolism, isn't it? All metaphor. Not actual visions of future events. You can get these Victorian dream books that explain what's going to happen to you based on what you dreamt about. I think one of them is that if you dream that you're walking around naked, it's meant to mean you're in for some bad luck… Yeah, it's all symbolism—not all that different to Freud, really!

I'm all keyed-up this morning.

I'm going to find out what's on that film! Yesterday, I handed the film in at Boots to be developed (the only place I know that still provides that service these days.) I chose the 24-hour service, so today I'm going back in to pick up the prints.

What's going to be on them? Something earth-shattering? Or nothing at all?

My mind's been spinning out of control with thoughts and theories since yesterday. One minute I'm sure that I've stumbled onto some major conspiracy, the next minute I fall back on the belief that I'm the victim of a practical joke… I know it would have been the sensible thing to meet up with a friend, talk the thing through, get the other person's perspective… I'm not like that. If I'm feeling bad, or I'm faced with a problem, my first reaction is to isolate myself… I went into town to hand in the film, but apart from that I've been alone in my flat since yesterday; I haven't seen or spoken to anyone.

My default setting is to just lie on my bed. If I'm feeling bad, or if I don't feel like doing anything else, I just lie on my bed and think and daydream, building castles in the air. I know that's just shutting myself off from the world: my bed is a small area in a small room; but sometimes I just have to retreat, retreat into that small space. I guess the trickcyclists (or the Freudian ones, anyway) would say I'm attempting to retreat into my mother's womb... And I don't even always feel better for it, this lying in my bed. Sometimes when I'm lying there my mood can suddenly drop like a stone, or I can have a sudden panic attack... But then, my mood can suddenly drop like a stone and I can have a sudden panic attack even when I'm *not* lying in bed.

Yeah, so I've just been lying there, and for once I had a lot on my plate to actually think about. Those men I ran away from: did I just imagine them, those dangerous vibes? I must have done, mustn't I? Unless those men were somehow projecting some 'menace' pheromone, they weren't actually even doing anything, were they? Just standing there looking at me... Was the whole thing just a flight of paranoia and wild imagination built on top of a crank phone-call?

I've tried calling Martin again. I went from getting his answering service to getting a message saying that the number I had dialled was no longer in service. That probably means the SIM card has been taken out of his phone. What should I deduce from that?

I don't know. Like I say, my opinions have been as unstable as my mood. Hopefully those photographs will settle this one way or the other...

'I've got some photographs to collect.'

I stand at the upstairs counter at Boots, and I feel like a drug-smuggler clenching his cheeks at Bangkok customs. What if there's something dodgy in those photographs? I mean Martin hasn't got a girlfriend he could take porny pictures of, and I don't think he's the kind to take upskirting photos on the sly of women in the street... But what would Boots do if there was something iffy in those snaps? Refuse to print them? Burn the negatives? Maybe even call in the police?

I hand over the receipt and the woman goes into the back room. I'm sweating and my heart is racing. I look suspiciously around the shop floor. There are customers about but I can't see anyone who looks like a plain-clothes cop waiting to pounce on me.

The woman returns with the photographs in one of those laminated card wallets and hands them over with a smile. And that's it. No suspicious looks, no alarm bells.

I take the escalator to the ground floor and go over to the food section. My plan is to buy myself some lunch and sit in the park to look over the photographs. I buy a bottle of coke, a sandwich and a bag of crisps. After paying for them I put the photos in the bag with the food.

At the Petty Cury exit of the shop I bump into Mel and Muriel, two pals of mine. Mel's the small girl with long hair, Muriel's the tall girl with short hair. Mel talks a lot, Muriel doesn't say much. They're an item.

'Ooh, what you got there? What you got there?' says Mel excitedly, prodding at my bag.

'Just my lunch,' I say.

'That's what we're doing,' says Muriel. (The two girls work in the same clothes shop; it must be their lunch hour.)

'You coming to the Portland tonight?' asks Mel.

'Are people going to the Portland?'

'Yeah. Didn't Esther text you about it? She said she would.'

'She might've. I haven't checked my phone.'

'Well, check it now,' says Mel.

'Haven't got it on me.'

Mel groans. 'That's *stupid*. What's the point of having a mobile phone if you don't carry it around? It's not mobile then, is it? If you're just gunna keep it at home you might as well only have a landline.'

'I wasn't expecting any messages.'

'*Esther's* messaged you, hasn't she?'

'Yeah, but now you've told me about going to the pub tonight, haven't you? And even if you hadn't, I'd've found out when I got home.'

'So? Are you coming?' asks Muriel.

'Yeah, I should think so...'

We exchange 'see you laters' and the girls go into the shop and I go out. I'm glad they didn't offer to join me for lunch; I want to be alone to look at those photographs. I feel better for seeing two familiar faces, though; feels like I've touched base with reality for the first time since yesterday.

I go to Christ's Piece, a little park behind the bus station. It's sunny today, and a lot of people are sitting in the park with their lunches. On weekend evenings, this park is a popular meeting place for under-age drinkers. (Not to mention legal drinkers who prefer a cheap alternative to going to the pub; my crowd comes here sometimes.)

I find myself an unoccupied shady spot under a tree and sit down.

Drum-roll, please! I take out the wallet and extract the photographs.

The first picture is of some trees.

So is the second and third. There are footpaths through the trees and I think I recognise the location as a nature reserve on the edge of town: Limekiln Close. The next picture confirms this: a shot looking down into a disused chalk quarry. The nature reserve is next to this quarry, which has a racing circuit for scramblers.

After this, more nature shots. Some of them show a water-filled quarry. I know where these were taken as well—it's an area of pits and wasteland between Romsey Town and Cherry Hinton. A path for cyclists and pedestrians runs through it, and people from Cherry Hinton use it as a shortcut into town. The path's fenced in on both sides and you're not supposed to venture into the wasteland because it's private property; but there are holes and places where the fence has been pulled down, so it's easy enough if you want to explore.

Just when I'm thinking that I've paid good money for a photo-diary of Martin's weekend nature rambles, I come across a picture of a man. A man getting out of a car in a street, obviously unaware that he's being photographed. The man is a stranger to me; middle-aged sallow-faced, dark grey hair, thin, Slavic features. He's a dead ringer for Doctor Jackson in Gerry Anderson's *UFO*.

The next picture shows the removal men. They're dressed in the same beige overalls I saw them wearing yesterday, they are loading furniture from a house into their unmarked van. I can imagine Martin crouching behind a car across the street as he takes this shot; that's just what it looks like.

Another shot of the removal men outside a house. This time I recognise the house: it's Frank's place! Martin said that Frank was one of the people they'd taken away!

The Sallow Man again. What's he got to do with all this?

The removal men. This time standing by a smaller van, a transit van, the same beige colour as the furniture van.

The next one shows removal men *and* the Sallow Man! So they are connected! Is he their boss? The evil genius behind all this? In all the shots he's dressed in black: black, trousers, black, jacket, black roll-neck sweater. Yeah, he must be the boss.

The last picture shows the furniture van and two of the matching transit vans parked outside a warehouse. Could this be their base? Had Martin found their headquarters?

I look up from the photographs and take in a much-needed dose of reality, like a diver coming up for air. Shoppers walking up and down the main path across the park; a girl, lying on her front, propped up on elbows, reading a book; a couple of toddlers playing with a ball while their mums look on; some homeless people sitting on a bench near the tennis courts; sunshine and birdsong, trees and grass…

The real world. The everyday world… And then, in these photographs: another world entirely: a world of conspiracy, of paranoia…

And me: where the hell am I? Which world am I inhabiting?

Chapter Three

Getting out.

The highest attainment of a young person's social existence, the pinnacle of having a meaningful life. Getting out. Or so they say. Technically. going to the shops to buy your groceries is 'getting out.' Going for long walks or bike-rides. Going to the theatre or the pictures. They're all 'getting out.' But somehow, for most people, for the young most of all, getting out means going to the pub. If someone is uptight, repressed, or anal about something, and you say 'that person needs to get out a bit more' you really mean 'that person ought to go out to the pub.' Somehow going to the pub is considered the acme of having a fulfilling social life.

I'm not really sure why that is.

I go to the pub quite a bit, but I go because it's something to do, not because I think it makes my life fulfilling and worthwhile. I mean, what do you do at the pub? You drink alcohol, get more or less drunk, and engage in casual conversation with your mates.

Not such a big deal, is it? You can get drunk in the privacy of your own home (and it costs a lot less money.) And you can talk to your friends almost anywhere. So why does it have to be over drinks at the pub?

I dunno. But nevertheless, here I am, at the pub, pint of beer in front of me, talking to my friends.

We're sitting in a booth in the courtyard of the Portland Arms, a pub and music venue, one of our usual haunts. It's a warm evening, and still light at this time of the year. It's a small courtyard, hemmed in by the pub buildings on three sides and by a wall on the other. Including ours, there are two wooden booths, a number of small metal tables with metal chairs and in the corner there's this structure that's something between a gazebo and a Polynesian grass hut. There are a few other drinkers beside our group, but it's a quiet night with no gig happening.

Let me introduce you to everyone.

I'm on the end of the bench and seated next to me (I'm happy to say) is Yuri, armed with a gin and tonic. She's the Japanese girl I've mentioned before. She's over here studying art. You seem to see a lot of Asian girls going in and out of the Cambridge School of Visual and Performing Arts on King Street, and Yuri is one of them. Our crowd met Yuri one night at this place a few months back, and when we 'went on' to Howard's place afterwards, she ended up tagging along.

I wonder if it's somehow racist to be attracted to a Japanese girl *because* she's Japanese? I sometimes think I'm guilty of that. I've never really known any East Asian girls before, and I never really had a 'thing' for them, either… But now that I've met Yuri… Her jet-black hair is long and straight, and she wears metal-framed glasses. She has a tanned Japanese complexion. (I'm not sure why people insist on calling it 'olive.' Olives are green, aren't they?) Apparently in her country pale skin (or *fair* skin as they call it) is considered more attractive for girls. Yuri is quite tall for a Japanese girl, five foot four inches. Her name Yuri means 'lily' which she tells me is also a term for lesbian in Japan. So, yes there is that undeniable sense of the exotic, of something new (to me, at least!) that draws me to her…

I could say a lot more about Yuri, but I ought to be moving on. The bench rightangles after Yuri, and the next member of our group is Howard. Howard stands out from the rest of us because we're all in our twenties and he's in his forties. He's bald, he's fat, and he sweats buckets in hot weather. Howard's wife left him about ten years ago, and that was when he suddenly cultivated an obsessive interest in alternative rock and the local rock scene in particular. Now he publishes an online fanzine and runs a label releasing records by local bands. So here he is—thriving in his midlife crisis. It's not that he's trying to recapture his youth by hanging round with younger people, but it's just that in the circles he moves he unavoidably comes into contact with a lot of younger people like us. The bands are in their teens and twenties, and so are most of the fans. It's only if you go to see some ancient band like Half Man Half Biscuit that you'll find an audience of middle-aged punters.

There's a sort of nervousness about Howard. He often talks in these quick, jerky sentences, blurting out whatever he wants to see and laughing awkwardly at his own attempted witticisms. His favourite drink is bitter. Since his wife left him, he has been completely celibate, whether through choice or not we don't know (and often speculate about.)

Sitting next to Howard is Hilary. Hilary is a guy. No, apparently this wasn't his parents' idea of an eccentric joke; apparently Hilary *is* a unisexual name. So maybe not a joke, but still a pretty lousy idea of his parents to lumber him with a name that these days everyone thinks of as a girls' name.

Although we haven't been here long, Hilary is already half seas over; this will be for the very simple reason that Hilary always gets himself tanked up before he even goes out. I don't know what it is: agoraphobia, social phobia, but Hilary doesn't feel he can go out at night unless he's already had a few. Hilary's the same age as me, but he's a lot more immature. No, he *acts* more immature, but I know he's not as stupid as he pretends to be. Again, I could put a label to it: low self-esteem, or a self-defence mechanism; but there are these people who like to act more dense or childish than they really are; and Hilary is one of them.

Hilary's still on his first pint since getting here, but he probably drank a four-pack before he went out, so let's call it his fifth.

Next to Hilary are Mel and Muriel, who I met earlier at Boots. As I said then, Mel is small and a chatterbox, Muriel's tall and taciturn. They're an item, and I'm pretty sure that in spite of appearances, Muriel's the one who wears the trousers in that particular ménage.

Mel's drinking a vodka and coke, Muriel is sipping a Southern Comfort on the rocks.

Last but not least, and sitting facing yours truly at the other end of the table, is Esther. I've known Esther since we were at school together, and she's as effervescent as she always was. There's something kind of wild about Esther, and this is illustrated by the fact that she's currently working as a stripper in Cambridge's 'indie' strip joint. (Not the one in town with the dress-code and inflated bar-prices.) I think you're supposed to call it 'erotic dancing.' We went to see her once, and I admit she looked good up there, with her boyish blonde hair and nice set of curves. Some might call her a plus-size, but she's tall, so it's well-distributed, and when she's doing her routine there's nothing awkward or heavy about her; she knows how to move.

Esther says she wants to follow a 'path of vice.' That's what she calls it. She started out doing nude modelling for art classes. Now, as I said, it's striptease. And from stripping she wants to move on to pornographic modelling and finally to pornographic films. It's just a whim of hers, really. She wants to follow an 'unpredictable path.'

So that's us. A pretty motley bunch, right?

Well, like I've already said, my crowd are people living on the sidelines of society. Many people would call us screw-ups. And yeah, we are, but we've also got our heads screwed on straighter than most 'normal' people. At least I think so. We're all pretty left-wing here. On the other hand, we drink too much, most of us smoke (Howard's the only non-smoker in this evening's group), and we occasionally do drugs.

This would be a typical evening of booze and small-talk, except that right now I'm sitting on a powder-keg. Yeah, that's how it feels. How do I even begin to tell everyone about what I've found out, what I *think* I've found out? Just show them those photographs? I thought of that, but I also thought how they could be received and perceived in other ways: a practical joke against yours truly, a symptom of Martin's paranoia… I dunno if it's fear of being disbelieved, but I left those photos at home. I want to somehow ease into the subject; some sideways approach rather than plunging straight into it.

At the moment the discussion is about Blu-ray players. Esther's is on the blink.

'I've only had it two years,' she's saying. 'They must make these things so that they pack up as soon as the guarantee's expired, so you have to buy a new one.'

'Of course they do,' says Mel. 'If things like that lasted forever, the companies that made them wouldn't sell enough of them to make a profit.'

'That's it. The pretty much tell you they're not going to last long when they only guarantee them for one year.'

'Yep. Everything's built to spill…'

'Built to Spill? That was a band, wasn't it?'

'Like lightbulbs,' says Muriel.

Mel looks at her. 'What's like lightbulbs?'

'Lightbulbs. Low energy'

'Oh yeah, there must have been a lot of opposition to them at first. Those old filament ones you had to replace all the time. But I guess the companies make their profit by making the new ones really expensive.'

'I dunno about being built to spill,' blurts out Howard. 'Y'know, smart TVs, Blu-ray players; they're complicated; inside, I mean. Old style TVs, VCRs: they had simple mechanisms. Less things to go wrong with them. The new stuff, it's all computerised; more parts. More that can go wrong with 'em.'

Having said his piece, Howard fortifies himself by taking a long swig of his pint.

'Yeah, I can see what you mean there,' agrees Esther. 'I remember when I was a kid, I'm sure we had the same TV and video recorder for about ten years.'

'That's why interstellar travel can't be possible,' declares

Hilary.

Esther laughs. 'Interstellar travel? Where did that one come from?'

'From what you said about things not lasting,' says Hilary. 'A journey to another planetary system would takes years and years, right?'

'What about wormholes or hyperspace?' speaks up Yuri.

'Those are science-fiction short-cuts. I mean a space journey with current Earth technology. It would take years and years and the crew would have to be in cold-sleep—'

'Like *Planet of the Apes*!' says Esther.

'Yeah. What I mean is, all sorts of things could go wrong with the ship and the equipment during those years in space. You can't guarantee that everything will keep on working like it's supposed to.'

'You could have a maintenance robot to take care of that,' says Yuri. You can see she's got all this sci-fi stuff at her finger-tips.

'Yeah, but who's going to maintain the maintenance robot? *That* could go wrong.'

You can tell it's quite early in the evening: Hilary's actually making a valid point and talking sense. Usually by the end of the night he's pretty much incoherent.

I notice Esther looking at me with an inquiring smile. 'What's up, Chad? You're strangely quiet tonight. Anything wrong?'

'Nah, I'm okay,' I say. 'You know Martin's gone?'

A frown. 'Martin? Gone where?'

'Out of Cambridge. Moved house.'

'That's a bit sudden. Where's he moved to?'

'Don't know.'

'What d'you mean you don't know? Haven't you asked him?'

'Can't get hold of him. His phone's dead.'

'That's weird. And you're sure he's moved?'

'Positive. His flat's empty.'

'Why should he go off like that and not tell anyone? Hang on a minute.' Esther fishes her smartphone out of her pocket. 'Let me try calling him...'

She places the call.

'Nope. "The number you have dialled is no longer in service." That's weird. Why would he go off like that and cut himself off from everyone?'

She thinks it's strange. And I haven't even given her the full story. It's an encouraging reaction. I decide to dip my toe in further. 'Don't you think that a lot of people we know have gone away suddenly recently?'

'Have they? I can't think of anyone else...'

'What about Frank and Fiona?'

'What *about* Frank and Fiona? Fiona moved back in with her folks, didn't she? Berkshire, I think. And who's Frank?'

'He was in Splinter,' says Howard, naming a former local band.

'Frank was not in Splinter; he was never in any band,' I tell him. 'You're thinking of Fred.'

'Fred? Fred who?'

'Fred who was in fucking Splinter,' I growl.

'I know Frank,' declares Hilary. 'Used to go out with Emma.'

'Which Emma?' asks Mel.

'Emma with the glasses.'

'I know two Emmas with glasses. Which one?'

'The Emma who used to go out with Frank.'

'And where *is* Frank?' I demand, keeping my lid on with an effort. 'Does anybody know?'

'Moved to London, didn't he?'

'Have you spoken to him recently?'

'No... I think he changed his mobile number.'

'And don't you think it's strange?'

'Not really,' shrugs Esther. 'People move on. I can think of some others who've gone recently: Laura, Peter... People move on. Sometimes they stay in touch, sometimes they don't. Yeah, it's funny how Martin upped sticks and left without telling anyone, but he must have had his reasons...'

I can't do it. I can't tell them about Martin's phone-call; how he said that *they* were coming for him. I can't tell them about the removal men. I can't tell them about the photographs and the evil genius who's behind it all. No, not in front of everyone. I need to speak to Esther alone. I've known Esther since we were kids. I can talk to Esther. Yeah, I'll arrange to see her alone. Not right now, I'll text her tomorrow.

I've got to tell someone. I'm going to go fucking crazy if I don't tell someone...

Chapter Four

Esther, like a lot of people in these overpopulated days, lives in a shared house; a three-bedroom place, part of terrace, and it's over in Romsey Town, which is quite a ways from where I live and so, being one of the few people in Cambridge who doesn't ride a bicycle, I've had to hoof it across town to see her this evening. Not a problem for me; I don't mind walking, at least I don't when it's not chucking it down, which it isn't today. I measure my journeys by the number of cigarettes I smoke along the way—from mine to Esther's is a four-cigarette journey.

So it's just getting dark and here I am knocking on Esther's front door.

Esther's two housemates are Patricia and Neil, and just my luck, it's Patricia who answers the door.

Her smile of welcome disappears when she sees it's me. 'What do you want?'

'To see Esther,' I say.

'And what makes you think she wants to see you?'

'Because she invited me over,' I tell her. 'Just let me in.'

Yeah, Patricia, the four-eyed bitch, doesn't like me; not

one bit. And is there a good reason for this antipathy? Have I ever said or done anything to upset or offend her? Something to earn myself an entire chapter in her bad books? Like buggery I have. She just doesn't like me—hasn't liked me since the day our paths first crossed; my pheromones must clash with hers or something. She seems to take the very fact that I exist as a personal insult; she begrudges me every cubic centimetre of oxygen I inhale in order to keep living. Not only does she not like me, but she does her best, at every opportunity, to try and convince me that nobody else really likes me either, and that I am universally unliked and unlikeable. Her antipathy to me has taken on the colours of a personal vendetta.

I mean, we've all got people we don't like; people who get our backs up one way or another—me, I've probably got more people I don't like than people I *do* like; I can be very fussy about choosing my friends. But the people I don't like, I dislike them passively; I avoid them as much as possible, and if I find myself having to sit at the same table with one of them at the pub, I just won't talk to them any more than I have to. I'm definitely not one of those 'the friends of my friends are *my* friends' people. So, when it comes down to it, I can be just as arbitrary about these things as Patricia—but it just pisses me off when somebody decides they don't like me before *I've* had a chance to decide I don't like *them*!

After I tell her to let me in, Patricia just turns her back on me and walks off to the kitchen, leaving me to come in and close the door behind me. The hallway here is poky, as you'd expect in these terrace places, with one of those very steep and very narrow staircases with creaking steps, which I now creakingly climb to get to Esther's bedroom door.

I knock.

'Who is it?' calls out Esther.

'Me,' I say, very succinct.

'*Entrée.*'

I walk in, and there's Esther lying on her bed listening to

music, lying there in just a t-shirt and knickers. (She'll often lounge around at home in this kind of casual undress.) She's got a proper bedstead in her room, not just a mattress on the floor; but then, this is a furnished place, private landlord, not like my council digs. She's got posters all over the bedroom walls; vintage cheesecake stuff: Bettie Page in a bikini, that tennis girl with no knickers—that sort of thing; they give you a good insight into Esther's character and interests. A kind of tomboyish bisexuality, you could call it.

I don't know if I would describe Esther's head as square or round; either way it's not one of those oblong, or oval heads. Her hair's short, pale blonde (natural, not dyed), with a choppy fringe. Her eyebrows are darker than her hair and she has these sparkly blue eyes which I've always liked. They're windows of her good-natured soul. Esther's one of those people who can get along with just about everyone—she even gets along with her housemate Patricia, which I'll admit kind of pisses me off; she ought to be showing me some solidarity by not liking the person who doesn't like me; that's what part of me thinks, anyway. But then, they are housemates, and it's probably better for the general harmony of the place that they get along.

'You're prompt as usual,' says Esther, sitting up on the bed. She switches off the music. 'You must know to the split-second how long it takes to walk from your house to anywhere in Cambridge.'

'That's how it is when you walk everywhere.'

'Well, how about a beer to refresh yourself after your long walk?'

'That'd be great, thanks.'

There's a four-pack sitting on her bookcase, still cold from the fridge. She passes a can to me and pulls the tab on another for herself. There's no chair in the room, so I sit down next to her on the bed.

Esther's giving me that encouraging smile of hers. 'So, what can I do for you, Chad Fenton? Something you need the oracle's advice about?'

'Yeah…' I say. I pause to take a swig or five of beer. 'You see… something's happened… and you're the only one I can talk to about this…'

Esther holds up a hand. 'Say no more! I think I can guess what it is.'

'Can you?' How can she guess? Was it something I said at the pub last night?

'Yes, indeedy,' she says, nodding sagely.

'Alright then; what is it?'

She pulls up the corners of her eyes. 'It's Yuri! Sexy Japanese Art student! Now, am I right or am I right?'

'You're wrong.'

Surprised look. 'Am I? You mean you don't fancy her?'

'Well, yeah I *do* fancy her, but that's not what I want to talk about. And incidentally: how did you know?'

'That you fancy Yuri? It's pretty obvious, Chad darling. You should just ask her out already… Okay, so if it's not her that's on your mind, what's up?'

I neck some more lager, take a deep breath, and then I launch into the introduction I've been rehearsing in my head all the way here. 'Something's happened; something weird. I know what I'm going to tell you is going to sound crazy; it sounds crazy to me; but it happened.'

I look at her, waiting for her reaction.

'You sound like someone who's about to say they had a close encounter with aliens. Is that it? You've had a close encounter?'

'No, it's not that…'

She squeezes my shoulder. 'Come on—spit it out. I can see you've got something that's worrying you; so, whatever it is, just tell me. I'm not gunna laugh at you or anything.'

'You might, you know. What's happened, it's really off the wall; it's conspiracy-theory stuff; that's how it'll sound, anyway.' I take another swig of my beer, and notice there's not much of it left. 'Okay: I'll begin at the beginning.'

'Best place,' agrees Esther.

'Well, this happened the day before yesterday. About five o'clock in the morning I get a phone call from Martin—he's sounding really scared and he starts telling me all this stuff; about how *they're* onto him; they're outside his flat. He says they're coming to get him.'

'Martin! Him who's suddenly upped sticks and moved?'

'He hasn't moved; at least, not by choice. You haven't heard the half of it yet. You see, he said he'd stumbled onto something; he said that there were these removal men who remove *people* as well as their furniture; and that they're operating around here, in Cambridge—he even gave me some names: Fiona and Frank; he said those two had been taken away by these removal men.'

'Ah! So that'll be why you were going on about them at the pub last night.'

'Yeah. The next thing Martin said was that he had proof about these people; and it was hidden in his drugs' stash.'

'His drugs' stash?'

'He calls it that; it's just a hiding place under his bathroom sink, behind the pedestal whatsit; it's where he keeps any stuff he's got. Anyway, just after he told me this we got cut off. I tried redialling but I couldn't get through.'

'What did you do after that? Did you go rushing round to his place?'

'Well, I didn't *rush* round. Not straight away. For a while I just sat there thinking about it; you know, wondering if he'd been bullshitting me, or whatever; but in the end, I did decide to go and see him. He wasn't in when I got there. The front door was open but he wasn't there. I thought he might have just stepped out to the communal bins or something, but I wasn't sure. So I went in and I went to the bathroom and I checked his stash behind the sink; and I found something: there was a roll of film there; camera film.'

'Camera film?' asks Esther, sounding interested. 'Oh yeah; Martin's a shutterbug, isn't he? Did you take the film roll? Have you still got it?'

'Yes. I took the film in and got it developed.'

'Ah! And what was on the pictures? Anything interesting?'

'Yeah, and I've brought them along to show you; but let me finish my story first; I haven't got to the important bit yet; the maddest part of the story: I was still in the bathroom when I heard someone come into the flat; I thought it might be him; lucky for me that I didn't call out, cuz it wasn't him at all; it was these two men in caps and overalls who'd walked in; and they started ransacking the living room, turning everything upside down. They hadn't seen me in the bathroom and I got out through the window. First thing I saw outside was a removal van parked there; and it hadn't been there a few minutes before when I first got there. So I was looking at the van and thinking about what Martin had said about 'removal men', when I saw the two men. I dunno if they'd heard me getting out through the window, but they'd come out and they were just standing there looking at me; staring at me with these blank, zombie faces. And I suddenly felt really scared; you know, threatened.'

'How d'you mean?'

'Well… It's like they were projecting these waves of menace or something…' I smile helplessly.

'"Waves of menace"? How close to you were they standing?'

'Not that close. About twenty metres away.'

'Hm. I can imagine you picking up vibes from someone standing right next to you—but not from that distance.'

'I know it sounds mad, but that's what happened—I suddenly felt more shit-scared than I can remember feeling in a long time. I mean *really* scared.'

'So, what did you do?'

'I legged it.'

'And did they come after you?'

'Nope. I mean I didn't look back till I was right down the

street, but they weren't following me.'

I look at Esther to see how she's taking it. She takes a swig of her beer and looks thoughtful. No sideways glances at me like she thinks I've lost it—just mulling it over.

'Do you believe me?' I ask desperately. 'You don't just think I'm bullshitting, do you?'

Esther gives me this heartfelt look that answers my question all by itself. 'Oh, Chad…' She strokes my face. '*Of course* I believe you! I've known you long enough, haven't I? I know you're not bullshitting cuz I know you're not a bullshit artist. And I can see how upset you are; I can see this has been eating you up… It might be *someone else's* bullshit, but… You haven't seen or heard anything from Martin since then, have you?'

'Nope. I went back and checked his flat again, later the same day: and like I said last night, it's been cleaned out.'

'So, if we're to believe what Martin said himself, he's been taken away. Taken away cuz he found out about these removal men who make people disappear. And he mentioned Frank and Fiona; said that they'd been taken away. But *why* take those two away? What's so special about them?'

'Well, from what Martin said, it's the fact that there's *nothing* special about them that's the reason they were taken.'

'So, we're looking at some sinister conspiracy to whittle down the number of NEETs and stoners in Cambridge? Is that it?'

'That's what it sounds like.' I lift up my t-shirt and pull the wallet of photographs from where I'd got them uncomfortably stashed in the waistband of my jeans. (I haven't got a pocket big enough for them and didn't want to bring them here in a bag.)

'Ah, the photographs!' says Esther. 'So, what's in them?'

'Plenty. I'll show you through 'em.' I open the wallet. The photos are still in the order they were taken, so the one on the top is one of the shots of the nature reserve.

37

'Trees,' says Esther.

'Yeah, I'm not sure if these first pictures are relevant. They're just shots of that nature reserve on Limekiln Road, and some are of that area of wasteland between the end of Mill Road and Cherry Hinton; you know, with the path going through it.'

'Yeah, I know that place; it's just down the road from here.'

'Yeah, but I dunno if there's anything important about it. Like I said: I'm not sure if these first photos are relevant. He might just have been out taking pictures. These next ones are where it gets interesting...'

And I show her the surveillance shots. The removal men.

'Now, this is definitely Frank's place they're outside here,' I say. 'But this one I don't know.'

'Jesus,' says Esther, 'That's Peter's house.'

'Who's Peter?'

She taps me on the top of the head. 'Idiot. I told you about Peter last night! When you were asking about people who'd moved away recently.'

I look at her. 'And this is where he lives?'

'Lived, yes.'

'So, they got him, too...'

The next photo is the first shot of the Sallow Man.

'This is the Sallow Man—I think this is the guy in charge.'

'Ooh, I think I know him!'

'Yeah, I know; he looks like Vladek Sheybal.'

'Looks like who?'

'Vladek Sheybal. Polish actor. He was in *UFO*.'

'*UF*—No, stupid! I don't mean I've seen him on TV; I mean I've *seen him* seen him. As in seen him in the flesh. I know I have...'

I wasn't expecting this. I feel my heart pick up its pace. 'Who is he, then?'

'I don't *know* him; I just know I've seen him

somewhere… Recently, as well… Was it at the pub…? Yes, I've got it—it was the Beverley Kills' last gig at the Portland; yeah, that's it. He was watching the gig, standing right at the back of the room. I remember noticing him cuz he was older than anyone else there, and I wondered if he was maybe the manager of one of the support bands…'

'And you're sure it's this guy?'

'Sure I'm sure. I remember those staring eyes and the Slavic cheek-bones. It's not a face you forget, is it?'

'No… Was Martin at that gig? Did he see the guy?'

'Umm… nope, I don't think Martin was there…'

'Hang on a minute—was *I* there…? No, I wasn't, was I…?'

'No, you weren't. But what makes you think he's the guy in charge? It might just be a random photograph.'

'No, cuz there are more of him. Hang on a minute… Here we are.' I show her the photo with the Sallow Man and the removal men together. Esther examines it. Next comes the photo of the vans outside the warehouse. 'And this looks like it might be their headquarters…'

'The villains' secret headquarters… Now, if we knew where this place was…'

'*If* we knew; I can't see any clues in the picture to say where abouts it is. It might not even be in Cambridge.'

'Hmm… No, I reckon it must be local. Think about it: Martin must have found the place to take this picture of it, and he hasn't got a car, has he…? Yeah, how *did* he find the place? He doesn't have a car, so he couldn't have followed one of those removal vans back to its base… But I don't see how else he could have found it… Unless he maybe followed someone there on foot…'

'Or he could've followed them in a taxi,' I suggest.

Esther laughs. '"Follow that removal van!" "Right, Guv! I've been waitin' all me life for someone to say that to me!"'

'Are you taking this seriously?' I ask, annoyed.

'I'm sorry if my levity was ill-timed, but you know, we've

got to keep our sense of humours… Or is it our senses of humour…? What I'm wondering is how did Martin stumble on this conspiracy in the first place…? Did he hear something online, or…? I know! Maybe those shots of the nature reserve and the wasteland aren't totally random; maybe he saw something when he was out doing his nature photography—saw something at one of those places!'

'That's an idea,' I agree.

'Yeah, he might have seen something…' says Esther. 'But the nature reserve's public, so—I know! Maybe one of these pictures is a clue to where that warehouse is!'

'I dunno… The picture of the warehouse is at the end of the film roll; the nature pictures are all at the beginning…'

'Yeah, but that doesn't mean he didn't see the warehouse when he took those first pictures; even if he didn't take a shot of it then. He might have gone back there later on… You know, that warehouse might be part of an industrial estate; and there's a few of those right around here in Romsey Town, and we're not far from where he took those pictures of the wasteland. We should check them out! See if we can find this warehouse!'

I look at her. 'You'd do that? You'll help me with this? You don't think this is all just me suffering from delusions, then?'

'Course I don't, and course I'm gunna help you. I mean yeah, the whole thing sounds completely mental—but, with everything you've seen, what Martin said, and what's in these photos, there's got to be something in it… Part of me thinks this has got to be some huge practical joke, but then I think, "Who'd go to all this trouble just to play a trick on you?" …No, there's got be something…'

'And if it *is* what Martin told me?'

'Then it's pretty fucking scary, isn't it? I mean, we can't even go to the police; we don't know if they're in on it… And why are they doing this? Making a bunch of nobodies vanish? And *what* are they doing with them? Have they killed them; the people who've disappeared? Or have they been sold into slavery and made to work in labour camps, or something? Or maybe they've been taken to a secret island and had their names replaced with numbers, like that TV series you're into.'

'Yeah, I've been thinking about that,' I say. 'I mean, it's gotta be the establishment that's behind all this, right? …There was something Yuri told me recently—apparently, in Japan there's a lot of college-leavers who aren't doing what the establishment there wants them to, and going out and getting corporate jobs. Instead of that, these people are preferring to just get parttime, minimum-wage jobs, so they can lead a kind of semi-slacker lifestyle—and there's a lot of people over there who think this is a major problem. I kind of wonder if that's what's behind what's happening here; the removal men and everything. Maybe they're taking the people like us away, brainwashing them or something, and turning them into productive citizens, so they can release them back into the community to go out and get proper jobs…'

'That would almost be the better explanation,' says Esther. 'At least then, they'd be still alive. But we don't know if they are, do we?'

'No, we don't.'

A pause. Esther sighs.

'And you've been sitting on all this since—when?—Monday?'

'Yeah.'

'Stupid! You should've told me sooner!'

She gives me this mock-angry punch on the arm, and then she's thrown her arms around me and she's hugging me tightly, and I'm hugging her, and I suddenly feel like everything's going to work itself out somehow.

Chapter Five

I have to go and see my GP this morning. A 'medication review.' It's just a formality, really. If I don't go, my prescription forms will start crying out in bold font 'Review Overdue.' So, every six months I see my GP, he asks me how I've been, I tell him that I'm feeling pretty much the same as usual, and he says to keep on going with the medication I'm taking. Short and sweet, isn't it? Which is fine with me. Our NHS staff are overworked as it is, so I don't like to take up too much of their valuable time.

I haven't had any counselling for years. I never really got that much out of it, and these days the mental health services are as overworked as the rest of the NHS, so they don't refer you for counselling unless they think you really need it.

So I'm walking to the surgery, and thinking how I'd hate to be a GP myself. My handwriting is bad enough to qualify me for the job; but, apart from the being overworked and everything, GPs have to frequently tell people that they're going to die! Now how the hell do you break a thing like that to someone? How do you say it? How do you tell someone that their life is about to be terminated? Saying 'sorry' would be pretty feeble in that kind of situation. And yet there are all these people who choose to become doctors knowing that telling people they're going to snuff it will be part of their job description! Do they get special training on what tone of voice they should use when breaking the fatal news? I could never do something like that. I could never tell someone their days are numbered and that they need to forget about any plans they had for the future. I think I'd rather just say nothing and let 'em carry on in blissful ignorance until the moment they dropped dead.

I arrive at the surgery. The entrance hall is empty. Just out of sight through a doorless doorway is the reception desk; there's no queue there at the moment, but even so they prefer patients with appointments to use the touchscreen to 'arrive' themselves, so's to leave the reception desk clear for people needing to book appointments or collect prescription forms. Above the open doorway they've pinned up a notice saying that last month there were 367 missed appointments. They put these up every month in an attempt to guilt-trip those douches who book appointments and then don't turn up for them; apparently missed appointments cost the NHS money.

So I go to the touchscreen. It's on the right as you come in through the doors, attached to the wall by a bracket, right beside door to the downstairs waiting room. Today, the screen, for some reason, is angled right down towards the ground. Who left it like this? Was the last person to sign themselves in a midget? Or was it some mum who canted the thing like that so that her kid could have the fun of using the touchscreen?

I try to push the thing back up to the vertical but it won't move. Is the hinge broken? Is it stuck in this position? So, what—am I supposed to use it like this? But I can't even see the screen at this angle; the image isn't clear. Am I supposed to squat down to use it? But then I'd look bloody stupid if anyone came along… The door to the waiting room opens and a nurse carrying a clipboard comes through and goes up the stairs. If she notices the position of the touchscreen, she doesn't say anything.

I look at the canted screen again. This is ridiculous! If someone tilted the thing down then it can be tilted back up again! Simple logic. I just wasn't trying hard enough.

I grab the screen firmly in both hands and push it towards the wall. It doesn't move. It feels like it's locked in this position. But it can't be! I push it harder…

Then I hear something snap and suddenly I've got the whole weight of the monitor in my hands. It's broken loose! It's broken loose from the fucking wall!

Now what am I supposed to do?

Try pushing it back! Yeah, maybe it's just slipped out of

a groove or something, and all I've got to do is push it back in. I try this, jiggling the screen around to try and get it in the right position... It won't go in! I can't feel it lock!

Someone else comes out of the waiting room—a patient. I freeze, facing the wall, the screen in my hands. I'm trying to make it look like the bloody thing is still attached to the wall. My heart is going like the clappers, and I know my face is bright red. I can see the woman looking at me as she walks past, but she doesn't say anything and goes out through the exit.

I try pushing the screen again. It's no good. Something's broken; it's not going to just reattach itself to the wall. Shit, am I going to have to pay for this? If I report it at the reception will they charge me with vandalism?

I'm still wondering what to do when someone comes in from outside. Bollocks! Are they going to want to use the screen?

No, thank God; the guy goes straight through the doorway to the reception desk.

I've got to put this thing down before anyone else turns up. I slowly crouch down, the touchscreen in my hands. Lower, lower... Gently does it... Then it stops. The damn thing won't lower any further! Then I see what's wrong: the cable connected to it is stretched taut!

I hear voices—at least two people coming down the stairs.

Sod this for a game of soldiers!

I let go and just leave the touchscreen hanging there—and I make a swift exit from the building. I'm just going to have to be one of the statistics on next month's 'missed appointments' bulletin!

One of the main misconceptions we have about anime in this country is that everybody in Japan watches the stuff. They don't. Only a certain section of the population regularly watches anime. I mean obviously there's enough of these viewers to sustain the industry, but even so the majority of

Japanese people not only don't watch the stuff, but they look right down their noses at it.

The majority of anime fans are male, but like I said before, there are girls who like the stuff, and Yuri, the Japanese girl in my life, is one of them. Does that make her a geek? I don't really see her as one. (But then, I don't really see *myself* as one and some people would disagree with me there.) I mean, she's an Art student; and no, she's not learning Art just to draw comics. As I think I've said before, Yuri is working at the College of Visual and Performing Arts here in Cambridge; and here I am waiting outside that very building. We're meeting up for lunch. I won't call it a date, because we're still not actually 'going out.'

The college is on King Street, which is about as near to the City Centre as you can get without being in the City Centre. There are pubs, restaurants and small shops here on Kings Street. The CSVPA inhabits a building that it's easy to tell used to be a retail unit. You've got two big plate-glass windows facing the street, either side of the recessed entrance doors. But now, instead of merchandise, you've got displays of students' artwork hanging in these windows. The display boards are nearly as tall as the windows, so you can't see what's going on inside the place.

The pavement right here is narrow, so I'm kind of in the way standing here waiting, treating the passers-by to my secondary smoke.

But then the door opens and out comes Yuri, smiling broadly like she always does. She's got an overbite and her upper teeth are slightly crooked; the second two incisors are slightly pushed back, making the canines look very long and sharp. This kind of dental arrangement is apparently very common in Japan and I'm not criticising it at all—I love Yuri's smile.

'Hi!' she greets me, singing the word.

She looks genuinely pleased to see me, but then a little voice always reminds me that for a Japanese girl its basic etiquette to be smiling and cheerful with people, so I still can't decide if that smile and that greeting are especially for me, or if they're the same as she doles out to everyone... Esther said it was pretty obvious that I fancied Yuri—I wish she could've given me a similar report about Yuri's feelings for me.

I know it's ridiculous for someone my age who's not a virgin, but whenever I meet Yuri alone like this, I start feeling kind of shy; unsure of myself. I don't think I've felt this way around a girl since I was an awkward adolescent at secondary school.

Today, she's dressed in a sort of pinafore mini-dress with a blouse and string bow-tie, black tights and buckle shoes. (I think there are a lot of Japanese fashions like this, that echo school uniforms—they're mad about school uniforms in Japan.) She looks great. More than great. And she says she's not good-looking; or rather, she says she's not considered good-looking back home in Japan. Not just because of her unfashionable 'tan' skin complexion, either; but she says her face is considered a plain-looking one by Japanese standards. Well, my standards are obviously not Japanese, because I think her face looks beautiful! (She says that another point against her is her flat chest—Japanese men are obsessed with big tits. Yuri told me Japanese men were like this because big tits aren't that common in Japan—so I had to tell her that men are just as obsessed with big tits here in the UK, where they *are* pretty common.)

I know I ought to tell Yuri how great I think she's looking... But instead, I just ask her where she wants to go for lunch.

'McDonald's!'

'Again?'

'Sure!'

So we set off for McDonald's, Yuri walking by my side. Yuri doesn't have any ethical objections to the American fast-food chain. (They have them in Japan, with the main difference that they have green tea on the menu.) I don't think she's very politically-minded, and apparently this is something else that's common with Japanese women. (Yuri's introduced me to some Japanese girl rock bands, and apparently it's very unusual for those bands to have any political lyrics in their songs. They prefer to sing about things like food and cats.)

We thread our way through the lunchtime crowds, passing that church on the corner of Market Street that everyone apart from tourists seems to have a blind-spot for. ('Oh! Is there a church there? I never noticed it!')

If you think its frivolous of me to be out on a lunch date with an exchange student instead of following up on sinister conspiracies, well a) I've still got a life to live and b) our investigations have reached an impasse. We checked out, Esther and me, the industrial estates in the Romsey Town area and we didn't find any warehouse matching the one in the photograph. We looked online to see if there were any industrial estates near to the Limekiln Road nature reserve: there aren't. So we're left wondering if those landscape photos are completely irrelevant after all; something that just happened to be on the same roll of film; or if they have some other significance…

McDonald's is located down a pedestrian mews called Rose Crescent. The restaurant—if you want to dignify McDonald's with that name—is one of those places that has a narrow frontage but is much bigger once you get inside. There's quite a queue when we get there, what with it being lunchtime, but we finally get served and we find a free table in the upstairs seating area. I'm a vegetarian so I have the veggie-burger meal; carnivorous Yuri has the cheese-burger meal.

'So, what did you think of *Black Lagoon*?' asks Yuri, as we unwrap our food.

Black Lagoon is an anime I've just been watching on Netflix (recommended by Yuri, of course.) It's this violent action series about this Japanese businessman who gets taken hostage by modern-day pirates, and after his bosses leave him out to dry, ends up ditching his former life and joins up with the pirate gang. The pirates—or I guess they're actually mercenaries since they hire themselves out—are based in this fictitious city on some island that's overrun by organised crime gangs from around the world.

'I really liked it,' I say. 'It was different to the others I've watched. It was a hell of a lot more violent, and the whole thing had this amoral tone to it.'

Yuri finishes swallowing her mouthful of food before speaking.

'Do you like Revi? I think she's cool.'

Revi is the foul-mouthed, blood-thirsty heroine of the piece.

'Yes, she was,' I agree, piercing the lid of my coke with a straw. 'I really liked the voice actress. Her voice was perfect for the character.'

Yuri nods her head. 'Megumi Toyoguchi. I like her.'

'Erm... I watched the English dub. I don't know what the actress's name was.'

'Sorry, I forget! Yes, you watch the English dubs.'

'Well, y'know, I speak the language pretty well.' Lame joke—so lame that, going by her (lack of) reaction Yuri doesn't even realise it was meant to be one. Quickly moving on, I say: 'I thought it was interesting how the characters all smoked all the time in that one; they seemed to really emphasise it in the visuals. It's like they were saying that because these people lived violent lives and they knew they could get killed any minute, that they just considered smoking another acceptable risk.'

Which makes me think: what excuse do we have? Me, and my crowd. Most of us smoke, and we're not all earning our livings as gun-toting mercenaries, walking shoulder to shoulder with the Grim Reaper on a day-to-day basis—but we still go and play Russian roulette with our lives by smoking cigarettes all the time. Ask any non-smoker and they'll say we're a bunch of complete fucking idiots.

'I think maybe they have the smoking because it looks cool,' says Yuri, taking the aesthetical point of view as usual.

'That island in the story; it's not a real place, is it?' I ask.

Yuri looks confused. 'What island?'

'The island where they all live. You know, where that city Roanupur is.'

'That's not an island,' says Yuri. 'It's on the mainland.'

This is news to me. 'Are you sure?'

'Yes.'

'I could've sworn it was an island in the South China Sea.'

'No, it's on the mainland.'

'What mainland?'

'The Malay Peninsula.'

'Is it?'

'Yes.'

'I could've sworn they said it was an island.'

'No. They show it on a map in the OVA.'

I frown. 'OVA? What's an OVA?'

'It stands for Original Video Animation; OVA episodes are extra episodes only on the DVD or Blu-ray release. In *Black Lagoon* there are five OVA episodes.'

'I don't think they had those on Netflix…'

'You should check.'

'I should.'

…And the conversation flows on as we eat our evil, corporate lunch. I tell Yuri about my misadventure at the surgery this morning, and it gets a big laugh from her. So, at least some good came out of that disaster!

I ask Yuri to recommend another anime for me to watch, and she tells me about this one called *Strike Witches*. It has the most insane premise: it's set in some alternative reality where World War Two is a war against aliens and Japan and Europe are allies. And it's also a reality where girls don't wear skirts or trousers, so their modesty is only covered by knickers or swimming costumes. The eponymous Strike Witches are a bunch of schoolgirl witches who sprout animal ears and tails when they engage their witch powers and they fly around with these aeroplane thigh-boots strapped to their legs.

It's at times like this you remember that 'Only in Japan' saying.

I don't tell Yuri anything about the conspiracy thriller I'm currently living in the middle of. I'd like to tell her; it's not like I'm worried about her not believing me or thinking I'm a lunatic—but… I dunno…

And I don't get round to asking her out, either. We're getting along so well, that I feel like I just don't want to go and spoil it. I should probably just wait till we're both drunk before trying to move things onto the next stage.

And then as we're leaving McDonald's I see the Sallow Man.

He walks past us as we come out the doors, looking straight ahead, wearing a black suit and a polo-neck sweater, just like he is in those photographs. I instantly recognise that Slavic profile; there's no mistaking him—it's the Sallow Man, in the flesh. He's here, he's real; he's not just an image in some photographs. For a minute my thoughts are all over the shop, but then the obvious course of action occurs to me: I've got to follow this guy; I mustn't let him get out of sight.

I turn to Yuri, place my hands on her shoulders.

'Look I'm really sorry, but for complicated reasons I can't go into now I've got to follow that man in the black suit who just walked past, so I'll have to say good-bye and once again I'm really sorry.'

And after getting out that mouthful, I take off without even waiting for a reply, walking briskly to keep the Sallow Man in sight. I realise—too late—that I've just ditched Yuri in a pretty crappy way, and she's most likely going to be very upset and/or pissed off—but I can't go back and explain to her now; I'll have to try and explain things to her later.

Out of the mews, the Sallow Man turns right towards Kings Parade and Trinity Street. Past the church he takes a left onto Kings Parade. There are a lot of tourists about as we're right in the middle of the 'historic city centre' here, with King's College right in front of us. I keep him in sight, walking a safe distance behind. Part of me worries that he might look back and see that I'm tailing him; but then I think, why should he look back? I mean you don't, do you? When you're walking along you don't generally look back over your shoulder; not unless you're either paranoid or you're attracted by a sound.

Actually, it's *me* who ought to look back, because I suddenly realise there's someone close behind, 'dogging my heels' I think the expression goes. I look round. It's Yuri.

'What are you doing?' I hiss, coming to a stop.

'Coming with you,' she says. 'This looks fun.'

I look up the street. If I hang around here, the Sallow Man will soon be out of sight amongst the crowd.

'Come on, then,' I say, setting off again, Yuri walking by my side.

'Why you follow that guy? Who is he?'

'Well, I don't actually know who he is. I just think he might be involved in something shady. And listen—I've got no idea where he's going; we could be following him for ages.'

'Ages?'

'I mean "a long time"; so if you want to just head off back to college…'

'No. I wanna stay with you.'

Bless her. And after I'd just ditched her like that. Most people would have thought, "to hell with you" after being treated like that, but not Yuri—she just comes straight after me!

The Sallow Man turns off the Parade, into a maze of

narrow streets. We're in old Cambridge with a vengeance now; all these big gothic buildings with rows of tall, narrow windows. Some of these buildings are actually museums, but they don't really advertise themselves. It's quiet here, off the tourist track; there aren't many people about; our footsteps are loud on the pavement. The Sallow Man walks on, walking quickly, like he's going somewhere specific. He crosses the road and takes a right into an even narrower street.

Is he going to lead me right to the warehouse from the photograph? It's hard to imagine there being anything like a modern industrial estate around here.

'Where's he going?' whispers Yuri.

'Beats me. I don't even know this part of Cambridge that well.'

Up ahead, the Sallow Man disappears through an open archway on the left. We run to catch up. Through the arch is a small courtyard; the walls around it all roofs, chimney, pipes and dormers; all thrown together in a jumble. The Sallow Man is climbing a flight of rickety fire-stairs to a door on the first-floor landing. He opens it and goes straight inside.

Yuri looks at me. 'Now what?'

A good question!

'Let's see if he comes out again...' I say.

We wait. He doesn't come out. Yuri wants to know why I'm following that man, and so I end up telling her the entire story—and she not only believes what I say, but she's impressed! Seems I've elevated myself in her eyes to spy story hero by getting myself into this mess. The Sallow Man still doesn't reappear, and in the end I tell Yuri she ought to scoot off back to college, and she agrees and scoots off. After that I hang around for another hour or so, and then frankly I get bored with waiting and realise I've been smoking far too many cigarettes. What's he doing in there? What's in that building...? Well at least I've got this courtyard marked. I'll tell Esther about it and we can figure out what to do next. I guess I'm just not cut out for long stake-outs.

Chapter Six

One of Chad's friends, as you may recall, glories under the name of Hilary, and he's generally looked upon as being the comedy drunk of the group by his immediate circle of acquaintance. One of these days Hilary might even realise this fact, and decide to do something about it.

Unlike a lot of binge-drinkers, Hilary doesn't just get drunk because he likes the pleasurable sensation of inebriety; for him, alcohol is a valuable social tool, one which he believes he just couldn't function without. Hilary has these communications issues: he's shy and nervous around people, especially girls; he always has been. But if he drinks, he comes out of himself; he becomes more talkative, more sociable. But because of his need to address phobia, Hilary always starts his evening's drinking at home, before he even goes out—because if he didn't do this, he wouldn't even feel confident enough to go out in the first place. This head-start over his friends invariably means that at the end of a night's boozing at the pub, club or venue, he is always going to be much more stupidly drunk than everyone else. And this is where the clowning comes in; the silly impersonations, jokes at his own expense… (And as for those late-night parties, he can rarely stay the full course without passing out—with all its marker-penned consequences.)

Another defining characteristic about Hilary (so he thinks) is his virginity. He still has it. Had it all his life and can't seem to get rid of the damn thing. For this reason, he's desperate to have a girlfriend and a sex life. And like a lot of people in his position, he always hopes, when he goes out of an evening, that tonight is going to be his lucky night, tonight will be the night when he meets that special someone. So far, that lucky night and that special someone have remained elusively out of reach. Like other twenty-something virgins of the male persuasion Hilary thinks that losing his v-card is the most important goal of his life; that his friends must be secretly laughing at him for never having had sex.

Recently, Hilary has started to blame his lack of success in finding a girlfriend on the social circles he moves in; it's a smallish circle and there aren't many girls he sees regularly, and they have one and all been crossed off his list of possibilities. Mel and Muriel are out of the question of course; they're gay and in a relationship. Esther he's always thought of as being way out of his league. Patricia is too snooty and superior. Kelly has a boyfriend. Liz turned him down... Yes, this crowd is no good; these people are holding him back. He needs to branch out and make some new friends.

And that's just what he's planning to do this very evening.

He sits in the living room of his flat, drinking a can of Fosters and watching *Red Dwarf*. He always watches TV while he's doing his pre-going out drinking, and *Red Dwarf* hasn't been chosen at random for this evening's viewing. You see, one of the reasons Hilary thinks he hasn't got anywhere with a girl is because he's not funny enough in his conversation; ever since school it has always seemed to him that it's the comedians who get the girls; that girls like someone who can make them laugh. And so Hilary is watching *Red Dwarf* because he thinks that if he goes to the pub armed with lots of witty lines from the sci-fi sitcom, he will be funnier and more entertaining. Unfortunately, no-one has ever told Hilary that this sort of thing is called 'second-hand humour' and, especially when used in excess, does not come across very well, and is no substitute for genuine, spontaneous humour. (Needless to say, Hilary only watches episodes from the first six series of *Red Dwarf*—there's precious little comedy material to be gleaned from any series after that one.)

His phone buzzes. It's a text from Esther saying the gang are going to be hanging out at Christ's Piece this evening. For a moment he's tempted; sitting in the park can be a good way to meet people… But no; his mind is fixed on him going his own way tonight; he is seeking pastures new, and doesn't want to hang out with the usual crowd. With this in mind he has determined to go to the Empress tonight—a pub that's way down Mill Road and not one that his crowd usually frequent.

And so, having downed four cans of Fosters, and absorbed the gags from as many *Red Dwarf* episodes, Hilary feels ready to embark on his quest.

Won't the gang be surprised if he turns up next week with a girlfriend! It won't be just Chad who can get any girl he wants. Hilary is getting fed-up with playing second fiddle to Chad Fenton; sitting there and watching him charm the knickers off one girl after another. Chad has clearly set his sights on that Japanese girl Yuri, at the moment. This really pisses Hilary off, because *he'd* liked that girl. Being a foreigner, he thought she wouldn't have judged him the same way an English girl would; and she isn't good-looking enough for him to feel like she's out of his league… But then Chad had gone and set his sights on her, and after that happened, Hilary knew he might as well just throw in the towel.

It's a longish walk to the Empress but he enjoys it—it's a warm evening and it can be very pleasant just to be walking along when you're mildly drunk like this. Buoyed up with anticipation and those ludicrously sanguine hopes which people like him often entertain that things will go right for them, in spite of that long history of them *not* going right for him, he enters the pub, buys himself a pint and goes out into the beer garden. The Empress has a fairly extensive beer garden, supplied with the usual picnic benches. There is also an enclosure housing a couple of piglets; the presence of these animals being a sort of gimmick of the pub's. Hilary has made sure to arrive early, before the place becomes packed, and he sits himself down at a vacant bench. His idea is that when the place starts to fill up, other people, hopefully some of them female, will want to sit at this bench.

He lights a cigarette and looks around. One bench nearby is occupied by a group of people who look to be in their late thirties; at another sits a giggling group of girls in their teens. They look a bit too trendy for Hilary's taste, these girls; they look like they listen to download chart pop music rather than alternative rock. (Hilary may be desperate, but he couldn't go out with a girl who doesn't like the same sort of music as him.)

More groups of people arrive, but they naturally move towards the empty benches rather than the one that has an occupant... And now Hilary finds himself facing a dilemma: he has nearly finished his pint; if he goes to the bar for a refill, he might return to find his bench taken up. Should he wait? Should he go without buying another pint until some people join him at this bench? In terms of his mood Hilary is more than drunk enough, but like plenty of people who are more than drunk enough, he still finds himself craving more booze. This phenomenon is known as 'alcoholism.'

And then, disaster: a group of five young men come up to his bench! Oh, great. This isn't what he wanted.

'Anyone sitting here?' asks one of them.

'No,' Hilary is forced to admit.

They men sit themselves down on the bench. Hilary doesn't like the look of them; they're slightly older than himself, and they look like wideboys; he's not picking up a good vibe from them. The 'one who appears to be the leader,' a man wearing a leather jacket who has sat down facing Hilary, introduces himself and his friends.

Hilary mumbles his responses.

'Well go on, then!' says leather jacket. 'Tell us your name!'

'Hilary,' says Hilary.

The inevitable laughter follows.

'Seriously?' says leather jacket.

'It is a boy's name as well as a girl's,' explains Hilary, patiently. (He has had to make this point a great many times in his life.)

'Your parents really had it in for you, didn't they?' laughs the man with slicked-back hair who's sitting next to him.

'Come on, leave 'im alone,' says leather jacket. 'Nothing wrong with his name… So, what you doing here, mate? Meeting up with some of your mates?'

'No…' admits Hilary.

'Solitary drinker, eh? Not good, not good,' shaking his head. 'Lemme tell you something: girls don't go up to blokes sitting on their own. Fact. So, if you're here wanting to pull something, you won't get anywhere sitting on your tod. Trust me.'

'Yeah, you should stick with us, mate,' says slicked-back hair.

'Yeah, we'll find you something,' agrees leather jacket. 'So how d'you like 'em?'

'Like what?'

'Girls, you wally.'

'I don't know, really…'

'Not too fussy, eh? Tell you what: I had a diamond last week; a real screamer, she was. Nice pair of tits as well.'

'Last one I had had bloody hair round her nipples!'

'Jesus Christ!'

'I remember one I had who didn't even shave her legs! She thought it was alright just cuz she was blonde and it didn't show up like dark hair!'

'They should shave it all off! Pubes an' all!'

'Yeah, but some of 'em won't do that!'

'Tell 'em you won't fuck 'em if they don't shave it off!'

'Or bring your shaving kit and do it yourself!'

'I'm just going to the bar,' says Hilary.

He breathes a sigh of relief when he gets away from those

guys. Like he wants to be taken under the wing by them! So now the whole beer garden is out of bounds for him! He can't exactly come back with his drink and sit at another table—not without those guys seeing him. He'll have to sit inside now, and somewhere out of sight of the bar.

He finds a quiet corner table and necks his second pint. Already his optimism has disappeared into a sinkhole, thanks to that encounter with the love-'em-and-leave-'em brigade. Is this evening just going to be yet another disaster like all the others?

It's somewhere around this time that the gaps start to appear; or rather the gaps that *will* appear the following day when Hilary tries to recall the events of this evening. This is a common experience with Hilary. Looking back on an evening out like this one, he can always remember the first couple of hours with perfect clarity; after this, his memories usually start to become sporadic; he cannot remember everything that was said; he cannot remember precisely when so-and-so arrived or when so-and-so left. Memories become disjointed; he will recall part of a conversation; he will recall something he said or did; he might even recall something random like a song that was playing on the jukebox. The longer an evening progresses, the more he drinks, the more pronounced will become these gaps; he might recall that they ended up in another pub, but will have no memory of actually walking from pub A to pub B; he will recall being in a fast-food restaurant, but will not recall what he bought and ate... And then, if the evening and the drinking goes on for long enough, the flashes of memory will give way to complete darkness; he will have no memories of subsequent events at all. Those are the worst times, because Hilary will often learn later that he became more annoying than funny, talking a load of bullshit; or that he persistently pestered some girl who wasn't interested; or that he became belligerent and got into an argument with someone; or that he threw up all over the place...

Hilary hates himself for his behaviour on those occasions, and whenever they happen, vows to himself that he will cut back on his drinking, if not abjure completely—but as Rousseau's Julie pointed out to her lover after he, also under the influence, had started talking dirty to her: these good resolutions only really merit praise if they are actually carried out.

So Hilary is sitting at the corner table, quaffing lager. He will remember he sat there alone for quite some time, but he won't be sure if it was during his third or still his second pint when the group of three people arrive and ask him if they can join him at his table. Of course he says 'yes.' The newcomers are two girls and a boy; they introduce themselves; one of the girls sits next to him and they start talking. He won't be able to remember the girl's name the next day (Hilary's not very good with names at the best of times.), but he will just about be able to remember her face though—at least he will retain a hazy impression strawberry-blonde hair and a pretty, painted smile. He will *think* that the girl tells him she's an Anglia-Ruskin student, but he won't recall what she said she's studying there. The details of their conversation will be patchy, but he will have a general feeling that the talk was flowing along nicely, and that the girl seemed to like him. He will recall that he rolled out some of his store of *Red Dwarf* gags ('So Rimmer says, "Step up to red alert!" and Kryten says, "Sir, are you absolutely sure? It does mean changing the bulb."'); they seem to go down very well!

And he will remember the disastrous finale as well. Why did he decide to get up and go to the bar? He will kick himself for this. It wasn't like *she* wanted a drink; it was only to get one for himself. Like he wasn't tanked up enough already! So he goes to the bar; and he will remember there being a huge huddle of people there; and he will remember becoming more and more agitated at the delay—especially when, after he finally gets his elbows on the bar counter, the two overworked barmaids seem to be serving everyone else except him. He will remember finally getting served. He will remember going back towards his corner table and stopping short when it comes into view. Two newcomers, both male, have joined the group; one of them has taken his chair, and is talking merrily away with the strawberry blonde.

There are people for whom this development wouldn't have bothered them at all: they would have just rejoined the group, said 'hi' to the newcomers and grabbed themselves another chair from somewhere. Hilary is not one of those people. He just sees that his place has been usurped, that the girl he'd just decided to fall in love with looks like she's already forgotten he even exists… His reaction to this development is an immediate one: capitulation and retreat. He puts down untasted the pint he has just bought and exits the pub.

He will remember crying as he walks away from the pub; he is quick to cry when he's drunk—but then, 'crying drunk' is another well-known phenomenon. And then he will remember a determination striking him, conquering his first impulse to just go home and go to bed: the last resort he has often considered when he's yearning for intimacy, for some kind of connection, and nothing else has gone right for him: there is a particular club at the Junction; this club is only held once a month and Hilary happens to know that it is taking place tonight. It's called the Dot Cotton Club, and it's the gay club. Yes, he'll go there. It's somewhere completely new and he might just meet someone… Hilary will not be the first essentially heterosexual young man to have tried this option.

Of walking to the venue he will have sporadic memories of the following day. Darkness has fallen, he is already very drunk, his head is buzzing, but he doesn't lurch and stagger; no, he walks with that focused, determined gait of the inebriate who knows that if he *doesn't* thus concentrate, he *will* start lurching and staggering.

The Junction, Cambridge's second largest music venue,

has been around since 1989, when it was officially opened by the legendary DJ John Peel. For years the venue stood forlorn in a wilderness of gravelled parking space and empty lot, but now the whole area has been redeveloped; buildings have sprung up all around the venue: a hotel, a bowling alley, a multiplex cinema…

Hilary will remember his arrival at the doors of the Junction, the contrast of the lights and the people after the darkened streets he has been navigating; walking up to the entrance guarded by the usual thickset, close-shaved bouncers, and doing his best not to look completely wrecked. Somehow he manages to succeed in this and is allowed inside.

What happens at the club is very hazy indeed. He will know he continues to buy drinks, in spite of the state he is in. Some, he will suspect, are purchased for him. He will remember being amongst a group of young men and talking God knows what bullshit. There is one boy in particular; he is wearing make-up but is not cross-dressed; he has this friendly smile and he seems to be concerned for Hilary and the state he's in. The boy seems kind and looks to be about his own age…

How long does he remain at the club? He will not be sure the next day; he might have stayed till the end; he might have been there not more than an hour; it's all a whirl of lights, and faces, and gaudy costumes and bad music. (He won't be able to remember precisely what the bad music is, but only that he didn't like it.)

And then he is out of the club, and walking arm-in-arm with someone. Is it a loving embrace, or just to stop Hilary from falling? A bit of both, he thinks… They walk, and they arrive at a car, and Hilary will remember being shocked to discover upon looking round, that the man he has been walking with is not that kindly young man in the make-up at all; the face he sees in the semi-dark is much older; a face scored with the lines of middle-age; and it does not seem like a kindly face. Who is he? How has this happened? How did he get here? What happened to the boy from the club?

What happens in the back of the car, Hilary will only remember vaguely, but he will remember enough to feel completely wretched and humiliated when he wakes up the next day, alone and in his own bed.

Chapter Seven

I remember that Esther once brought this 'alternative' astrology book into school; a sort of streetwise teens' astrology book which told you things like what kind of sex the different star-signs preferred. Esther read some of it out to us during lunchtime, telling us all what it said about our various star-signs, and one thing it said about my star-sign, Taurus, was (and I can't remember if this went for all Tauruns or just male Tauruns), it said that we preferred a hug to a shag. At the time I was still a virgin, so I couldn't really confirm which I preferred. In fact, being a virgin as I was, at that time getting laid seemed a much more important milestone to pass than getting hugged—but now, in my experience and maturity, I think that there might have been something in it. It's not that I'm one of those people who find sex to be a complete let-down; but I know I'm not as crazy about it as some people are... But yeah, a hug, an embrace, with someone you have strong feelings for, to have their arms around you and your arms around them, to embrace that other person's warm, responsive body and to know that that person cares for you... Yeah, I think I do get more out of that than from a bout of sex; I mean the sex is pretty much just an instinct, a bodily function, however much you try to dress it up; but a hug is much more than that...

Another thing that book said that I *don't* agree fits me is that Tauruns prefer reading about sex to actually doing it. Can't say that's me—I'm no connoisseur of erotic fiction.

Thinking about them though, the funny thing about those books (and I guess the same applies to porn movies, at least the ones that pretend to have a plot) is it's always about illicit sex; spur of the moment casual sex, promiscuous sex, infidelity... I mean if you think about it, a porn writer could be just as explicit writing about a monogamous couple's first bedroom activities; or even a happily married couple's sex, as long they're still adventurous and get fired up—but that's not what people want when they read that stuff, apparently. It has been sudden, gratuitous sex; raw, brutal sex; dishonest, cheating sex—that's what gets the one-handed readers fired up. Seems the context is important as the pornographic details.

This evening we're sitting in the park, having a cheap night out. I've mentioned that we do this sometimes of a Friday or Saturday night, haven't I? It's Saturday tonight and we're sat in a circle under our usual tree on Christ's Piece; and we've got carrier bags full of cans of beer or spirits-with-mixers bought from a nearby supermarket. Yuri is here (sitting next to me), and there's Esther, and Errol, Muriel and Mel... Howard's not here; he never comes out on our 'cheap nights out.' I think he considers himself too old for drinking in the park. As I said before, this park is a haven for homeless drinkers, under-age drinkers, and people like us, who want to avoid paying pub prices, while enjoying the nice weather. It's gone eight and starting to get dark now.

 Me and Yuri are both on the Fosters. Yuri's telling us about this anime called *Negima*. '...It's about an English boy wizard, age ten, who goes to Japan to teach in a girls' middle school.'

 'A boy wizard?' says Esther. She's sipping a can of Jack Daniel's and coke. 'So, it's like an anime Harry Potter, is it?'

 'Yes, he's like Harry Potter. All the girls in his class fall in love with him.'

 I laugh. 'So, you've got a ten-year-old boy being lusted

over by a classroom full of thirteen/fourteen-year-old girls? I'm not sure JK Rowling would approve.'

'What's the wizard's name?' asks Esther.

'Negi Springfield.'

'Negi Springfield? What, does that sound like an English name to Japanese people?'

'No, the name is a joke. "Negi" is the Japanese word for spring onion—So, Negi Springfield.'

'Where's Hilary?' I ask Esther. 'Did you text him?'

'I did, but he didn't reply,' she says. 'Maybe he's down in the dumps.'

'All the more reason to come out, I would have thought.'

'Yeah, Hilary's alright when he's just slightly pissed,' says Mel. Mel and Muriel are both drinking canned gin and tonic. 'But then when he overdoes it and gets bladdered, he can be a real pain in the arse… Did I tell you, I met him in town one time, during the day? I think that's the only time I've seen him when he's sober; and it was weird, because he was like a totally different person. He seemed really shy and embarrassed and he talked differently; talked in this really quiet voice.'

'That's cuz he only comes out of himself when he's drunk,' I say.

'He's dependent on it,' says Mel.

I met Hilary at this young people's therapy group I was going to a few years back. He'd hardly say a word during the sessions. He'd just sit there, staring at the floor. Everyone knows what therapy groups are like: they've been sent up enough in films and TV shows—and quite rightly. You just sit there, in this circle of chairs, and talk about whatever's on your mind, whatever's happened to you recently; every little thing. Now, I'm not going to say the whole thing is worthless—there must be some people who get something out of going to therapy groups like that—but I don't think it ever did anything for me, and I don't think it did anything for Hilary, either. For me, going to that group was more like a social thing; just chatting to the other 'clients' (that's what they called us) in the common room between the sessions, and when we went outside to smoke our fags—that was the best part for me. Hilary talked more outside of the sessions, and that was how I got to know him.

I sometimes think that kind of therapy—and I mean individual as well as group therapy—might actually hinder more than it helps. It's like it encourages you to be morbidly self-analytical; to focus on every little thing that's happened to you, to dissect and analyse every little thing you've said, every little thing that you've done, in a way that most normal people don't. It encourages you to be introspective.

We used to think that the therapists at our group had a cushy job of it, too—they just have to sit there and listen and make occasional comments. Not very taxing for them. Still, I doubt they got paid much for their trouble.

Some people you meet in those therapy groups have had seriously crappy lives. There was this one girl when I was there; she seemed to have spent most of her childhood being raped and abused; it was like she seemed to attract it like a magnet. There was something about the girl's eyes… I don't know if I was reading it into them on account of what I knew about her, about her life, but I always thought she had this haunted look in them—a victim's eyes. Some of the things these people have gone through; you wonder how they manage to carry on. This girl didn't—she topped herself in the end.

'Hey, let's change the subject,' Esther says. 'Shouldn't be talking about our friends behind their backs.'

'Why not?' asks Yuri bluntly,

This makes me smile—and I agree with her, as well. 'Yeah, it's natural, isn't it?' I say. 'People do it all the time.'

'Yeah, it's natural,' allows Esther. 'But it can be pretty mean, can't it? You know, if you start slagging someone off; saying things about them you wouldn't say to their faces.'

'Yeah, but even that,' I argue; 'even being critical of our

friends behind their backs: that's natural, too. There's that saying: "Eavesdroppers never hear anything good of themselves." Shows we do it all the time.'

Muriel laughs. 'So, eavesdropping's a crime—backbiting isn't!'

'Well, "backbiting" is putting it strong,' says Esther. 'We weren't backbiting Hilary just now. We were just talking about his alcohol problem. Backbiting's when it's malicious. We weren't being malicious.'

'Yeah, backbiting's when you let off steam about someone you don't really like, but pretend to like them to their face,' says I. 'Now, that one I *do* hate. If you don't like someone, you should just be upfront about it—let 'em know you don't like 'em.' (Yes! Just like Patricia does with me!) 'That kind of two-facedness really pisses me off—being nice to someone to their face, and then just showing how you really feel about them behind their backs.'

'Yeah, but sometimes it can be diplomatic to be friendly to someone you don't really like,' argues Esther. 'You know, if it's a friend of a friend; someone you're going to see a lot of when you're out and about.'

'You should tell that to your housemate,' I say. 'She doesn't display much "diplomacy" in her dealings with me.'

'Oh, yeah; Patricia... Well, I've tried to talk to her, y'know... but she can be stubborn...'

'Ha! Yeah, Patricia hates your guts!' crows Errol.

This seriously pisses me off. 'Shut up, Errol. She doesn't like you much either.' I reach for my cigarette packet.

'Not as much as she hates you!' persists the dorky git. 'You know what she said—?'

Esther raises an imperious hand. 'Time out, Errol; time out.'

'What? I was just going to tell him—'

'Yeah, well don't. That's called snitching, Errol. That's called telling tales. Telling people what someone else said about them behind their back is the worst.'

Errol withdraws into sulky silence. The sight of this pleases me.

Yuri snakes an arm around me, leans her head against my shoulder. 'Don't worry what that girl thinks about you,' she says, confidentially. '*I* like you.'

It's next morning and I wake up to find Yuri lying next to me. It startles me for a second. It's been a while since I've shared my mattress with anyone else. There she is, lying on her side, facing me. Her eyes are closed, her lips are parted and she's snoring softly. She looks different without her glasses…

It all comes back to me. My recall of the previous night is very good, so I must have paced myself with the drinking. Actually, I *know* must have paced myself with the drinking, because of the incredible sex I was able to have with Yuri when we got back here…

Yeah, it all seemed to work out well at the park last night… I can't take all the credit on myself, though; it must have been Yuri, as well; it must have been mutual; Yuri must have thought it was time to take things a few steps further, as much as I did…

We acted like a couple of kids, really. We teased each other, traded insults and good-natured racisms; giggling, prodding each other, playfighting… All touchy-feely, you know. It was a stupid, adolescent way of courting (especially for me, a guy who's pushing thirty), but it was still courting and it was fun and we enjoyed it and it worked, cuz by the end of the evening we were snogging. Even without the sex that came later, I would still have rated this the best night out I'd had in a long time.

As for the sex when we got back here, that was the best I've ever had. And I'm not just saying that; I mean it. It was Yuri that did it. As soon as we both got naked, she was all over me, like she wanted to eat me up or me to eat her up or something—and her being like that; it soon got me worked up into the same state. No-one's ever turned me on like that before. We just clicked, we just ignited each other. It was like our two bodies were made for each other, and we were frantically making up for the lost time, for all the wasted years we should have been together but weren't.

The duvet is already half off us; I pull it back all the way, gently, so's not to wake her. I want to look at her while she's still sleeping, look at her beautiful yellow body. Like I say, she's lying on her side, one hand resting on the pillow close to her face, palm upwards. She looks so peaceful, her eyes closed, her face relaxed, breathing softly and regular... I can smell her. This mattress only stank of me until last night, but Yuri's scent has asserted itself, marked out its territory. I just love the smell of her body... She's lying with her left leg bent, raising her hip, accentuating its curvature. I let my hand glide down the side of her body, over the ribcage, up and around the jutting hip and onto the smooth thigh. Her body responds to the contact; it twitches and she mutters something in Japanese, but her eyes stay closed; she hasn't woken up. I look at her breasts, small, pointed, with large, purple nipples and aureoles—those nipples and aureoles basically *are* her breasts. Now I track my vision down to the thick patch of pubic hair at the base of her abdomen, jet black like the hair on her head. My finger traces the line of downy hair extending from her thatch to the hollow of her belly-button... The bikini-line. That's what I used to think until embarrassingly recently—I thought that shaving the bikini-line meant getting rid of that 'line' of hair situated in-between the top and bottom halves of the bikini...

She is so fucking beautiful. Every little centimetre of her. If her body wasn't my ideal of physical perfection before, I know it is now. Yuri's body is the only body for me.

My fingers play with the thick curls of her pubic hair, and then move deeper, between her legs, rubbing her, arousing her. She starts to moan in her sleep...

And then her eyes open, focus on me. A smile, like the

rising sun, spreads itself across her face.

'Chad…' she says, slowly, in a broken half-whisper. She stretches out a hand, caresses my cheek. I kiss her palm, lick it. And she looks at me… she looks at me with these adoring eyes, looks at me half imploringly, like she loves me so much it hurts her… And me, I'm overwhelmed by it; I'm so fucking grateful and I wonder what I ever did to deserve having someone look at me with eyes like this…

Chapter Eight

There was a TV series back in the '90s called *Millennium*. It was produced by the makers of *The X-Files*, and was born from the serial killer episodes they'd made in that show. The premise was that the proliferation of serial killers in the States at that time was somehow connected to doom-and-gloom prophecies about the approaching millennium. The show ran for three seasons, but only just, because it was never actually that popular; they'd probably hoped the show would just be able to ride on the back of *The X-Files'* success, but it didn't; it was very dour, and it was never going to attract the same youth audience *The X-Files* had. And on top of that, they kept changing the format to try and make it more successful, but that just resulted in the series having an uneven feel to it, what with each of the three seasons having different people at the helm, trying to steer the show in different directions. As the show ended in the spring of '99, for the actual millennium a crossover episode with *The X-Files* was made to round off the story. In this country *Millennium* totally bombed. ITV bought the first season, but they pulled it from the schedules about half-way through, because people just weren't watching it. And the third season wasn't shown in the UK at all, at the time; it ended up getting its debut screening on the Sci-fi Channel, a few years post-millennium. These days you can watch the whole thing on

Amazon Prime.

Anyway, in the second season, there was this really good episode called 'A Room with No View' or 'A Room Without a View' (I can't remember which, off hand.) The episode was one of the ones with this sexy demonic woman called Lucy Butler—she was kind of a nemesis for Frank Black—and she was kidnapping high-school kids; kids that showed any spark of individuality, of originality, of non-conformity; and she was keeping these kids locked in bare rooms in this house in the middle of nowhere, and she was slowly grinding them down, breaking their spirit so that they'd just cave in and become regular people who would fit into society…

I'm mentioning this because I've got this idea in my head that something like that might be going on inside that building I saw the Sallow Man walk into; that Martin, Frank and Fiona, and whoever else has been taken away, are being kept prisoner in that place, and going through some sort of brainwashing. That's my theory. But then, this really huge ego I've got hidden away inside me (at least, I think it's hidden) says to me: 'Don't be a dick! If they were kidnapping all the originals, all the rebels; they'd have taken you first! Not people like Martin and Frank!'

I can't help feeling my ego might have a good point here. Still, the Sallow Man must've gone into that building for some reason; there's got to be something there.

It's now Monday and I'm with Esther and we're walking through town, on our way to that street and that courtyard I followed the Sallow Man to. (That's bad grammar, isn't it? Finishing a sentence with a word like 'to'? I should have said 'the courtyard to which I followed the Sallow Man,' shouldn't I?)

'So, is it true what they say about Japanese girls?' Esther asks me.

'I don't know. What do they say about Japanese girls?'

'Y'know, that in the sack they act like the pleasure's half-killing them, and they make the guy who's fucking her feel like he's a total sex god. Is that, Charles dear, a correct assessment?'

'Well, I can't speak about the entire female population of Japan,' I answer, letting the 'Charles' slide. 'But what you just said pretty much sums up how it was for me with Yuri.'

'Ooh, yeah!' whoops Esther. 'You the man! So, did she do that thing with her feet?'

'What thing?'

'You know; that Oriental thing: making you lick them.'

'Yeah, she did, as a matter of fact. I didn't get it at first, when she put her foot in my face; I thought she was trying to push me away.'

'Ha! That's good! Did you work it out for yourself or did she just say, "Rick!"?'

I look at her. 'That's exactly what she said. Have you got my place wired for sound and vision or something?'

'No, I was just thinking of the Japanese prostitute in *Lost in Translation*: "Lip my stockings!" ...Actually, is that right? Do they R their Ls, or L their Rs in Japan?'

'The kind of do both, really...'

Yuri stayed round mine all day yesterday; she stayed naked all day as well; and not just when we were fucking—no, I mean she watched TV with me naked, ate her food with me naked, smoked her cigarettes and drank her coffee with me naked. The idea was mine, I'll admit; but she was happy to go along with it, keeping her clothes off all day. She even said that from now on she'd always strip off ('disrobe,' she put it) whenever she came to my flat, as soon as she got in through the door, as a sign of her love for me. She said it made her happy because it made me happy—and Jesus Christ, I really don't know what I've done to deserve a girl like Yuri.

We're walking through the centre of town. There are people about but not too many. It's easy for someone like me to forget that it's quite a luxury to be able to go into town on a weekday morning, when the place isn't crowded—unlike the people who actually have full-time jobs, and who can only do their shopping on Saturdays when the place is jam-packed.

'So where is this place we're heading to?' asks Esther. 'What street's it on?'

'I don't know the name of the street.'

'You didn't think to look at the name? You could've googled it when you got home!'

'Look, I can find the street again, alright? It's off a street that's off the street where all the museums are. I don't need to know its name to find it again.'

'And our guy went into this courtyard and into one of the buildings.'

'Yep. Up a flight in stairs and in through a door.'

'And he didn't come out again.'

'Not for at least an hour, he didn't. Yuri had to go back to college, but I hung around to see if he came out again.'

'And he didn't come out.'

'Like I said; not for an hour.'

'What happened after an hour?'

'Well, I got bored with just standing there so I went home.'

'Not much of a detective, are you? They have to stake-out places for days on end, detectives do.'

'Yeah, but they get paid for doing it. That's an incentive.'

'And isn't your curiosity to find out all about this Sallow Man an incentive?'

'Well, yeah. But I still can't help getting bored just standing there on my own.'

'So you want me to stand with you this time?'

'If you want to stand and wait; but I thought you said you wanted to take the bull by the horns and go right up to the door he walked in through?'

'Well, that's the plan that will avoid all the standing around and waiting.'

'I agree. Let's do that.'

Soon we're walking through those gothic streets. We find the side-street and then the courtyard.

'That's it,' I say, pointing. 'The door at the top of those fire stairs.'

I look at Esther. She's looking round the courtyard. 'It doesn't exactly look residential,' she says. 'I doubt this is where the guy lives. Look there's a garage there. Maybe this place is a depot or something.'

'I thought we'd decided the warehouse in that photo was their depot.'

'Well maybe this is a smaller depot. Come on.'

We run across the courtyard and climb up the metal stairs. The stairs are rusty and rickety. I look back at Esther. She doesn't look nervous; she smiles at me. I know *I* feel nervous. What are we going to find up here? I feel like if I'm not already in this over my head, then I'm about to be in this over my head.

We arrive at the door. The door has peeling paintwork and glass in the upper panel. You can't see anything through the glass because there's a net curtain. The net curtain makes it look domestic, somehow; not like the entrance to some sinister brainwashing centre. There's a window to one side of the door, right over the garage. The window has net curtains too.

'Well, go on, then,' says Esther. 'Open the door.'

I take hold of the doorknob; it feels loose, like these old doorknobs usually are. I turn it; the door opens. I push it open.

Expecting a corridor, I'm surprised to see instead what looks like a shabby bedsit. There's a truckle bed, a chair, a table and a wardrobe. Everything looks old. The wallpaper is peeling, the furniture is old, the floor bare boards. There's no-one in the room.

'Looks like I was wrong,' says Esther. 'We've found the Sallow Man's digs. You'd have thought he would go for something posher than this.'

We step inside and look around. There's a small bathroom and a kitchenette adjoining the main room, both with old-looking fittings. A third door opens onto a stairwell.

'It doesn't look like the home of an archvillain, does it?' says Esther, after we've finished our survey.

'I dunno,' I say. 'Maybe the Sallow Man's one of these frugal, self-denying guys who doesn't believe in luxury and worldly possessions and he does what he does out of dedication, not for money.'

I see that Esther's grinning at me. 'Which would explain why he's sallow, right? Building up the guy's backstory, I see…'

I shrug. 'Well, you can't help doing that, can you?'

'Y'know, this might not even be his place. When he came here that day, he might have been visiting whoever lives here.'

'He walked straight in like he owned the place,' I say. 'And anyway, there's that.'

I point to a black jacket hanging on the partly-open door of the wardrobe.

'See? It's like the one he's wearing in the photos; the one he was wearing when I saw him.'

'Yeah…' Esther walks up to the wardrobe and takes hold of the jacket. Something falls out of it. She stoops and picks it up. 'Hello—what's this? A diary or something…? Ha! You might be right about this guy! Most people would have a digital notebook these days; but our Sallow Man likes to be old-fashioned.'

Before I can reply to this, I hear the sound of a heavy vehicle outside. I rush over to the window, pull back the net curtain. A beige van is pulling up in the courtyard below. It looks like one of the vans used by the removal men; it's the same colour as their pantechnicons.

'Shit!'

Esther joins me at the window.

Out of the van gets the Sallow Man and one of the removal men. The Sallow Man is wearing his black suit, complete with jacket identical to the one hanging in this room. The removal man is in the usual beige overalls and baseball cap. Are they going to head for the stairs or the garage?

The stairs, of course.

'Shit! They're coming!'

'Don't panic,' says Esther quietly. 'There's another way out of here, remember?'

Of course; the back stairs!

We cross the room to the stairwell. Once we close the door, we're in pitch darkness. We keep hold of each other as we descend the steep wooden stairs, treading carefully, trying to make as little noise as possible. Above us, I hear the outside door open.

We stop at the foot of the stairs. We hear voices above. Short, clipped sentences. We can't make out the words.

'Now what?' I breathe.

'There's a door here,' comes Esther's voice.

She opens the door and there's light. I follow Esther and see that we're in the garage. Dim light filters through the dirty windows of the garage doors; double rows of square panes along the top of each door. There's enough light to see that between us and those doors the room is full of junk; machine parts, piled up boxes. We weave our way through it.

We pause at the doors. I look at Esther's face in the dim light.

'Should we wait here till they've gone?' I ask.

'Nah, let's get out of here now if we can,' says Esther.

The garage doors are secured by a bar held by two brackets. Taking one end each, we quietly remove the bar, put it to one side, and Esther cautiously opens the door. I look over her shoulder. The courtyard is empty. From this angle we can see the fire stairs; the door to the apartment is closed.

'They're still inside,' says Esther. 'Come on—now's our chance!'

We slip out through the doors and dart across the cobbled courtyard, stopping when we've put the van between ourselves and the door above.

I'm all nerves, but smiling Esther just looks like she's enjoying herself.

'Now what, captain?' she asks.

'Don't ask me. I could say hide somewhere and wait for them to come out, but there'd be no point, really. We can't exactly follow this van.'

'Yeah, if this was one of your cheesy TV shows, then we'd have a handy tracking device to slap on the rear bumper and track the villains to their lair…' She reaches for the handle of the van's rear doors. The door opens.

'What are you doing?' I hiss, looking anxiously up at the door at the top of the fire-stairs.

'Looking for clues.'

She opens the door wide and steps into the back of the van. The interior space is almost empty; just one cardboard box, up near the partition dividing the back from the cab. Esther kneels beside the box and looks inside.

'Nothing interesting,' she reports. 'Just some of those beige overalls…' She starts shuffling through the clothes.

Then I hear a noise. The door above has opened and the two men are coming out.

'They're coming!' I hiss. 'Quick, get out!'

Esther looks through the window in the partition, then ducks down.

'Get in and shut the doors!' she hisses.

'What?'

'Just get in, you lummox! This is the perfect opportunity!'

There's no time to think. I jump into the van and close the door. I scuttle up to Esther.

'This is crazy!' I tell her. 'What if they open the back doors?'

'Why should they?' she argues. 'They're not carrying anything, are they? Just keep down and be quiet.'

Doors open in front of us and the van shakes as the two men get into the cab. And then the engine starts and we're reversing out of the courtyard.

And then we're off. There are no windows back here apart from the one looking into the cab, and after a couple of turns I've lost any idea of where we might be heading. And so, once again, just like that morning round Martin's, my life is turning into a spy thriller. It's different this time though, because there's Esther crouched right next to me. I feel reassured by her presence, but then a little voice pipes up: *You* feel reassured? It's supposed to be the over way round, isn't it? I mean if you find yourselves in danger, threatened with violence; it's you who's supposed to protect *her*, isn't it? You, the rugged and manly man.

And archaic stereotypes and perceived gender roles aside, I do still feel like there's truth in that; that I *am* the one who's supposed to protect the girl I'm with. I dunno if it comes from within me, this feeling; or if it's a result of external influence—but that's how I feel: that I'm the one who has to be the strong one, the protector. And right along with that feeling comes the awful knowledge of my complete inability to fulfil that role. How can I protect anyone from physical threat? I don't work out; I don't know any martial arts; and I have this strong suspicion that when it comes down to it, I'm a complete physical coward... Of course, lots of people walking around are probably physical cowards, but they never realise it, let alone have to feel bad about it, because they pass through life without ever getting into any situations that require from them physical bravery.

The realisation that I'm not alone in my pusillanimity doesn't make me feel any better though.

I look at Esther, crouched down beside me. She looks back at me with an encouraging smile.

So where are we headed? The obvious guess would be

that our destination's that warehouse that was in one of Martin's photographs. Good. Then we'll have learnt where their headquarters are. If only they park outside the warehouse and not inside it—then we should be able to get out and make a quick escape.

We've been driving for about twenty minutes when the van pulls up and honks its horn. The two men in the front cab haven't spoken a word; not a single word for the whole length of the journey. It doesn't seem natural. Now, we hear what sounds very much like the sound of a warehouse shutter door being raised. So we *are* at the warehouse from the picture! And we're not stopping outside; we're being taken inside the warehouse. The van moves forward again and then stops. The light shining through the narrow window above us is now yellow artificial light. The two men get out of the cab. The sound of the automatic shutter being lowered again. Then footsteps climbing hollow metal stairs.

And then silence.

'I think it's safe to go out now,' says Esther.

'Yeah.'

We open the back doors and step out. Right before us is the corrugated door. We move out from behind the van and see to the left, a flight of metal stairs, to the right, a wall with a door in it. Beyond the loading bay, the rest of the warehouse is in darkness. There are vague shapes in the gloom that look like stacks of boxes or crates.

'Let's try that door,' I say. 'We can probably get out that way.'

'I think we should look around first,' says Esther. 'Now that we're here.'

'And I think we should get out while we've got the chance.'

'Oh, come on.'

She heads off into the darkened part of the warehouse. I reluctantly follow her. As our eyes adjust, we see that there are indeed stacks of crates and cardboard boxes, and that's not all: there's furniture. Armchairs, sofas, beds, wardrobes, bookcases; piles of household furniture, all carefully stacked and secured with ropes.

And so it's all true. Here's the proof right in front of us. The disappearances. The removal men. It's all true. The last doubt, the last hope that there might be nothing to it, has evaporated.

I turn to Esther; I can see her face in the gloom.

'So this is where the removal men remove the furniture to,' I say. 'Now we know for sure those people haven't just moved away. Here's the proof. And all these boxes and crates here must be full of their belongings.'

'Yeah, but look at all this stuff, Chad. How many people have they removed? There's a lot more than just four people's stuff here.'

'Yeah, and what *about* the people? What's happened to them?'

We make a complete circuit of the warehouse. Apart from a fire-door in the rear door, there are no more doors, no more rooms. We arrive back at the parked van.

'Doesn't look like the people anyone's being held prisoner in this place,' says Esther.

'Do you think they're dead, then?'

She shrugs helplessly. 'I dunno. Let's take a look upstairs.'

'Are you insane? The Sallow Man's up there!'

'Come on, Chad. We should at least have a look while we're here. We might not get another chance.'

'Alright then.'

We return to the loading bay and, treading very softly, we climb the metal stairs. At the top of the stairs is a door with a window in it and what looks like normal daylight shining through from the next room.

Creeping up to the door, we peep through the glass panes. What we see is a large open-plan office. We can't see all of it from where we are, but the room seems to take up the entire upper floorspace on this side of the warehouse. A row of windows along the far wall let in the daylight. Filling the room are rows and rows of computer workstations. And at each one of them sits a removal man, headphones clamped to his ears, staring into the monitor screen, completely motionless, face expressionless. Several dozen removal men, all just sitting like statues, staring at the screens. The only exception is the Sallow Man, sitting at a desk right in front of us, like a teacher at the head of his class, flipping through some printed documents. I see his profile from where I am. His face is also expressionless, but there's life in it; he looks human, not a zombie like the others.

There's nothing else to see, so I nudge Esther, and we creep back downstairs.

'I dunno what the hell that was all about,' says Esther; 'but I don't think the missing people are being kept anywhere up there.'

'Doesn't look like it,' and returning to my favourite theme: 'Let's get out of here.'

I lead the way to the door on the other side of the loading bay. As I suspected, it opens into a front office; an unused office; carpet on the floor but no furniture. The door and full-length windows are screened by vertical blinds.

The door—thank God—is unlocked and we step outside. I feel a sense of relief, being out of that building and out in the sunshine again. Yes, this is the place in Martin's photograph. There's even one of the furniture vans parked outside. There are other warehouses around, some parked cars, but no sign of life.

'This definitely isn't one of the industrial sites we checked out,' says Esther, looking around.

'Let's get going,' I say. 'There're windows up there. Someone might look out and see us.'

'Okay. Looks like the exit's over there.'

I light a much-needed cigarette and offer one to Esther. We make our way out of the industrial estate and following an access road we find ourselves out on the main road. Hedgerows on both sides; no footpaths. It looks like we're out in the countryside.

'I think we came from that way,' says Esther, pointing to the right.

'Yeah,' I agree. 'Come on. We can't be too far out of Cambridge.'

We set off along the road; and it's not long before it becomes a street of houses. There's a church tower visible up ahead.

Esther chuckles.

'I know where we are,' she declares. 'This is Coldham's Lane. We're in Cherry Hinton. Just back thataway is that wasteland from Martin's photographs. We're a pair of prawns, aren't we? We were looking at the wrong end of it for warehouses.'

I smile. 'Yeah, well, at least now we know where the warehouse is.'

'Yeah, and we might know a lot more besides.'

'How'd you mean?'

'We've got this!'

Esther pulls a pad from her back pocket. And then I remember—the notebook that fell out of the Sallow Man's jacket. And Esther's still got it!

Chapter Nine

Ten people!

That's how many people have been Disappeared by the removal men. At least, that's what it looks like, going by the contents of the Sallow Man's notebook. Martin's name and address is there, crossed off. So are Frank and Fiona's. And seven other names and addresses, including Laura and Paul, the two people Esther mentioned. People I only vaguely knew, some of them, but all of them still people who could be roughly described as being part of our 'set.' And all ten of them are just thought to have moved away from the Cambridge area. Nobody misses them and nobody cares. The Sallow Man knows how to select their victims. It's like this Disappearing project fits right into the scheme of things; like it's not a rogue element but something that's meant to happen; part of the movement of the social mechanism. Maybe it's always been happening; maybe the removal men have always been at work, moving from one town to another, quietly filling their annual quota of Disappearances; removing the required number of statistics from the columns of the electoral register...

Does the Government know about this? Or is it something bigger than governments? Governments come and go, but behind them there's this vast mechanism that keeps this country in motion; and it's a machine that keeps on running the same way, and it doesn't matter which party happens to be in power; the machine just keeps on running...

We're sitting in the beer garden at a pub in Cherry Hinton, Esther and me. It's a nice day and we're eating sandwiches and drinking beer, and I at least, am trying hard to feel like there's still a normal, everyday world around us.

There are other random jottings in the Sallow Man's book: the names of local bands, the dates of gigs at local venues. Has he been at all of these gigs, the Sallow Man? Esther saw him at one of them. Why does he go to them? Is he a music fan? Or is he spying on us?

'Look at this,' says Esther, showing me a page of the book. The Sallow Man's handwriting is small, and neat; the handwriting of a very meticulous, very organised person. '"Herschell House."'

'Where's that?' I ask.

'I dunno... But I've heard of it; I'm pretty sure it's in Cambridge... There's no name with it, though; just "Herschell House." I'll have to Google it later.'

'Can't you do it now? You've got your phone.'

'Yeah, but I'm out of credit.'

I drink some more of my beer, while Esther leaves through the notebook. We're the only ones out here in the beer garden; this pub doesn't seem to get much of a lunchtime crowd.

'Oh fuck,' says Esther.

'What is it?'

She looks at me. 'Another address; and this one's not crossed out. Dwayne and Vicky's address.'

Dwayne and Vicky live in Romsey Town, just a few streets away from Esther's place. They're married and they're anarchists—and I mean in the serious, card-carrying UK Anarchist Party membership way. They call themselves 'activists,' although I'm not sure exactly what 'activities' they get up to, and they boast that their post gets screened by the police.

'Dwayne and Vicky? Just their address? Are there any more?'

'Nope, there aren't any more; it's the last entry in the notebook—see? After that the pages are blank.'

'Then it's got to mean that they're going to be the next victims!' I declare. 'They're going to be Disappeared!'

'Yeah, if they haven't done it already,' is Esther's response. 'I'll ring them up. If they're in, we can go over there and warn them. Those two: if anyone's gunna believe our story it's them!'

'Bullshit.'

Yes, that's Dwayne's response. I'm sitting next to Esther on one sofa in Dwayne and Vicky's front room; Dwayne and Vicky are sitting on the other sofa. They're a pretty bland and boring couple, really. Don't expect them to look eccentric and alternative just because they're anarchists—they take themselves way too seriously for that. I remember them once proudly showing everyone an interview with them that was in some underground magazine. The feature opened with Dwayne proudly saying, 'We, of the Cambridge Anarchist Party, are opposed to capitalism and all forms of government.' Oh, *really?* Well, stick a daffodil up my arse and call me Wilfrid Hyde-White—who would've thought that a bunch of anarchists would be opposed to capitalism and all forms of government? I think Esther was expecting too much from these idiots when she said they'd believe our story.

'I detect scepticism,' she says. Dwayne's someone who doesn't particularly like me (and the feeling's mutual), so I've been leaving the talking to her.

'Well yes, I am a tad sceptical,' says Dwayne. (His brand of sarcasm is very mainstream for a so-called extremist.) 'I'm an activist; I'm not one of those loony conspiracy-theorists who believes every stupid story they hear—removal men who act like robots and take away people as well as their furniture—Go'n tell that one to David Icke.'

'Look, I know it's a bit out there,' says Esther, still being diplomatic. 'But it's not like we haven't got any proof.'

'Oh yes, your *proof*,' sneers Dwayne, trading smug looks with his wife. 'Chad follows this 'Sallow Man' back to his house. You both go there and very conveniently find this notebook that tells you about all the people who have disappeared, and that we're next on the list.'

'But we've *shown* you the notebook,' says Esther, brandishing the book in question. 'You don't think we faked this, do you?'

'Actually, we *do* think you faked it,' says Dwayne.

'But why would we do something like that?' persists Esther.

'Say, "Why would *he* do something like that."' (Meaning me, of course.) 'Why *you're* going along with it, I don't know. I never thought you were like him.'

'And just what are you accusing me of?' I speak up.

'I'm accusing you of making this whole thing up.'

'And why would he do that?' asks Esther.

'To trick us, of course. Yes... you think you're better than us, don't you?' says Dwayne, actually condescending to look at me and address me in the first person. 'You look down your nose at us, don't you? Just because we're serious about our politics, and actually get things done—but you think you're more of a rebel than we are just because you're bone-idle, unemployed and you watch *The Prisoner*.'

'I think you might be overestimating your own importance, here,' Esther tells him. 'I think Chad here would consider it a complete waste of his valuable time to play some elaborate prank on you two.' Turning to Vicky: 'You've been letting Dwayne do all the talking—do you agree with him on this?'

'Well, yes,' she says. 'This story of yours has got to be a put-on.'

'Look, if you want more convincing,' says Esther; 'we've only got to go down Coldham's Lane and have a look at that warehouse.'

Vicky looks at her husband. 'Actually, yeah... If I saw that warehouse, I'd have to think there was something in their story. What do you think?'

'They faked it,' says Dwayne.

'We couldn't fake a warehouse full of people's furniture and belongings!' says Esther.

'She's got a point,' says Vicky.

Dwayne slaps his hands down on his thighs. 'Alright then. Let's go there; let's go there now and have a look at this place. We'll go in the car—that alright with you two?'

'Wouldn't it be better for us to wait till after dark...?' I suggest.

'No, it wouldn't,' is the firm response. 'We'll go *now*.'

So we get into Dwayne's crappy old car. He's at the wheel, with Esther in the passenger seat to show the way, and I'm in the back with Vicky. We get out onto Coldham's Lane—a process which involves crawling along a maze of narrow one-way streets with frequent speed bumps and other 'traffic calming' measures—and head towards Cherry Hinton.

'Shouldn't we stop and park somewhere before we get there and walk the rest of the way?' I suggest.

'No, we'll just drive right up to the place,' says Dwayne. 'No messing around.' He's in a pig-headed mood, so I don't waste my breath arguing with him. He won't be copping an attitude in a minute, when he sees we've been telling the truth.

'It's the first right just before we get to Cherry Hinton,' says Esther.

We arrive, we turn onto the access road, and when we get to the warehouses, there's our warehouse—except there's no removal van parked outside and there's a sign over the office entrance saying 'Jacobson Printing'! There wasn't any signboard up there a few hours ago.

'What the fuck?' says Esther.

'Have we driven into the wrong place?' I demand, looking around.

'No; this is definitely the right place…'

'What's wrong?' asks Dwayne, stopping the car. 'Where's this sinister warehouse?'

'Well, it's this one,' admits Esther. 'But it's changed. There was no sign saying 'Jacobson Printing' there before.'

'I thought you were only here a couple of hours ago.'

'We were. Three at the most.'

'Oh, I *see*,' says Dwayne, oozing more of his commonplace sarcasm. 'So, the sinister conspirators have covered up their tracks since you were here three hours ago and they've turned the removal men's warehouse into an innocent printing factory! Now why didn't we guess that was going to happen?'

'Well they must have done that…' Esther doesn't sound convinced herself.

I get out of the car.

'Come on,' I say. There's got to be some clue…'

Esther joins me.

'Yeah, we should look around, they might—'

Her sentence is cut off by the slamming of doors, and the revving of an engine. Dwayne's car performs a neat three-point turn and disappears back down the access road.

I look at Esther.

'I think we can take that as their final answer,' I say. 'Nice of them to leave us to walk back.'

'Well, we tried to warn them…' says Esther. She turns towards the warehouse. 'I don't get this. They didn't even know we were here, did they?'

'They must have known,' I reply. 'They must have seen us leave, and they must've guessed we'd come back, so they quickly hid the removal van and put up that fake sign.'

We walk up to the warehouse which now says it's the home of 'Jacobson Printing.' Below the sign is the empty front office we walked through before, with the same vertical blinds—except that now the blinds are open and the office isn't empty; there's a man working at a desk inside. The shutter door is partially raised, and Esther ducks under it. I follow her.

All the lights are on in the warehouse and where three hours ago there were stacks of boxes and furniture, now there's a printing machine going at full throttle and several people in overalls working at it. I see it but I don't believe it.

We stand there gawping for a bit, then Esther walks up to the nearest employee, a woman in her thirties. The woman smiles when she sees us.

'Can I help?'

'Yeah, we're looking for a removal company…' says Esther. 'We thought their warehouse was here…'

The woman shakes her head. 'No… There's no removal firm on this estate. You must have the wrong place, love.'

'I suppose we must have… What about you? Has this place been here long?'

'Well, I've worked here about three years, but the firm's been here about ten years I think…'

There's nothing more to say, so we make our excuses. The woman is lying of course, but there would be no point trying to take her up on it.

We're walking back across the loading bay. Esther grabs my arm.

'Come on,' she says. 'Let's have a look upstairs.'

The woman has turned back to the printing machine and we scamper up the metal stairs. The same pair of doors face us at the top, but when we look through them the scene has completely changed. It's still an open-plan office, but the rows of her terminals have gone; and the floorspace is smaller because at the back of the room there are now a number of partitioned-off offices. The office has a small staff; two women sitting at desks, one of them typing, the other talking on the phone. A third woman is standing at a photocopying machine. Through the window of one of the partition-walled offices a man is visible seated at a desk, also talking on the phone.

My eyes meet Esther's. Silently we descend the staircase and leave the warehouse.

'This is impossible,' declares Esther when we're back outside. 'They couldn't have just cleared out like that and set up this fake printing company; they *couldn't*—not in three hours. *Chad*.' I look at her. She looks scared now; for the first time today, she looks scared. 'It's not possible…'

'It's got to be possible,' I reply. It's not much of an answer, and I look away from her when I say it.

'And have they cleared out for good?' says Esther. 'Or have they just cleared out from this place?'

I see what she means. Have they abandoned their project because we found their base? Have they packed up and gone home? Or have they just set up shop somewhere else?

'We'll know the answer to that one if Dwayne and Vicky disappear,' I say.

Chapter Ten

A round, brick building, with a cone-shaped roof, flattened at the top. Walking through a gap in the hedgerow, I come upon it suddenly. The building stands in a small field, surrounded by trees. It has an open, doorless, doorway, and looks old and unused. The walls of the building are made of yellow bricks, the roof is dark brown.

I remember a building similar to this one from my childhood; but I don't think this is the same one. What *are* these round buildings? You see them all over the countryside… Are they grain silos…? Or those places where they used to keep doves…?

Well, I can't stop here and investigate; I've got somewhere to be.

Leaving the building behind, I move on through the still, silent countryside. The sky overhead is colourless, neutral. The air is warm and still. I haven't seen a soul or heard a sound.

I come to a stream with a hump-backed bridge with a sluice-gate. The bridge is very old. After this, I cross a harvested corn field. On the verge at the far side is the rusting wreck of a car; from the shape of the bodywork, the fenders, it looks very old—from the fifties at least. The paintwork that still clings to is a sickly pink colour; probably it was once a bright red. Back in Mepal when we were kids, we knew where all the wrecked and abandoned cars were supposed to be; some of them were legendary.

I pass through a copse of trees and there it is—the thing that I'm looking for. It's way out across the flat fields—the building, the enigmatic building; a white rectangular box standing alone in the cheerless landscape.

That building again. The one I keep dreaming about…

Am I dreaming right now? There's something there, something waiting for me in that building; an answer; the solution to a mystery; something… I don't know how I know it, but I know. I know I have to get to that building; I have to get to it before I wake up or else everything will just fade away…

I set off across the fields, walking fast, keeping my eyes fixed on my target.

Easy… easy… Just keep going… You can make it…

And then I wake up. I'm lying on my mattress in my bedroom. It's daylight and I'm alone. I get out of bed, go to the window and pull back the curtain.

He's there, down in the street below: The Sallow Man. Dressed in black as usual, leaning against the bonnet of a black car, arms folded, staring right up at my window. Our eyes meet…

I wake up with a start. I'm lying on the mattress in my bedroom. It's daylight and I'm alone. The dream-images are still clear in my mind.

I smile, almost laugh: I've never had a dream with a false ending before. At least, I don't think I have. And am I really awake now, or is this another false ending? I get up and go to the window. When I pull back the curtains, there's no-one in the carpark below.

It's raining this afternoon, so I'm wearing my parka with the hood up. I turn into the industrial estate off Cherry Hinton Road. Nope, I'm not here looking to see if this is where the removal men have relocated to, and yes, I am getting pretty sick of looking at industrial estates; but this particular industrial estate happens to be the location of the headquarters of the philanthropic foundation who I'm currently a client with, and today I've got an appointment with my keyworker.

Nothing's happened since that day we found the Sallow Man's headquarters. Dwayne and Vicki haven't been whisked off the face of the Earth. There's part of me that wishes they *do* get taken away; that it would be their well-deserved comeuppance for not believing me and Esther and for driving off and leaving us like that. But no... Esther's friends with them on Facebook, and they're still around. (And a nice pair of anarchists they are, using Facebook! You can bet they'll have some excuse ready, though; like they're 'Hijacking the System' or something...)

And another thing about that adventure: when I told Yuri all about it, I didn't get the reaction I was looking for at all; she seemed really pissed off. Insensitive man that I am, it took me a while to work it out; but I finally got it—she was jealous; jealous that I'd had this adventure with Esther and not with her. I've got to keep Yuri in the loop about this business...

I think I said before that this foundation I'm with is devoted to finding work placements for the terminally unemployable. And by terminally unemployable I don't mean those shiftless people who are always on and off the dole because they're bad workers and can't hold down a job—I'm referring to the long-term mentally ill; that's who these people specialise in helping out. They find voluntary work or work placements for us, and then they monitor our progress. The idea is that a successful placement might become a permanent parttime or even a fulltime job. I think some anonymous millionaire finances the foundation. Perhaps he's sympathetic cuz he's had mental illness in the family or something...

I told you about what happened at my last work placement, didn't I? How I got fed-up of being bossed around by this arsehole office junior; and I started swearing and throwing things around...? This will be the first time I've seen my keyworker since that incident; I'm wondering what she's going to say. The place I was at is bound to have made a complaint about me, which means I've probably caused some embarrassment to my keyworker and to the foundation. (I think Yuri would say that I've 'shamed' them.) It's not like I'm expecting a bollocking from my keyworker;

not from Susan. Susan's not the type to administer bollockings. She's not exactly what you'd call assertive. Mousy, is the word I think of for her. I don't mean the colour of her hair; I mean she's like a mouse: all quiet-spoken and timid.

I arrive at the foundation building, a small one-storey building dwarfed by the warehouses around it, and I walk into the front office.

'Hello, Chad,' the receptionist greets me. 'Still raining is it?'

The receptionist's name is Alice, and she looks like someone's cheerful old granny. I don't know if she's actually past retirement age, but she must be getting close.

I confirm that it is indeed still raining.

'Well, they say it won't last long. Just a passing shower. Sit yourself down. Susan will be with you soon. She's just with another client at the moment; they're running a bit late.'

I take my parka off and sit down. There's nowhere to hang it up so I just throw my coat on the empty chair next to me, wet side up.

'There's another thing about that missing airliner in the news,' proceeds Alice, typing on her computer while she speaks to me. 'They're saying all sorts of things about it; like the passengers have been sold into slavery; taken to a forced-labour camp somewhere...'

The fate of Flight 714 is still the big mystery of the day. It's been more than a year now, since the plane disappeared on a regular flight from Djakarta to Beijing. At first they thought that it must have been engine failure and that the plane went down in the South China Sea; but they've been searching for a year and they've never been able to find the wreckage. Usually when planes go down in the ocean they find 'em pretty soon, because the black box flight recorder's supposed to send out a tracking signal; so the fact that it hasn't in this case has sparked all kinds of wild theories about what might have happened to the plane and the people in it. And they're not just coming from the conspiracy nuts, but also from relatives of the crew and the passengers; these people prefer to believe that their loved ones are alive and in trouble than that they're just fish food—and so there are all these theories like that they've been sold into slavery by pirates, that they're being held captive on an island that's not on the map, or that they've gone through a time-warp into a parallel universe; theories that remind you of that TV series *Lost*. (And don't get me started about the last episode of that one…)

'It's all nonsense, isn't it?' says Alice. 'Mind you, I know they've got those forced labour out there. You hear stories about it happening in China, don't you?'

'China's like one great big factory,' I say. 'But yeah, they'll probably find out that plane just crashed off course or something…'

Speaking of plane crashes, I always wonder about that famous Concorde disaster in France. It's always seemed to me that the pilot must have deliberately crashed his plane into that hotel. I mean, it was an isolated hotel, wasn't it? Open countryside all around it. Surely they could have avoided it? But maybe when the plane was going down, the pilot, knowing he was a dead man, just went completely off his rocker and decided if he was going to die, he'd take as many other people with him as possible—and so he deliberately aimed his plane at the one big building in sight. I can imagine him speaking over the intercom: 'This is your pilot speaking. As you will see on your left, the port engine is ablaze, we are losing altitude, and we are all going to die when the aircraft hits the ground. So please feel free to unfasten your seatbelts and run up and down the aisles panicking and screaming in terror. Thank you for flying with Air France…'

I shared this theory of mine with Esther one time, and she said it said more about my warped imagination than it did about anything else.

Susan, my keyworker, now walks into the room, seeing off her last client. The client is a girl I know from some group activity sessions we've had here; I forget her name. She's one of those neurotic, quick to fly off the handle types. I can't deal with that sort. Girls like that are the last kind of girl I'd want to be going out with. I think it's attraction of opposites—I'm messed up, so I know that the best girl for me is one who's got her shit together.

After seeing the girl off, Susan comes up to me. 'Good afternoon, Charles,' she says. (She insists on calling me Charles, and for some reason, I actually let her.) She's a small bespectacled woman, is Susan. Usually wears a woolly cardigan. I don't know her age, but I reckon she's a few years older than I am. I'm looking for signs of disapproval, but her greeting is the same, and her expression as bland, as usual.

I follow her along the corridor to her cubbyhole of an office.

We sit down, and Susan takes up my folder.

'How are you this afternoon, Charles?' she begins.

'Okay, I guess,' I reply.

'And I understand that you've stopped attending your current work placement…?'

'Er, yes… yes, I have.'

'In fact, there was a bit of an incident there, wasn't there?'

I look at her. Her voice and expression are both still neutral.

'You could call it that,' I agree, forcing a smile.

'Would you like to talk about it?'

I take a deep breath. 'It was that git Darren,' I say. 'He kept bossing me around every chance he got; all the bloody time. I was always working too slow, he said. Even if I was doing photocopying, he'd tell me I was working too slow—like I could make the machine run any faster! Nobody else said I was a slow worker, cuz I bloody wasn't; it was just him; he was just always on my case. And I know why he was on my case as well: it's because he was the one at the bottom of the office ladder before I came along, and he's just one of those sad gits who'll boss someone around whenever they think they've got a chance to—and I bloody well wasn't going to stand around and let him boost his sad little ego at my expense.' Another deep breath. 'So, that was it; I decided to quit.'

'I see…' says Susan. 'And don't you think you could have perhaps calmly explained the situation and your concerns to him, instead of becoming violent and abusive?'

She had me there. 'Well, yes, I suppose I should have…' I concede. 'But he was such a total cunt! (Pardon my French.) If I'd tried to be reasonable with him, he would've probably just said I was giving him lip or something.'

'Well, trying to talk it through is still better than flying off the handle. You know I had to apologise to the people there,' she tells me, trying to sound firm. 'And they say they won't take any more clients from this foundation.'

I thought it was going to be something like that.

'Sorry,' I say. 'But at least I didn't hit the guy, did I? And Christ knows I felt like hitting him.'

Susan heaves a sigh. I sympathise with that sigh.

'What are we going to do with you, Charles? Do you have any ideas where you would like to try next?'

'Not another office,' I say firmly. 'I just don't like the whole set-up of offices. The hierarchy. The having to smile and be nice to people you don't really like.'

'We all have to do that Charles…'

Hang on a minute; is she saying she doesn't like me? No; probably just being paranoid.

'I know most people say doing that's a normal part of life, but I don't like it. It just seems so insincere to me. Being nice to someone's face, slagging them off behind their back. I think if you don't like someone you should just not talk to them at all.'

I know I'm repeating part of one of our conversations from Saturday night at Christ's Piece here—but Susan wasn't with us then, so it's not a repeat to her.

'We all have to interact with people we're not that fond of, Chad,' she tells me. 'It's just good manners to be polite to people, whatever your personal feeling for them might be.'

'Well, I don't like it,' I insist. (Stubborn, aren't I?) 'So, like I say—I don't want another office placement.'

'Then what else do you want to do? A placement in a shop? We could start you off volunteering in a charity shop, perhaps...'

'Nah, I don't fancy that,' I say. 'You've still got people who boss you around. I think I've got authority issues. I don't like being told what to do.'

'That's something else most people have to put up with in life,' says Susan. 'Don't you think that perhaps you're being a bit too picky, Charles? Don't you have any dreams? Any goals?'

I have to think about this. I tend to be a 'one day at a time' person—at least, I have been lately. I don't like to think in terms of long-term goals. 'I dunno...'

'There must be something.'

'Well, there was the band...'

'A band? What sort of band?'

'A rock band. I was the guitarist. This was a few years back. I was all fired up about it at the time; I was sure we were going to be big...! But then the vocalist left and we couldn't find a decent replacement. I had a go at being the singer myself, but I couldn't get the hang of singing and playing at the same time...'

'You could start another band, couldn't you?'

'Nah... Don't feel like it at the moment.'

'How about working in a music shop or a record shop?'

'*What* music shop or record shop? They've all closed down! Anyway, I said I don't fancy working in a shop.'

'Well, is there anything else, Charles? If you could pick anything, is there anything else you'd like to do?'

'Wouldn't mind being a scriptwriter,' I say. 'You know; for television. *Doctor Who*'s really been going downhill lately…'

'That's something. Have you written any scripts and tried sending them off?'

'Well, no… I haven't been inspired recently…'

I hear another deep sigh.

'Then what *do* you want to do, Charles?'

I wish I knew myself.

Chapter Eleven

Most people in Cambridge who don't drive cars have bicycles. Cambridge is famous for being a city of cyclists. Everybody commutes by bicycle, so it seems—which means that bicycle theft is a thriving local industry. Not being in possession of a bicycle, our hero Chad Fenton is one of a stubborn minority.

Esther owns a bicycle, and this fine morning, she makes her way to Muriel and Mel's house by means of this conveyance. Like Chad, Mel and Muriel live in Kings Hedges; they share a house on one of the newer estates on the edge of town, close to Kings Hedges Road.

Arriving, Esther parks her bicycle outside the semidetached house, and locks it up. (The bike wouldn't be there when she came out, if she didn't take this precaution.)

Muriel, tall, short-haired and taciturn, answers the door.

'Hello come in,' she says in one breath, while something like a smile briefly intrudes upon her expressionlessness.

Esther follows Muriel into the living room where Mel sits on one of the sofas, a seat she shares with two cats. These feline siblings, one black and white, one ginger and white, are named Buffy and Dawn, and in common with most cats who cohabit, they do not get along. The cats are named after characters from *Buffy the Vampire Slayer*, a television series with which the two girls are completely obsessed. (This is a common complaint amongst women, and in the case of heterosexual couples has been known to lead directly to the breakup of many a relationship.) Mel is superficially Muriel's opposite, being short of stature, long-haired and garrulous.

'Hey!' says Esther.

'Hey yourself,' says Muriel. 'Haven't you got a bag with you? Where's your stuff?'

'I'm wearing it!' is the cheerful reply.

After making a brief fuss of the cats, Esther stands to survey the room. It's naturally a small living room, but furnished and decorated with an aesthetic eye in a medley of pastel shades, it looks light and airy.

'Yeah…' she says, taking stock. 'This'll do nicely.'

'Oh, are you sure?' says Mel. 'Cuz if you don't like it, we'll just redecorate the whole room for you…'

'No, I'll let you off.'

Mel changes the subject. 'You'll never guess who I saw.'

'Who did you see?' dutifully inquires Esther.

'Dexter.'

Esther frowns. 'Dexter…? Dexter…? Dexter's Laboratory…? Ooh, I've got it! Your stalker from way-back-when.'

'That's him. He was in the Champion, and he actually had a girl with him.'

'That's good, then. If he's got himself a girlfriend, he can start becoming more normal. Did you say hello?'

'Nope. He looked dead embarrassed when he saw me there—like he was dreading I was gunna come up to him and badmouth him to his girlfriend or something. So I let him off the hook and just pretended I didn't know him.'

'Probably for the best,' says Esther. 'Can we use this sofa then?' indicating the second, and unoccupied, long sofa.

'Yes, if it's alright for you.'

'Ooh, and what about that chair over there?' pointing to a

corner of the room. 'Can we bring that over?'

Muriel brings forth the chair under discussion, an antique-looking mahogany chair with an upholstered seat.

'Yeah, that'll be perfect,' says Esther. 'You haven't got net curtains,' she observes, looking at the window which takes up most of the length of the front wall. 'Do we need to worry about the neighbours?'

'Fuck the neighbours,' says Mel. (You don't find much community spirit around these parts.)

Esther sits down to pull off her trainers, revealing the feet inside them to be encased in blue tights or stockings.

'I guess he wasn't actually a stalker,' says Mel, reverting to the subject of Dexter. 'He was just annoyingly persistent. He was always like, "We'll look back on this and laugh in years to come!" and I was like, "No, we fucking won't!" He just wouldn't get it through his thick head that I wasn't interested.'

Esther pulls off her jumper, under which is a very expensive brassiere, sky blue in colour. 'Yeah, I know the type,' she says. 'Those guys just get the idea stuck in their heads that you'll start to like them when you see how much they like you. They're just convinced that the only problem is that you don't know them well enough, and that once you *do* get to know them better, that you'll like them more. They just get fixated like that.'

'Yep, he was a real pain for a while back then,' agrees Mel. 'I ended up having to threaten him with a restraining order and if he didn't back off.'

'Would you really have done that?' rising to take off her jeans.

'Only as a last resort.'

'I remember once this girl saying to me, and real boastfully as well, that she'd had restraining orders put on three different blokes, and I thought, "Yeah, well that probably says more about *you* than it does about the three blokes."'

Having shed her outer clothes, Esther now stands wearing a very stylish lingerie set: bra, knickers, stockings and suspender-belt, all lacy in design, and sky blue in colour. It's the kind of underwear you'd expect to find lurking under an expensive evening gown, or a designer business suit, rather than under a pair of well-worn jeans and a jumper.

'Well, are we all ready?' she asks.

'I am,' says Muriel, camera in hand.

Yes, it's a photo-shoot; and the purpose of this shoot is that Esther wants to compile a 'profile': a set of professional-looking images she can submit for approval to some of the top-shelf magazines. She yearns to see herself on those glossy pages. 'Anyone can just post their porn-pics online,' argues Esther. And that's just not enough for her: Esther aspires to the distinction of actually being featured in one of the printed magazines. She knows she's a 'plus-size'—at least by the standards of the fashion industry—but the porn industry is much more politically correct than the world of fashion when it comes to size; there's not nearly as much in the way of body-fascism. As you will remember Chad telling us, she has already scored a hit as a striptease artist, and she is now eager to branch out into other areas of the sexual exploitation industry.

Mel and Muriel have very kindly offered their living room as a venue for this endeavour, with Muriel very eager to take upon herself the duties of photographer.

The shoot begins, with Esther taking to the sofa for the first set of pictures. She poses herself, and Mel and Muriel suggest poses. For the first group of shots, she remains 'fully' dressed, but then, inevitably, the bra and knickers have to go, and she retains only the stockings and suspender-belt.

Seated on the chair, she lifts her leg and she turns her foot to the camera. 'This is the big fetish in Japan, at the moment,' she announces. 'The soles of the feet through tights and stockings. Chad heard that one from Yuri.'

'Yeah, how are those two getting on?' asks Mel.

'Like a towering inferno,' replies Esther. 'Can't keep their hands off each other, from the sounds of things. I'm glad Chad's got himself another girlfriend. It's what he needed.'

'Yeah, but she won't be around forever, will she?' says Mel. 'She's only got a student visa.'

'Well, if it works out long-term, she can move over here, can't she? Or Chad could move to Japan… He'd need to learn the language, though…'

The posing continues. Esther goes back to the sofa for some rear-end shots Muriel, down on one knee, takes shot after shot.

'The camera loves you,' she says. It's unclear whether this is addressed to Esther in her entirety, or just her buttocks.

'How about a turtle's head shot, while I'm here?' suggests Esther.

'Don't you dare!' yells Mel. 'You'll stink the room out!'

'Only kidding!'

Presently, they pause for a coffee and cigarette break, Mel doing the honours in the kitchen.

'You really want to go all the way with this porn thing?' asks Mel, when they have settled down with their drinks.

'Yeah, I'd like to try everything at least once,' says Esther.

'Even the films?'

'Yep!'

'You know you'll have to work with some really sleazy people in that industry…'

Esther just shrugs. 'Comes with the territory, doesn't it?'

'Gunna draw the line at anal?'

'Nah… I'm up for that.'

Mel looks studies her friend. 'Did you have a really strict upbringing?'

Esther laughs at this. 'Ha! No, I'm not rebelling against anything, doing this. It's just something I thought I'd like to try.'

Mel takes a drag of her cigarette. 'What about

prostitution?'

'No, I'm not interested in that.'

'What about BDSM? Dominatrix stuff?'

'No, not that, either. I mean yeah, I'd do it if it was for a film or a photo-shoot; but not as a service. I'm only interested in the performance art side of the sex business; not the, y'know, the one-on-one retail service kind of thing.'

Muriel, meanwhile is studying Esther's crotch. 'You're not blonde,' she says. 'Down there.'

No, I'm not,' agrees Esther, looking down at herself. 'I don't mind; I like my beige bush. Some blond people have blond pubes, but it seems to be the minority...'

'So, you think Chad's calmed down now?' asks Mel. 'He really lost it at that place he was working at, didn't he?'

'Yeah...' says Esther, pulling a face. 'He did. But it does sound like this other guy was a real arsehole who was really giving him a hard time. Things like that can set him off.'

'Keep taking the tablets,' says Muriel.

'He does,' says Esther.

Thinking of Chad makes Esther think of the Sallow Man, the Disappearances; all that insane stuff... She looks at the two women facing her, and she wonders what it would be like if she told them about it. But maybe just to even tell them about it would be to drag them into it...? She likes Mel and Muriel; she likes the whole 'it's you and me against the world' thing they've obviously got going... Should she...? Should she mention it...? Maybe not. She knows that Chad, aside from telling Yuri, doesn't want to tell other people about it, wants to keep a lid on it... She was the one he came to first. He had this problem weighing him down and he came to her... She's known Chad since they were at secondary school together; back when they used to read Camus and Dostoevsky, while all the other kids were reading Harry Potter and Stephen King...

Nothing's happened since Monday; nobody's come and spirited away Dwayne and Vicki. She's Googled Herschell

House: it's not actually in Cambridge, but out in the countryside, towards Grantchester; it's a big place, like a stately home, or something. She hasn't been able to find out who lives there…

Switching her mood, Esther drains her coffee cup, noisily smacks her lips.

'Thanks for that!' she says. 'Back to the photography. How about I do some shots with your cats?'

Mel's eyes saucer—so do the cats'.

'Forget it!' she snaps. 'You're not dragging Buffy and Dawn into your sordid world!'

Chapter Twelve

Yuri showed me a music video of this Japanese girl band (who were actually based in London, but were still Japanese girls); and they were walking along this footbridge, and they were walking in single file, they were wearing identical black dresses, and they were walking along in this exaggerated marching kind of way, with big smiles on their faces—and somehow, it didn't seem silly at all. It was like it just seemed totally natural that this trio of Japanese women in their late twenties (they might even have been in their thirties; you can't always tell with Jap women) should be walking along a footbridge like that. But then, imagine if it was some white English girl band doing the same thing—the effect would be completely different; it would look totally embarrassing; you'd just want to tell the women to stop making complete tits of themselves. Only Japanese women can walk along a footbridge like that and get away with it.

Actually, there are a number of things that only Japanese women can get away with: flat chests, major overbites, and falling arse over tit without losing their feminine dignity.

There was this television historian (and I mean an historian *of* television, not an historian *on* television) who once put his foot in it by saying that the reason all the best UK sitcoms (ones like *Porridge* and *Dad's Army*) had all-male casts was because only men were funny. That's what he said. Well, this guy has obviously never been to Japan, cuz then he would know that Japanese women are absolutely hilarious. Japanese women are the essence of comedy. I mean, look at anime: those shows are packed full of funny female characters; but in most of our comedy over here, it's like only guys can be klutzes and eccentrics; if there's a woman in the cast, she'll just be the token sensible one, the 'straight woman.'

My point? I'm not sure, really—except that I'm forever singing the praises of Japanese women, what with me being a total convert now, thanks to one particular example of that race who has become the most important thing in my life.

The Q-club is on the corner of Station Road. When you go inside, you're immediately confronted with the cash register where you pay your entrance fee and, if necessary, produce your ID card (fake or genuine as the case may be) for inspection. The bouncer in his ubiquitous black bomber jacket, also stands just inside the door, and he may decide to frisk you are rummage through your bag if you've got one. Are bouncers a necessary evil? I dunno, but I really wish we could do without them. I don't like 'em. They're burly and surly and when you've got a whole bunch of them at the door, the act like they own the place. (It's a small mercy that they make do with just the one here at the Q-club.) Is it the jealousy of the brainy male to the brawny male at work here? Do I envy them their physiques? Not consciously, I don't— and I definitely don't agree with those people (Plato was one of them) who declare that a healthy body always equals a healthy mind. It doesn't. There are lots of people who work out but are still fuck-ups. Take the bouncer we've got here: he's obviously a social inept; I've heard him once or twice making very clumsy attempts to chat up one of the barmaids here.

So, the ground floor of the venue is pretty much just a railed-off gallery, with the ladies and gents' toilets leading off it, and when you've paid your entrance fee and hung up your coat if necessary, you go down this broad flight of stairs to the basement and into the club proper. On your left, when you come down the stairs, you've got the 'chilling' area; the booths with those sofas with chipped plastic upholstery, and the low wooden tables. Right in front of you is the bar. And then, to your right is the actual dance-floor, modestly-sized (this is a smallish club) and adjacent to the bar, there's the saloon area, which is equipped with those tall round tables with tall round stools, all chrome and glass and fixed to the ground. (I have, on more than one occasion, seen a patron find out the embarrassing way, by trying to pick one up, that the stools are fixed to the ground.)

Tonight is the indie nightclub Club Hot Rock, and yours truly happens to be one of the DJs. This particular indie club is a kind of a local institution, organised by Howard, our bald, forty-something fanzine editor. As for the clientele: it's mainly student indie-kids from the sixth form colleges and the local polytechnic. They'll even be some students from the 'posh' universities—they're not all toffee-nosed privileged-class snobs in those places these days. Quite a few of our patrons will be under eighteen, but we wink a blind eye at that one. Aside from the students, it's just us aimless twenty-somethings; the ones, with jobs or without, who basically act like teenagers. (Or is it that the teenagers act like twenty-somethings?)

What music do we play here? That word 'indie' covers a multitude of sins. Well, we'll play all sorts: everything from 60s rock 'n roll to 70s punk, to 90s grunge and Brit-pop, to the contemporary bands—the only major rule we have is that we've got to play the songs that you can actually dance to; so, no slow or uneven stuff.

Myself, I'd like to be playing more tracks from those

Japanese girl bands Yuri's been introducing me to; I'm getting severely into those bands now. But the trouble is availability. There's no USB port on the decks here for playing downloads—just the traditional turntables and CD players. Yuri didn't bring her CD collection to the UK with her, and I've only managed to buy a few. I'd like to buy more of them, but Japanese CDs can be very pricey online, and I happen to be in the 'work-related activity' group, which thanks to the valiant efforts of David Cameron, means I don't have much money. In fact, we get the same amount as the people on Job-seekers' Allowance, and that weekly pittance is supposed to be just a stop-gap for people who are in and out of temporary work. But old David Cameron, he was a determined man; he even invented a new law so he could override the House of Lords' veto on his bill, just to get it through—so convinced was he that disability benefits were the single biggest unnecessary drain on the annual tax budget.

But I'm digressing.

Another feature of the Q-club is the flat-screen TVs bracketed to the walls around the seating area; and there will always be some cult film, b-movie, or anime showing on them (without sound of course.) Yuri has contributed to tonight's entertainment by selecting an old anime from the 90s called *Kekkou Kamen*, and it's on right now. At the moment there's this schoolgirl who's naked to the waist and manacled to this giant revolving swastika in the school assembly hall. This is her punishment for falling asleep during a late-night exam. This is an evil school, you see, with pervert teachers who inflict BDSM punishments on underachieving students; and it's this one girl whose grades are always bad, who always gets singled out for the punishment. This cartoon may seem gratuitous exploitation to the uninformed, and it is, but let me tell you, it's also a bold and satirical commentary on the harsh regime of the Japanese education system. It's not that discipline is really strict in Japanese schools, but there's a lot of pressure on students to succeed; a hell of a lot—it's like failure is not an option in Japanese schools.

There's none of our crowd sitting in the booth with us right now. I'm surprised that Esther, Mel and Muriel haven't shown up; they usually come along to this club, and they usually get here pretty early. Howard is DJing at the moment, and I'm not on till later, so I'm sitting here with Yuri, and we're talking sporadically, listening to the music and watching the TV. Kekkou Kamen has just arrived on the scene. The titular heroine of this anime is a naked superheroine; well, naked except for her mask, boots and gloves. She always turns up to rescue that underachieving student; usually waiting till the very last minute to make her appearance.

Yuri nudges me and points with her head. I look round. It's Esther. I smile and say 'Hello,' but I can see something's wrong because she looks upset, and Esther doesn't usually look upset. She says something to me, but I can't hear her over the music.

'What?' I shout.

She leans close to my ear, speaks slowly and clearly: 'I need to talk to you. Right now. Come upstairs. It's important.'

She sounds like she means it. I make my excuses to Yuri and follow Esther upstairs. She leads me straight into the ladies' room as the venue for our conversation. I've never been here before (toilet cubicle sex is the main reason for invading the opposite sex's domain at nightclubs, and that's never happened to me in this place.) And it turns out to be pretty much the same as the gents' facilities next door: two cubicles, two hand-basins. The only difference here is the absence of urinals, and the presence of a vending machine for tampons.

In the clearer light in here I can see that Esther really does look upset. She's not wearing any make-up and her eyes are red round the edges, like she's been crying.

'What's wrong?' I ask.

'It's Mel and Muriel,' says Esther. 'They've gone. They've been taken away by those removal men.'

This floors me. Mel and Muriel? 'But I thought—we thought—Dwayne and Vicky were going to be Disappeared next. I mean if the removal men haven't just given up completely.'

'I know that's what we thought, but they must have changed their plans. They've taken Mel and Muriel.'

'But… Hang on a minute… You only saw them on Saturday, didn't you? When you went round to do your photo thing… They were alright then, weren't they? How do you know they've gone?'

'Because I went round there again, today—this afternoon. And their house was empty; furniture gone and everything. I spoke to one of the neighbours; they said removal men had come along and taken everything away first thing this morning. The neighbour was surprised; said she hadn't even known the house was on the market. I asked her if she could remember who the removal company was—she said it was an unmarked van, and it was beige and so were the overalls of the removal men. It was *them*, Chad.'

I can't take it in. Mel and Muriel…

'But… but why would they change their plans like that?'

'I've been thinking about that,' says Esther; 'and I think I've worked it out: it's the Sallow Man. He must have realised it was us who took his notebook.'

'How could he have worked that out?'

'Well, he's not stupid, is he? Think about it: he must know his notebook's missing. It might have been what he went there to pick up that day. And we know from what happened next that they must have seen us leaving their warehouse. I reckon the Sallow Man must have worked it all out—the whole thing: that we were in his room and took his notebook, and that we got to the warehouse by hiding in the back of the van. I mean he's clever, isn't he? He'd be able to work these things out…'

'Yeah… Yeah, I guess he would…'

'Right. So they changed their plans and they took Mel and Muriel instead of Dwayne and Vicky.'

A girl walks into the room. She gives me a funny look, but says nothing and goes into one of the cubicles.

'And I feel like it's my fault…' says Esther, in a lower tone.

'What d'you mean your fault?'

'I feel like they deliberately chose Mel and Muriel to get back at me,' says Esther, looking despondent again. 'Because I was sticking my nose in…'

'Yeah, but so was I, wasn't I? You make it sound like this was some kind of reprisal for us finding their base and making them have to abandon it; but that's stupid, Esther. If they thought we were in the way or knew too much, they would've taken *us*, wouldn't they?'

Esther sighs. 'Well, maybe the Sallow Man's vindictive; maybe he's got a twisted sense of humour…'

'And that's why you're saying you think this is your fault?'

'Yeah… I almost told them—when I was round there on Saturday; I almost told them about all this that's been going on… I thought about it, but then I didn't tell them; and now it's like I think if I *had* told them, then maybe they would've been on the alert, you know? Like when we tried to warn Dwayne and Vicky. Maybe they would have been on the alert, and they might've avoided being taken away; they might've got out of it.'

A toilet flushes, the girl comes out of the cubicle and leaves the room.

'No,' I say. 'That's just… Look, I don't know exactly how they carry out these Disappearances, but knowing that these people are out there doesn't stop you from being taken away by them. Martin knew about them, but he still got taken away.'

'Yeah, I suppose... This whole thing's insane. I mean, *why* are they targeting us? Why us? We're not important.'

'Well, I told you what Martin said; he said it was *because* we're not important that we're being targeted. We don't really fit into the equation so we're easier to take out of it.'

'Yeah, but *why*, Chad?'

'Christ knows... Maybe it's when the numbers don't add up... Yeah, they have to balance the books, get the numbers right, and if the numbers are wrong, they have to make some subtractions. So they choose who they think are the best people to subtract; people like us.'

'But how can just removing a few people balance the books? I mean people get "subtracted" all the time—people die suddenly; accidents, murders, illnesses; people are being subtracted all the time.'

'Yeah, and people are being born all the time as well; new statistics; additions as well as subtractions... And maybe all the accidents, all the sudden deaths; maybe they're all somehow taken into account.'

'They can't predict sudden deaths, Chad.'

I shrug. 'These people... Maybe they can...'

Mel and Muriel. Two of the people I saw the most of. And now they've been taken away like Martin was; Disappeared; extracted from the mainstream of life and either eliminated or transposed to some other location; somewhere that's not on society's map.

I've been drinking more heavily since Esther's bombshell. She's still here, and Howard and Hilary are sitting with us as well. Neither of us has said anything to those two, but I've told Yuri all about what's happened; she suggested we call the cops. All very well, except we don't know if we can trust the police; they might be involved. If the removal men *are* officially sanctioned then the cops will be either in on it, or it'll be completely above their heads and if we went to them with our story, they'd just be ordered from above to drop the case. And what would we have to tell to the cops anyway? You can't really list someone as a missing person when—to all outward appearances—all they've done is just suddenly moved house.

Kekkou Kamen has got to the episode about the Samurai Cameramen who's 'terrorising the school with his naughty Polaroids.' When they invented those cameras in the '70s, they became synonymous with dirty pictures. Before that, there was only the old type of camera, with films that needed to be developed in a darkroom; so unless you happened to have your own darkroom, you couldn't really take your own dirty pictures, because you'd have to send the film off to be developed. But now, digital technology has come to the rescue, and we can take all the dirty pictures we like—I was doing that with Yuri only yesterday. Esther had emailed me the results of her photoshoot with Mel and Muriel, and Yuri straightaway offered to pose for me. I think it might have been jealousy in part; she wanted me looking at pictures of *her* and not Esther; but even so, she was totally up for it. And so we just did the photoshoot in my bedroom; me with my smartphone camera, and Yuri posing herself like a pro; she was really into it. (She was so good, I asked her if she'd done this kind of thing before—she said she had, but only by herself, in front of a mirror.) We just took dozens and dozens of pictures together, and both of us loved it. And people do it all the time, these days, don't they? They do it because they can; the technology is available, so we use it.

Smartphones make pornographers of us all.

A classic from Nirvana has just started playing. Yuri gets up from the sofa. She stands over me and holds out her hand.

'Come on. Let's dance.'

I can see she wants to cheer me up, so I take her hand and we go onto the dance floor. I don't dance that much at these clubs. I can dance well enough to pass muster; I'm not exactly John Travolta, but I can at least remember to move my feet as well as my upper body. Yuri's a girl, so of course dancing is built into her DNA. (I guess there must be *some* girls who have two left feet, but you don't see many of 'em.)

There're a lot of people on the dance-floor for this song. 'Smells Like Teen Spirit' is a rock anthem; it's a song about teenage rebellion; more specifically about the Riot Grrrl movement that happened around that time. Bikini Kill were the band most identified with the scene; and another band to come out of it, Sleater-Kinney, are still going as well. Apparently, Kurt Cobain went out with quite a few of these Riot Grrrls before getting hitched to that flaky pastry Courtney Love. You hear very mixed accounts about Kurt Cobain; that he was a nice guy, that he wasn't a nice guy... But hey, he blew his own brains out, and everyone loves a tragic rock star...

Yuri smiles while she dances; smiles with pure lust for life; her own teen spirit. She's got her hair up in twin-tails tonight and she's wearing a denim mini-skirt with a white belt, a sleeveless top, hold-ups and sneakers. She's here and she's dancing with me, and I feel like why can shit even be allowed to happen in a world that's got someone like her in it?

And then suddenly everybody but me is dancing in slow-motion and the music has slowed to a heavy rumble, like a tape winding down because the batteries are dead. It's so sudden I feel dizzy; I'm so out synch with everyone else, I nearly fall over. What the hell? I would think I was coming up on something, except that I haven't taken anything except alcohol tonight. I look at Yuri, dancing in slow-motion. Her body moves in this slow, sinuous way; everything's fluid and coordinated, but slowed right down... And it's not just that: her smile has gone; her face is expressionless, and there's this glassy, vacant look in her eyes. I can't make eye-contact with her; it's like her mind is somewhere else and her eyes are staring into infinity... I look around the dance-floor; all the other slow-motion dancers have got that same look in their eyes. Nevermind *me*; it looks more like *everybody else* has just come up on something.

What the hell is going on...? Is everybody else—?
And that's when I see him. The Sallow Man.

I'm looking at the seating area next to the bar; the saloon with the stools and round tables. The Sallow Man. He's there; sitting in the corner of the saloon, at the furthermost table. There's a green light shining right down on him, and he's sitting there and he's staring right at me; those bird-of-prey eyes are boring right into me from right across the room.

This is all his doing. He's behind this. Somehow, he's taken me out of synch from everyone else. What does he want with me?

The only thing I can read in that face over there under the green light, is intense concentration; like he's studying me; like he's trying to see into my mind.

I start walking towards him. I leave Yuri, and walk past all the slow-motion dancers… Away from the dance-floor people aren't moving at all: they're sat motionless in their chairs, standing motionless at the bar… The Sallow Man isn't affected. I see his eyes blink, so I can see he's moving in real time. He keeps his eyes on me as I step off the dance floor and advance towards him…

And then he's off his stool and opening the door in the wall behind him; a door marked 'private.' He's through the door and gone. I lunge for the door. The music suddenly speeds back up to normal speed; people are moving and talking. I'm at the door and I grab the handle, and I push it and pull it, but it's no good: the door is locked.

I turn and look around. Everything is back to normal in the club; the song's playing, the people are dancing, and everyone's acting as though nothing has happened. I guess for them nothing *has* happened; it's only happened to me.

Yuri, looking hurt and confused, comes up to me and wants to know why I suddenly just walked off the dance-floor…

Chapter Thirteen

Yuri Yamanaka grew up in the Wakayama Prefecture of Japan. It's part of the Kansai region, which the big-city Japanese look upon as hick country, and the local dialect is very rough and ready. (In English dubs of anime, which are usually produced in the States, Kansai dialect is always represented as an American hillbilly accent.) Right from grade school, Yuri showed a talent for art; and she decided pretty early on that an artist was what she wanted to be when she grew up. She was a shy girl back then, but not unpopular. Yuri's introduction to sex came at the age of thirteen, when she was raped by one of her middle-school teachers. In Japan, the school year starts in the spring, which actually makes more sense, if you think about it. In the UK our given reason for starting the school year in the autumn is that statistically, more kids are born at the end of the year than at the beginning. Maybe the statistics aren't the same in Japan. Yuri told another teacher, a female teacher, about being raped, and the school, understandably concerned about its reputation, proceeded to hush the whole matter up. Yuri wasn't actually expelled, but it was suggested that she might do better in another school in another district; this school obviously wasn't quite the right one for her; what she needed was a new start. And so, along with her family, she relocated to Yokohama. Yuri has never been able to find out for sure, but she suspects that her family may have received some 'financial assistance' from the school to help with the move. Yokohama is a city on the southern side of Tokyo Bay. Once it was just a fishing village, but it was expanded into a busy international port during the nineteenth century, when Japan decided to end its isolationist policy and began trading with other countries. Yuri settled into her new life and her new school, making friends with a group of girls who were sexually-abused misfits like herself. It was around this time she picked up her nicotine habit. Yuri still pursued her art studies, improving all the time, and was later, on account of her obvious talent, accepted into a high school which specialised in the subject. One other subject she excelled at was English; some Japanese people find English a difficult language to pick up, but Yuri just took to it, and now she can speak English fluently. Yuri graduated from high school with honours and, backed by her teachers, applied for a place at the Cambridge School of Visual and Performing Arts. She was accepted, and she came to the United Kingdom to study for her master's degree in Art.

And thanks to this, our paths chanced to cross, and Yuri became a part of my life.

I'm woken up this morning by Yuri sucking on my cock, and with the smell of her cunt and arsehole filling my nostrils.

My foggy eyes open to the delicious sight of her looming over me, humid, pungent, rank with hair. I let her know that I'm awake and she lowers herself onto me…

And then afterwards, Yuri's got her head back on the pillow and we're hugging and kissing each other, eyes expressing our mutual satisfaction.

'We came together…' she says.

'Yeah, we did,' I say, smiling. 'It's like that Beatles song: "Come Together." …Is that what that song's actually about? Bit rude for the 60s.'

'We came together because our hearts beat together,' says Yuri. She can be poetic like this sometimes. 'We're like John Lennon and Yoko Ono.'

'Hey; you're right!' I say, surprised. For some reason, the comparison has never occurred to me before. 'Yeah, and you're an artist, same as her—! But then, I'm not so much of a rock musician…'

'You used to be!'

'Yeah, but it didn't come to much, did it?' Looking back on all my stupid hopes from that time is always a downer.

'Hey, don't be sad!' says Yuri, stroking my face. 'You could start up a new band!'

'I'm not really motivated at the moment…' I tell her. 'Besides: I'm nearly thirty; getting a bit long in the tooth for a rock star.'

'You're never too old to have dreams.'

'Well... At the moment, my dreams are mostly about you.'

A smile spreads over her face. 'You say such nice things,' she says.

'Although, come to think of it,' I say, feigning a contemplative tone; 'it's just as well I'm not in a band—you'd probably do a Yoko Ono and ruin the whole thing!'

Mock anger and a shower of playful fists are her response to this.

'Oh, *you!*'

I grab the flailing wrists, pin them down. I move in to steal a kiss.

'No, no, no!' she says, petulantly shaking her head to avoid my lips.

But I'm insistent, and I get my way in the end.

'You're so mean...' says Yuri, when our lips finally part, and making it sound like a compliment.

'You know... I reckon we must be the best working example of Anglo-Japanese cooperation since Pearl Harbour, you and me.'

I get the puzzled reaction I was looking for. 'Pearl Harbour?'

'Yeah; we gave you directions how to get there.'

'Why would you do that?'

'Cuz we knew it would get the Yanks into the war on our side; and that's what we wanted.'

'I've never heard this.' A smile wipes away the confused look. 'You're making a joke.'

'No, I'm not! Well... it might not be true; might be just a conspiracy theory. Still, I wouldn't have put it past old Churchill.'

'You don't admire Winston Churchill?'

'Him? Just a big, overgrown, cigar-smoking baby, wasn't he? "We will fight them on the beaches...!"'

Yuri laughs. 'So... You're still going to that house today...?'

'Herschell House, yeah. And like I said, you're welcome to come along with us.'

She shakes her head. 'No... Too much work to do... You'll be careful, right?'

I assure her that I will.

Trumpington and Grantchester are at the posh southern end of Cambridge; it's where all the privileged class people live. Grantchester is also famous for its Grantchester Meadows, an established rendezvous for university students after graduating—they light up fires and get stupidly drunk; the worst cases usually end up in A&E. As well as being immortalised in a song by Pink Floyd (a band with local connections), it was on Grantchester Meadows that an invisible spaceship, belonging to the evil alien Skagra, landed in the unfinished *Doctor Who* serial 'Shada.' The author of the story was Douglas Adams, who would have known the location from his own student days. 'Shada' has had a colourful career. Production was halted on account of a strike and the serial never was never finished or transmitted; the location filming in Cambridge had been completed, and they were in the middle of the studio recording when the strike happened. Douglas Adams recycled some of the story for the first of his *Dirk Gently* novels—but he also rehashed some of the plot to another *Doctor Who* story 'City of Death', which was a bit of a cheek. Then in 1983, the 'Punting on the Cam' scene from the location footage was shoehorned into *Doctor Who*'s 20th anniversary story 'The Five Doctors'; this was done after Tom Baker decided he didn't want to reprise his role and take part in the new production. Ten years later, the recorded footage from 'Shada' was assembled and released on VHS with Tom Baker narrating the missing scenes. And then, after another ten years, the script was adapted into a radio adventure with Eighth Doctor Paul McGann taking Tom Baker's place. This one still had Lalla Ward as Romana, but

I think the rest of the cast was different. And now finally, the original recorded material has been resurrected again for DVD and Blu-ray release, this time with all of the missing scenes animated, with the voices dubbed by the original cast (except for Denis Carey, who's dead.)

And if all that wasn't enough, the scripts have also been turned into a rather crappy novel. Author Gareth Roberts—he's that *Doctor Who* writer who went and got himself cancelled for posting some transphobic tweets—seemed to exhaust his writing talents on a very funny first paragraph; after that it was downhill all the way. And one thing that's very obvious about that book to any Cambridge resident, is that the author clearly didn't bother doing much in the way of location research. In the book, which was written back in 2012, Grantchester Meadows are just referred to as 'the water-meadows outside Cambridge.' Which is funny, because these days everyone's heard of Grantchester, on account of being the titular setting of a television detective series, which I've never bothered watching but understand is very popular.

We're out in the Grantchester countryside right now, Esther and me. We're walking along a quiet road; there are driveways leading to unseen properties on one side of the road, and what looks like a sizeable tract of woodland on the other; probably some landowner's shooting preserve. It's a lovely sunny day; Esther looks like a ray of sunshine herself. She seems like she's managed to cheer herself up a bit since last night.

'How much further is it?' I ask. 'We must have been walking for an hour now…'

'Yes, we have,' says Esther, pointedly; 'and we could've saved a lot of time by cycling here, couldn't we? Except, somebody just has to be different and not have a bicycle.'

'Yes… point taken,' I say wearily.

'Anyway, it's just past this wood,' announces Esther. 'That's where Herschell House should be.'

Herschell House. What are we going to find there? Anything at all? The name of it was written in the Sallow Man's notebook; that's all we know. It can't be the address of a potential victim; someone lined up for Disappearance… It's a bloody great mansion; I've seen a picture of it. Not the kind of place where one of our crowd is going to be living. What we've been thinking is it might be the place where they're keeping the Disappearers. Lots of rooms in a big house like that. Esther, though; she's only really latched onto that idea since Mel and Muriel got taken—she wants to think that those two are alive and well and waiting for us to come and rescue them. *I'd* like to think that was true as well. But then I think: if Esther's right in her theory that the Sallow Man knows we've got his memo pad, then even if Herschell House *was* where they were keeping the Disappearers, they might have upped sticks and left by now; evacuated the place, like they did the warehouse… And there's also another possibility: they might be still there and they might be expecting us.

Of course, Esther didn't see the Sallow Man at the Q-club last night. No-one did, apart from yours truly. She thinks I must have just imagined it.

The woods end suddenly and now there's a tall brick wall facing the road. Further on, and we come to a pair of gates— a plaque on the wall beside one of the gate-posts tells us we've reached our destination: Herschell House.

'Well, we're here,' I say.

'Yep,' agrees Esther.

We look at each other.

'So, what do we do?' I ask.

'Go inside, I s'pose.'

The gates are ajar so this is easy enough. Just inside and on the left is a gatehouse. It looks locked up and disused. I know from old books I've read that back in the day there'd have a whole family living in that pokey building, who would be employed and maintained for the sole purpose of opening and closing the gates. That sort of thing would probably be considered a needless expenditure these days, even by the rich. (Especially now when we've got gates that can open themselves.) There's a broad gravel driveway in front of us; and on either side of it are gardens with lots of trees and shrubbery. We can't see the house from here.

'I suggest we make a stealthy approach,' I say. 'Across the garden.'

Esther agrees and we set off.

There's plenty of convenient cover, and we make our way across the garden. I've made a vow to myself to be less overly-cautious this time. When I look back on that previous exploit, our trip to the removal men's warehouse, I feel like I didn't acquit myself very well. Esther was the bold one, all for exploring the place, while I was all for getting out of there as quickly as possible. Not very good, Chad. I don't want Esther thinking I'm yellow. (And by 'yellow,' I make no reference to East Asian skin tones—at least I think I don't! I hope that the expression 'yellow' for 'cowardly,' is not some racist defamation of Asian people! I'll have to look up the etymology of that one.)

The house comes into sight now. The garden ends at a gravel forecourt fronting the mansion; we squat down behind some ferns to survey thee place. It's a big redbrick house, with lots of windows, tall chimneys, an arched portico—just like in the photographs. Don't ask me which monarch it was built under; it could be Elizabethan, Georgian, Queen Anne, or a combination of all three for all I know. There's no-one about, but the place looks inhabited and well cared-for; so do the grounds.

'So, what do you want to do?' I ask Esther. 'Just go up and knock on the front door?'

'No, I don't think that would be a good idea. Let's go round the back. See if we can get in that way.'

'Right.'

Keeping under the cover of the trees, we make our way

round to the side of the house. There's an archway leading into a courtyard. We go in. On our left is the wall of the house, and in front of us and to the right what look like old carriage houses converted into modern garages. One of the doors is open and we cross the yard and take a look inside. What we find are a couple of vintage cars; an open-topped Bentley and an old Jaguar; both cars are polished and spick and span; they look like they might be for show more than for use.

'I dunno about this,' I say. 'I don't see the Sallow Man as a vintage car collector.'

'Then someone he knows is,' says Esther. 'There's got to be some connection—'

'Whaddaya think you're doin'?'

We spin round. The owner of the interrogative voice is a man dressed in tweeds and a flat-cap, and wearing a truculent expression on his face. More importantly, he is pointing a shotgun at us.

'This is private property,' proceeds the man. 'What're you doin' 'ere?'

'We want to speak to the owner,' declares Esther. First I'd heard about it.

'Do you now? And what would you want to be speaking to them about?'

'I'm looking for some missing friends of mine.'

'And what would anyone 'ere know about any friends of yourn?' challenges the man.

'Well… I sort of have reason to believe they might be here.'

'Oh, do you now? "Reason to believe," eh? Well, 'ow about we step inside and see if we can't sort this out.'

The invitation is obviously a command, and the man indicates with his gun that we're to walk in front of him.

He directs us to a side door into the house, and then along a passageway. We're ordered to stop and the man knocks on a door. A voice bids us enter, and we are led into a parlour where an oldish man dressed as butler sits at a table drinking tea, a silver tea-set on the table before him.

He stands up. 'What's this, Perkins? Who are these people?'

'Intruders,' says Perkins. 'Caught 'em nosin' around the garages. They *say* they is lookin' for some missin' friends. Wants to speak to the missis, they say.'

The butler gives us a suspicious look. 'Who are you people? Journalists?'

'Why should we be journalists?' asks Esther.

'Journalists snoop around,' replies the butler; 'and apparently that's what you were doing.' To Perkins: 'I'll inform the mistress.'

He goes to a telephone set, fixed to the wall behind him; it's one of those retro jobs: just an ear-piece on the cord, and a sort of funnel to speak into. 'Inform the mistress,' he said. So, a woman owns this place... Are we barking up the wrong tree?

The butler concludes his brief telephone conversation and turns back to us.

'You will be conducted to the guestrooms,' he announces. 'And there you will remain until my mistress is ready to see you.'

'We don't want to wait in any guestrooms!' I tell him. 'Either let us go, or let us see whoever's in charge around here.'

I feel something dig into my back. It's Perkins and his shotgun. 'You'll do what you're bloody well told,' he says. 'Now, hands up!'

I look at Esther. She looks at me. We raise our hands.

Chapter Fourteen

We're escorted along the passageway and out into a huge hallway, obviously the main entrance hall, which is dominated by a staircase of the imposing variety. The hallway is all wood panelling, antique furniture, houseplants and Chinese vases. Perkins still has his gun on us, and the butler acts like it's the most normal thing in the world to be escorting guests around the house at gunpoint. We've been searched, but the only thing they've taken away from us is Esther's mobile.

We go up the stairs and along a corridor with so many doors it looks like a hotel. Oak-panelled walls and ornate little tables, busts on plinths, painted vases, standing in the alcoves between the doors. Everything is on such a large scale here; wide corridors and high ceilings… I'm not used to this. My only experience of mansions like this place is a few school trips to stately homes.

We stop in front of a door no different to all the others, but apparently this is the advertised 'guestroom' because the butler opens the door and politely beckons us to enter. What with the invitation being backed up by a shotgun in a pair of wellingtons, it seems wise to accept. I walk in first—and suddenly there's a rush of movement behind me and the door slams shut. I hear a key turn in the lock.

I pounce on the door and even though I heard that click of course I try to open it, twisting the doorknob this way and that. Then I start banging on the panels.

'What's going on?' I shout. 'Esther? Esther? Are you alright?'

'Shut your noise!' comes the voice of Perkins.

'It's alright, Chad,' comes Esther's voice. 'I think they just want to put us in separate rooms. I'll be alright.'

I subside, but I'm not happy. What if they're going to keep us forever in these 'guestrooms'? My 'Room with no View' theory returns with a vengeance. What if there are a lot of 'guestrooms' in this place—we passed enough doors before we got here. And what if some of them are already occupied? What if Muriel, Mel and all the other Disappearers really are here? We came here to rescue them, and all we've done is joined them...

I look around my prison. It's an ornately furnished one, the décor in-keeping with the rest of Herschell House. In the *Millennium* episode the rooms were more spartan; in fact, if I remember correctly, they were completely bereft of furniture and even carpets. I light up a cigarette, a) because I need one, and b) because it will be a small gesture of defiance if smoking is not allowed in these posh rooms.

I throw myself on the king-sized bed (not bothering to take my shoes off), and, bouncing on the soft springs, I find myself looking up at myself. The ceiling above the bed is mirrored.

What the hell kind of 'guestroom' is this? What the hell kind of house is this?

I also notice that the bedside table is equipped with a cut-glass ashtray. So much for my gesture of defiance...

I've smoked three cigarettes now, and I'm still locked in this room. I've inspected the drawers and wardrobes, all empty; I've inspected the window, which opens easily enough, but the first floor of this place is so far above the ground it can't really be considered as a viable escape-route—But mostly I've been wondering what's happened to Esther. Is she locked in another room like this, or is she being questioned by the owner of the house? Why did they have to split us up? Even if it's not what we thought it was, something is decidedly off about Herschell House: locking up intruders instead of turfing them off the premises; guestrooms with mirrored ceilings. Or is this how the other half live?

I'm back to lying on the bed when the key turns and the door opens. I expect to see Perkins or the butler, but instead a woman in a fur coat slips through the door. Can't tell if it's faux fur or the real thing. The woman looks to be in her thirties and she's looking at me with a very intense look on her rather popeyed face. Her hair is auburn and tied up with clips. She's got a big, beaky nose. Beneath the hem of the fur coat, I espy a pair of very shiny black boots with spiked heels.

She just stands there leaning against the door, giving me that intense look.

'Well?' I say, sitting up on the bed. 'Who are you? Are you going to take me to where Esther is?'

'Your friend Esther is occupied right now,' says the woman. She sounds posh.

'What's that supposed to mean?'

'I've come to talk to you, Charles,' she says.

'How do you know my name?'

'Because Esther told me, of course.' When she speaks, she shows a set of big, horsey gnashers. (Overbites only work well on Japanese women, remember.)

'Yeah? Then she should've also mentioned I prefer to be called Chad,' I tell her.

'She did mention something of the sort, but "Chad" sounds so vulgar, doesn't it? I'll just call you Charles.'

'Fine, but how—'

'Don't interrupt me, Charles,' says the woman, interrupting me. 'I said I've come to talk to you. This will involve you having to listen to me.'

'Alright, I'm listening. But can you at least tell me who you are? Do you own this place?'

'Not exactly; I'm the daughter of the house. My name is Constance.'

'I'm guessing from the look of your boots that you're wearing something kinky under that coat.'

'How very observant of you, Charles! Shall I show you?'

'No, you don't have to bother.'

'Oh, I think I *will* bother, if it's all the same to you.'

She drops the coat and I'm not altogether surprised to find that she's wearing full dominatrix gear: thigh-boots, knickers and basque, all in shiny black PVC. I don't think much of her figure; it's all gawky and angular.

'Well? How do you like my togs?' she asks.

I shrug. 'Not really my scene.'

'Really? You're not into BDSM?'

'Nope.'

'Yes, it is a rather stale scene, isn't it?' she says, ruminatively. 'I mean, it's all so contrived, isn't it? After a while, it starts to pale. I mean, it's easy enough to dominate someone who *wants* to be dominated; someone who's willing and passive. But where's the satisfaction in that? It's just playing games, isn't it? Yes, the *real* challenge is to subdue someone who doesn't want to be subdued. Someone who's going to put up a fight.'

'Yeah, but that would be illegal, wouldn't it?' I point out. 'You can't go around whipping people into submission.'

'That's just a small detail, Charles. All it takes to overcome these obstacles is money. Money can buy one whatever one wants: willing subjects; *un*willing subjects. People who've been bought and sold. People who have run away or been taken away and stripped of their human rights. There's nothing one can't buy if one has enough money. But then, you wouldn't know about that, would you, Charles, darling? You're just one of the oiks; the poor, deprived peasantry; haven't got two brass farthings to rub together.'

I'm not liking what she's saying—and I don't mean the bit about oiks. 'What do you mean by "people who have been taken"?'

'I mean what I say. It happens all the time. Are you thinking about your friends? That's what brought you here, isn't it? All those friends of yours who have gone missing... Hm... Wherever could they be...?'

Her voice is calm, matter of fact.

'What have you done with my friends?' I demand. 'Are

they here?'

'No, not any more,' is the answer. 'They've been moved on.'

'Where to? Moved on to where? What have you done with them, you bitch?'

'Oh, they've gone to Eastern Europe. Travelling by freight, of course. They're going to end up as film stars— *Posthumous* film stars, you could say. I told you money can buy anything; and there are people in this world who are willing to pay a lot of money to have some time alone in a room with a helpless human being in it; chained to the wall, completely at their mercy…'

I can't believe what I'm hearing. All my old theories have just been thrown out the window. The Sallow Man. The removal men. I'd pictured some sinister conspiracy orchestrated by the establishment for the quiet removal of unwanted people; I pictured those people either being eliminated or moved to some secret location… Instead, now I'm hearing about that sick underworld of torture killings, snuff-porn; people taken away and dying protracted deaths just for the entertainment of certain wealthy people who've got the money to act out their sick fantasies. And this house, from the sounds of it, is one of the dispatch centres. From here the Disappeared are smuggled out of the country like cargo, and never heard from again.

I spring from the bed. 'You sick fucking bitch! What's to stop me from wringing your fucking neck?'

I'm closing in on her fists clenched; she starts to look alarmed. 'Stop! You're not allowed to be like that!'

'And how do you expect me to be, you sick bitch? After what you've done to my friends… How do you fucking expect me to be?'

She holds out her arm, palm towards me. 'Stop! Stop this at once! This is not part of the game! You can't do this!'

'I'm not playing your sick games. I'm going to throttle you!'

'Perkins!'

The door bursts open and the groundsman springs into the room. He lunges at me, but I'm ready for him and he runs his face straight into my fist. He staggers backwards, and he's got blood gushing from his nose.

'Oh, stop it!' cries Constance, wretchedly. 'It's all gone wrong! You've ruined the game!'

Perkins gets to his feet; he looks all set to pay me back in kind. I bunch my fists.

Constance steps between us, holding us at arm's length.

'Stop it!' she wails. She looks at me, her face tearful. 'I was only *joking*, you silly man!'

'Joking about what?' I demand.

'Everything! Selling your friends to Eastern Europe to be killed; everything! Don't you see? I didn't think you'd react like this! I just wanted to see you looking upset.'

'You made it all up...?' say. 'Just to get a reaction out of me?'

'Yes...' contritely.

My anger turns to relief. It was all a lie...

'Then what have you done with my friends?'

'We haven't done *anything* with them; honestly! We haven't got them. We don't know anything about your friends.'

'And where's Esther?'

'She's downstairs with the Mater. I'll take you to them. She'll explain everything.'

Perkins is staunching the flow from his bloody nose with a handkerchief, and still looks like he'd like to pay me back for the injury—but Constance dismisses him and she takes me downstairs.

What's with this woman? I wonder. As an S&M queen she's a pretty pathetic specimen. More of a wannabe S&M queen, I guess.

She leads me into a living room—or don't they call them 'drawing rooms' in these mansions?—where I find Esther, naked but alive and well, sipping a cup of tea. She's sitting at the feet of a grey-haired woman dressed in a sort of PVC Nazi uniform; trousers and jacket, boots, swastika armband and peaked cap with eagle insignia. She looks like she's in her fifties, this woman, and you can see the family resemblance; she's got the exact same bulging eyes and beaky nose as Constance. A maid in a frilly uniform stands in the background.

Esther gives me a smile to show that she's okay.

'You took your time,' speaks up the woman, addressing Constance. She has a brisk, fruity voice. 'You were supposed to bring the lad straight here. Have you been messing around with him?'

'Oh, Mater!' wails Constance. And rushing to her parent's feet, she pours out the story of her woes.

'You silly, addlepated baggage,' is the mother's reaction. 'What on earth made you tell him such an outrageous story?'

'Because I'm a *sadist*, Mater. I was being *sadistic*.'

'You were being a bloody fool,' retorts the mother crisply. 'I keep telling you you haven't got what it takes.' She fixes her eyes on me. 'Sorry about my daughter. The name's Letty. Take a pew.'

I sit down in an armchair.

'Cup of tea?'

There's a tea-set on the table between us.

'Um… Okay.'

The maid steps forward and pours a cup for me.

'Your friend here's told me all about why you're here,' says Letty. 'And let me tell you, I've heard some stories in my time… But I'm afraid we can't help you. We have nothing to do with any scheme to make people vanish into thin air, I can assure you of that.'

'But then, why was the name of this place—'

'—In that fellow's notebook? Not sure about that. One possibility, though. We have parties here; I'm sure you can imagine what kind. Nothing nasty, though. All within reasonable bounds and with consenting adults, etcetera, etcetera. It's possible this chappie you call the Sallow Man has been to one of 'em. Didn't recognise him from the filly's description, but he might've been here. I don't know everyone who comes here personally, you understand. Friend of a friend; that sort of thing. Also, you have to remember, at these parties of ours, a lot of people choose to wear masks.'

'Letty says she'll let us know if he does turn up here again,' speaks up Esther.

'Pity I haven't got one of those photos of him with me,' I say.

'I know what look for, young man,' Letty tells me. 'Esther here says he looks like Vladek Sheybal; and I know what Vladek Sheybal looks like. He was in that film *Kanal*. I'll look out for the fellow. Our next do is this weekend.'

So this is the secret of Herschell House. A dotty old woman and her airhead daughter hold BDSM parties for the idle, rich and perverted. Now I can understand why that butler was worried about journalists snooping around. *The Cambridge News* would have a field-day if they found out about this.

Proceeds Letty: ''Course, you're welcome to come along yourselves, if you're that determined to catch the fellow. But like I say: can't promise that he'll be here.'

I look at Esther. 'What do you think?'

'I dunno… It's an idea. Let's think about it…'

And so, we finish our tea, Esther puts her clothes back on and we say our goodbyes to Constance and the Mater. We set off back to town.

Chapter Fifteen

Snakes bother me.

I mean the poisonous kind, the ones that can sink their fangs into you and wham! you drop down dead. I know we don't have snakes like that in this country (or do we?), but from what I've heard, in those countries that do have them, those jungle and desert countries, being fatally bitten by a snake is seen as being just one of those unavoidable day-to-day hazards, the same way we look at traffic accidents. I can't get my head round that. It doesn't seem the same to me. I mean there are things you can do to avoid car accidents; like crossing the road carefully, or never getting into a car; but if you live in one of those snake-infested countries, there's not much you can do to avoid snakes, short of shutting yourself up in your room and never coming out. The things can pop up anywhere at any time; they can slither in through your doors or windows or even come up out of your toilet bowl and bite you in the arse… And it's not just snakes: there're also scorpions, and venomous spiders and centipedes… In England, we don't really have anything like that; we don't even have any dangerous wild animals…

But I guess in the countries where they do have these things, they're just used it; they're just a fact of life that they accept. And it's not just natural hazards, is it? What about all those countries where there's pretty much permanent civil unrest or wars going on all the time? The people who live in those countries still manage to get on with their lives somehow. It seems like us human beings can get used to almost anything…

I've walked all the way to Esther's again this evening, cuz I haven't been able to get through to her on the phone. She hasn't answered my texts and if I ring her, I just get through to voicemail. She's either got her phone switched off or it's out of juice.

I want to talk to her, cuz I want to know what she wants to do next about the Sallow Man. Does she want us to go to that BDSM party at Herschell House on Saturday? Yuri's up for it, anyway; and I'll admit, whether it leads us to the Sallow Man or not, it would be an experience... But will he be there? Is that the reason he had the house's name written in his notebook? Is he a regular attendee of those parties? Him being into that kind of thing doesn't fit in with my mental image of the guy: committed to his job; never off-duty... But then, my mental image is based on a backstory that I just invented for him... And anyway, you can't always tell which people are going to be into that sort of thing; some people wear it on their sleeves, but some people keep it hidden; a kind of secret double life...

When we were walking back yesterday, my first reaction to that farce we'd gone through was that we'd been led up the garden path—that the Sallow Man had sent us on a wild goose chase as revenge for our pinching his precious notebook. I thought that, because that was how it felt—that we'd been tricked.

It was Esther who pointed out the serious flaw in my reasoning: 'Chad, we got the address of Herschell House *from* his notebook—so, how could he have sent us there as revenge for us stealing it?'

You can't deny that one.

I think I've mentioned before that I measure the length of regular journeys I make by how many cigarettes I smoke, haven't I? From mine to Esther's, it's a four-cigarette journey: one as soon as I set off, one when I get to the service station on Elizabeth Way, one when I get to the corner of Coldham's Lane, and one when I turn onto Ross Street, which lasts me pretty much to her front door.

Naturally, it's Patricia who answers.

'What have you done with Esther?' she demands, before I can even get a word in.

I don't like the sound of this. 'What do you mean what have I done with her? Where is she?'

'That's what I'm asking you. She went out with you yesterday afternoon, and she hasn't come back! What have you done with her, you psycho?'

'But she must have come back...' I say (rather pathetically, because I'm struggling to get my head round this.) 'I left her on Hill's Road; she was coming straight back here...'

'Yeah? When was that?'

'I dunno... fourish...'

'Well, she didn't come back here at "fourish" yesterday, and she still hasn't come back today. You've done something with her, haven't you?'

'I haven't done anything!' I retort. 'Why d'you assume I've "done something"?' An idea occurs to me. 'Is her stuff still there?'

She looks puzzled.

'Her what?'

'Her stuff. Her belongings; are they still in her room?'

'Of course they're still here! She hasn't moved out, has she?'

'It can be them, then...' I murmur. 'Then where is she...?'

Yes, where is she?

Esther has disappeared, or has *been* disappeared. She left me on Hill's Road that afternoon, intending to walk straight back home; but somehow, she never made it. Somehow, right in the middle of Cambridge, in broad daylight, she vanished into thin air. She hasn't been in an accident: we've checked that. She isn't staying round any friend's house; at least not any friend of hers that anyone knows about. She's just disappeared.

It *has* to be the removal men, doesn't it? Who else would want to make Esther vanish? The only trouble is, her disappearance doesn't fit their particular *modus operandi*.

The removal men usually come along in one of their big vans and cart off all the furniture and belongings along with the victim... Of course, Esther lives in a shared house, so they couldn't really have been able to take her stuff without being questioned by her housemates... But then, the removal men have got those small vans, as well; like the one me and Esther hitched a ride in. Maybe the removal men grabbed Esther off the street and bundled her into one of those vans... Could they have done that? In broad daylight, could they have done that; and with no witnesses...? In my mind's eyes, I follow the route Esther would have taken home after I left her on Hill's Road... I can't think of any likely spot where an abduction could have happened... But then again, these kinds of things *do* happen, don't they? You hear it in the news; people get abducted all the time; they just get grabbed in broad daylight and no-one sees it happen... Just because you're walking down a residential street doesn't necessarily mean you're going to be seen if someone jumps you and bundles you into a vehicle; not every house is going to have people in it all day, and the people who *are* at home aren't going to be spending all their time looking out of their front windows...

Actually, it's not just the biters; those great big fuck-off constrictor snakes that squeeze you to death and swallow you whole creep me out as well. The size of those things—you think, why are they even allowed to exist on the same planet as human beings? Whose bright idea was it to put us and those things together on the same lump of rock? The existence of those snakes is a very strong argument against any divine being having been involved in organising things on this planet—clearly *no-one* organised the set-up here; it's a complete, chaotic shambles.

You sometimes hear about someone getting swallowed whole by one of those big snakes. They're usually found, because the snakes go dormant after they've eaten someone;

they have to rest while they're digesting the poor bastard. You see the pictures and you think how did that guy let himself get caught by the snake in the first place? You think he ought to have been able to outrun the thing; but you'd be wrong about that. Those great big snakes might look slow; but they're not—they can move as fast as the small ones when they want to. It's a disturbing thought.

I wake up without Yuri sleeping next to me this morning. She didn't come over last night cuz she's busy with one of her art projects. (You should see her stuff. She's going to be famous, that girl.) I remember that Esther is missing and that puts me in a low mood. I wish Yuri was here so I could talk it over with her…

I turn over in bed and bury my face in Yuri's pillow; it's redolent with the smell of her lovely long black hair. One of the benefits of not washing the bad linen too often. She's become indispensable to me, Yuri—she's become part of my home; she's imposed her naked presence on every room in my flat. She's fit herself into my native environment. I just love every single thing about her—even the smell of her shit when she's taken a dump in my bathroom. You know how it is: the smell of other people's shit can often be highly offensive to you—if not downright intolerable. But, Yuri; her shit smells okay to me… Further proof we were made for each other, of our complete physical compatibility. You know when someone's really the right person for you, if you don't mind the smell of their shit…

I just lie there, breathing in the smell of Yuri's hair, thinking about what I'm going to do when I get up…

I looked up the meaning of the term 'yellow.' Seems it's got nothing to do with East Asian skin-tones; it's actually short for 'yellow-bellied,' and no-one seems to know exactly what it means… Would someone with jaundice have a yellow belly…? No, they'd be yellow all over, wouldn't they… That reminds me of a guy I saw in town once; just some random person who happened to walk past me in the street; in his fifties, he looked to be—I remember him because his skin was this really sickly yellowy-grey colour, and he had the most miserable look on his face; completely dejected. Seeing him like that, I just thought: 'Dead man walking.'

When I finally stop thinking about getting up and actually do get up, the first thing I do is pick up my phone. No messages or missed calls from Esther. I try calling her, and get put straight through to voicemail again.

I pull on the clothes lying beside my mattress, go to the bathroom for a slash and then go to the kitchen, take my pills, and put the kettle on for my first cup of coffee of the day. Armed with this, I go into the living room, sit in my usual place and reach for my cigarettes. I've just finished this breakfast of caffeine and nicotine when there's a knock at the door.

I don't like people knocking on my door—not when I'm not expecting anyone to be knocking on the door; and this knock I especially don't like. It's a loud knock, an imperative knock, the knock of officialdom. I think about ignoring it, but I get the feeling this knock isn't going to take no for an answer, and anyway it might be something about Esther.

I get up and I answer the door; and I'm right about it being the knock of officialdom, cuz it's two uniformed coppers.

There's something about police uniforms that sets off alarm bells. You don't have to have done anything wrong to get this feeling. Your conscience can be clean, you can be aware that you have not been guilty of any violation of the law, but still the sight of those uniforms can trigger that alarm. I think it's because as human beings we value our personal freedom second only to our continued existence, and we carry around with us that knowledge that those navy-blue uniforms are worn by people who have the power to deprive us of our freedom... Yes, I know that ultimately, it's a man in a silly wig and a jury of a dozen of our fellow-countrymen who have the power to deprive us of our liberty, but in the first instance it's the police; they're the ones who can arrest us, detain us, and lock us up in a prison cell.

Like I say, there's two of them, a sergeant and a constable; they're wearing peaked caps, which means they've come by car.

'Mr Charles Fenton?'

'Yes…'

'I'm Sergeant Wilde and this is Constable Boon from Parkside. We'd like to have a few words if we may.'

'About what?'

'About Esther Laurence.'

'Has she been… found?'

'No, sir; she hasn't been found. She has been listed as officially missing. We understand from her housemates that you were the last person known to see her. May we come in and talk for a moment?'

Of course you can't come in and talk for a moment! Fuck off! is what I'd like to say. I'm very selective about who I let into my domain; I'm very territorial. But these are the fuzz, and if I don't let them in it's only going to look suspicious.

So I let them in.

I don't like these two cops from the get-go. They're both young—about the same age as me, they look. I can't really accept them as capable representatives of authority. I'm just thinking what kind of morons of my generation would want to go'n join the police force in the first place. There's something laddish about these younger cops. They're like the boys you knew at school who always played football during break-time…

I sit in my armchair, and leave them to occupy the sofa, because I don't want to be sitting next to either of them—so I'm pissed off right from the start to see one of them planting his arse on my usual seat on the sofa. I can smell their aftershave. I can smell hostility as well. This isn't going to be a friendly visit.

'So, Mr Fenton,' begins the sergeant. 'I understand that you last saw Miss Laurence on Tuesday afternoon?'

'Yeah.'

'Could you give us more details, sir? When you met her, where you went, what time you left her...'

'I met her in town about midday, I guess. And we went for a walk.'

What else can I say about what we did that afternoon? I can't tell them that we went to Herschell House, because then I'd have to explain *why* we went to Herschell House, and that would mean having to launch into the full story about the Sallow Man and the Disappearances—and right now I feel like I just want to take the shortest conversational route.

'You just went for a walk?' echoes the sergeant, emphasis on the last word, as though going for a walk is the most improbable and unlikely thing in the world. 'And where exactly did you go for this walk, sir?'

'Just out Trumpington/Grantchester way,' I say.

'Really? All the way out there? And was there any particular reason for this walk, sir?'

'It was Esther's idea. She thinks I don't get enough fresh air.'

I reach for my cigarettes. I want a fag.

'Would you mind not smoking, sir?' says the sergeant.

I look at him. 'This is *my* flat, you know—'

'Nevertheless, sir, I am asking you if you would kindly refrain from smoking in our presence.'

Should I stand on my rights? I want to, if only to piss these two off... But then, maybe *they're* in the right; I'm a bit hazy about the laws on secondary smoke... Oh, sod it. I throw the fag packet back down on the table.

'Thank you, sir,' says the sergeant, in a way that I don't like. 'So, you just went for a walk, did you? On a weekday afternoon...'

'Why not on a weekday afternoon?' I demand. 'I don't

work and Esther had the day off.'

'And did anyone see you taking this walk, sir?'

'Well, yes, I suppose people must have seen us... There were cars... We didn't speak to anyone we knew, if that's what you mean.'

'I see. And how long were you out walking, sir?'

'A few hours, I guess. It was around four in the afternoon that we got back into town.'

'Four in the afternoon... And you told Miss Laurence's housemate that the two of you parted company on Hill's Road, I believe?'

'Yeah, that's right.'

'And you haven't seen or heard from her since that time?'

'No.'

'Have you known Miss Laurence long?'

'Yes, I've known her since we were kids; we were at secondary school together.'

The sergeant looks at the constable. 'Well, I think that will be all for now, Mr Fenton. We may have some further questions to put to you at another time.'

They get up from the sofa, and I show them to the door.

And then the sergeant fires his parting shot. 'I understand, Mr Fenton, that you have a history of mental illness? That you have been an inpatient at Fulbourn Hospital?'

'Yeah; so what?' I retort. 'Lots of people go to Fulbourn. It's not like I was ever sectioned or anything.'

'I was only asking, sir. We'll be in touch.'

I shut the door on them. How did they know that? I wonder. Do they have records telling them about everyone who's on the mental health list? Then I realise they must have heard it from the same person who put them onto me in the first place; the person who must have told them I was the last person to see Esther: Patricia. That bitch would say anything to drop me in it.

Do they really suspect me? If they come back for more questioning, I'm going to have to tell them the full story if I want to clear myself. I'm going to have to tell them we went to Herschell House, and that in turn will mean giving them the full story about the Sallow Man and the removal men. And it's going to be a hard story for them to swallow.

Fortunately, I've got some proof. The photographs I got from Martin's place. I wish I had that notebook as well, but Esther kept hold of that... I've hidden the photographs under my mattress. I go through to the bedroom and lift up the top corner of the mattress on my side of the bed. My fingers don't make contact with the wallet. I feel around some more... Then panic choke-holds me and I yank the mattress off the ground and tip the whole thing over.

Gone. The photographs are gone.

Chapter Sixteen

They came back alright. They came back and they took me in to the station. To 'help them with their inquiries.' Forty-eight hours. That's how long they can keep me without charging me. They planned it from the start. I know they did. After that first visit this morning, I bet they were keeping my flat under observation; they wanted to see if they had spooked me into making a move—like returning to the scene of the crime; going back to wherever I'd disposed of Esther's body, to make sure I'd buried it properly. But then, when I *didn't* do anything like (I didn't go out at all after that visit), they just came back and hauled me in for questioning.

I'm in a small cubicle of whitewashed brickwork, and I'm lying on a truckle bed covered with the regulation itchy grey blanket. The room also boasts a toilet (with no lid) and a hand-basin. I'm in hell. This is what hell looks like. My personal hell. I have been deprived of my liberty and separated from my home, the only place I really feel safe in. It's getting dark outside (there's a small window, too high up to look out through) and the light has been switched on; I'd like to switch it off, but I don't have that luxury. *They* decide when the lights go out.

My interview was with the same two officers who came to my flat: Sergeant Wilde and Constable Boon; and as before Wilde did most of the talking. Things have changed since the days of *The Bill*; interview rooms these days look more counsellors' offices, with those low-seated cushioned chairs. A CCTV camera up in the corner recorded the proceedings for posterity (and presumably also to make sure the examining officers didn't try any strongarm interrogation tactics.)

'Have you ever had sexual relations with Esther Laurence?'

'What's that got to do with anything?'

'Just answer the question, please.'

'No, I haven't.'

'When you went for that walk on Tuesday, you didn't have sex with her then?'

'I've just told you we've never had sex!'

'Did you want to have sex with her that day?'

'No, I didn't! D'you think I raped and then murdered her? Is that it? And I suppose I also just happened to have a spade on my person, so I could bury the body afterwards!'

'You could have returned to the scene later.'

'I haven't got a car! I'd've had to have lugged the spade through the middle of Cambridge!'

'Yes, but bodies don't have to be buried, do they, sir? They can be dropped in a pond or in the river.'

'That's just speculation! Where's your proof, for Christ's sake? You haven't even got any circumstantial evidence!'

'We've got the fact that you were the last person to see her.'

'Yeah, but that's *all* you've got! Jesus, why would I want to kill Esther? We've been best friends for years.'

'Just friends? Are you sure you didn't have any stronger

feelings for her? Feelings that you never told her about; that you've kept bottled up? By your own admission you were alone with her in the countryside; nobody else around…'

'Oh, for—Look I'd never do anything like that to Esther!'

'And you've never been violent towards any other woman then, Mr Fenton?'

'No…'

'You don't sound too sure, Mr Fenton.' Wilde opened his notebook. 'I understand you were once in a relationship with a girl named Alicia Drummond. About five years ago, wasn't it?'

I sighed. 'Yes, I was. Patricia told you about that one, didn't she?'

'We're not obliged to divulge our sources, Mr Fenton; all you need to know is that we have it on very good authority that you used to beat this girl.'

'What? That's a fucking lie! Once—I hit her once, that's all! I was stupidly drunk and I got angry with her about something, and I lashed out. I mean I was that drunk I don't even remember it happening…'

'And you think that makes any difference, does it? You're being drunk?'

'Yes! When it's something I wouldn't do when I was sober; something I wouldn't do normally. And Like I said, it only happened *once*.'

'Only once? Are you sure about that, sir? Our information is that you hit the girl on a regular basis.'

'That's because Patricia Yarrow's a lying cow! Don't bother—I know it was her! She doesn't like me; she hates me; she'd say anything to drop me in it.'

'Really, sir? Well, it seems to me that people don't have to lie to give you a bad name. It seems like you've done a very good job of doing that yourself…'

I'm beginning to come round to Dwayne and Vicky's opinion about the cops. Or at least those two coppers I've got on my case. ('On my case' in every sense of the word.) Obviously, they don't like me, but apart from that I'm not sure what they're thinking… Do they honestly think that I've murdered Esther? Or are they just enjoying putting me through the wringer…? Or worse, are they trying to fit me up? To pin the crime on me just to save them from having to look for the real culprit?

That Wilde guy especially pisses me off. He's only the same age as me, and he's one of those coppers who seems to think he can be as personal and insinuating as he likes, just so long as he tags the word 'sir' onto the end of the sentence.

The idea that I might end up being charged with this crime… That scares me the most. What would happen to me then? Up before the magistrates and committed for trial. I couldn't just go home; they don't set bail when it's a murder charge. I would have to be 'remanded in custody' until my trial. Do they have special 'remand' prisons for people awaiting trial? Or do they put you in the same prisons as all the convicted criminals?

Either way, I couldn't cope in a prison.

And what if I'm tried and then found guilty? That would mean being inside for years. In a prison: nothing but men around you, no privacy because you have to share a cell, pissing and shitting in a bucket, communal showers, horrible food, bullying and intimidation… I wouldn't last five minutes.

Should I tell them? I don't have one shred of evidence to back it up, but should I tell them the truth? Tell them the whole story…?

It's the middle of the night. An eternal night. A night that's never going to end. I think I'm going insane. I haven't been able to sleep; I still can't sleep, and I can't keep still. I haven't had a fag for so long I think I'm starting to get nicotine withdrawal. It's my thoughts. They won't let me sleep. They keep running wild; running around all over the place and round and round in circles. My face feels itchy; I keep scratching it. And my body's so restless the muscles in my arms and legs are starting to cause me agony. I keep turning over in my bed, thinking it will be better if I change position; but it isn't. The bed's so fucking small. No-one can sleep in a bed like this—it's not a bed: it's a coffin; it's a torture device. My throat's dry and parched, but I don't want to get up and go to the sink. The bed won't let me go; I'm chained to it.

Round and round my thoughts keep spinning. Yuri, Esther, Herschell House, the Sallow Man, Martin, Patricia, Sergeant Wilde, everyone hates me, everyone suspects me, dirty pictures, BDSM clubs, yellow-bellied wagtails... My thoughts and memories are getting all twisted into knots, tighter and tighter, inside my head; the pain literally makes me wince...

And then the lights come on.

I pull the blanket off my head. The glare hits my eyes, they tear up. Through the blur I can see there's someone there; someone sitting on the toilet. My vision clears.

It's Esther. Esther dressed just like she was when I last saw her, sitting on the bog like it's a visitor's chair, and smiling at me.

'You're awake then?' she says. 'I've just been thinking about when we first met. You remember that? First day of big school. You'd only just moved to Cambridge and you didn't know anyone. We were in the same class and I sort of took pity on you, didn't I? You were a lot more shy back then than you are now. You weren't really opening up to people, and I was the one who persevered with you. Wasn't that noble of me?

'We ended up sticking together all through secondary school, didn't we? Remember how we all thought it weird that even though you came from a turnip-country village like Mepal, you didn't talk like a fenny? You never did have much of an accent at all...

'People like us, the misfits, we always found ways to make ourselves feel superior to the trendy set. That's how it is. Remember how we used to hang around in the library at lunchtime? And we started reading some of the classics they had there, didn't we? I can't even remember which one of us thought of it first. And there we were, wading through books like *Nausea* and *Crime and Punishment*, when everyone else was reading Harry Potter…'

What is she doing here, I wonder? She's supposed to be missing, isn't she? Has she been found then?

'No, I'm still amongst the missing,' Esther tells me. 'It's like the first episode of *The Invaders*, isn't it? What is it that cop says at the end? 'He would've still been alive if he hadn't wanted to believe your crazy story!' Something like that… Don't get me wrong: I'm not blaming you. I walked into this with my eyes open. I knew we were taking risks. You don't have to blame yourself…

'But you need to start standing up for yourself, Chad. You've always leaned on me for support, haven't you? I dunno—maybe it's partly my fault; but you need to start having more faith in yourself. Stand on your own two feet. Especially now that I'm not around…'

I open my mouth to ask her what's happened to her; but then the light cuts out, and I know that she's gone. I'm alone again…

…

The light comes back on and now it's Martin sitting on the toilet seat; stocky, tousle-haired Martin.

'I know what you're thinking, dude,' he says. '"Thanks for dragging me into this shit" right? I don't blame you. I'd feel the same. Funny, isn't it? I always believed in all those conspiracy stories, and then I went and found one right on my doorstep. Disappearers, removal men, the Sallow Man… Or did I just dream it all up? Did it all start off in my head, and then somehow it ended up getting out into the real world…?

'A dream, or something. A crazy idea… And I went and passed it on to you, didn't I? It's like I infected you with just that one phone-call. Like a relay race and I passed the baton on to you…

'Why do people believe in this crazy shit? I should be asking myself that one, shouldn't I? Is it just cuz we're all paranoid? Or does it somehow make us feel better to think that there are all these covert operations, all these cover-ups going on? People pulling the strings from behind the scenes? …Or is it all just our overactive imaginations? Looking for patterns that aren't there?'

He looks around the whitewashed room. 'And now here you are in the cop shop… You've gotta tell 'em everything, dude, if you wanna get out of this. You got no choice, man. They're just gunna keep on thinking you offed poor Esther unless you tell 'em the whole story…'

The lights go out again.

…

When they come back on, it's Patricia sitting there. She's giving me this look of total contempt; eyes narrowed, lips curled.

'I can't begin to tell you how much I hate you, Charles Fenton. Look at you lying there, hiding under your blanket. You're the most spineless, gutless yellow-belly ever, aren't you? You can't stand up and face anything, can you? You always run and hide, like the chicken-shit you are.

'And don't think I don't know what goes inside that head of yours, that cesspool you call a mind. You sick, degenerate fuck. You want everyone to feel sorry for you just because you're depressed, don't you? Huh. No-one would feel sorry for you if they knew what went on in that mind of yours; they'd all run a mile. The only reason you've got any friends at all is because they don't know what you're really like; you make sure of that, don't you, you little turd? Put on an innocent act, don't you? Huh! If they knew what you were really like, they'd all drop you like a shot.

'Yeah, I figured you out from the start, that's why I hated you from the start. I saw right through you at once and you knew it, didn't you? That's why you were always sucking up to me, trying to placate me, wasn't it? You were worried I'd tell the others what I knew about you. You want everyone to like you, but you know deep down, that you're a completely unlikeable person.

'Nothing, to say for yourself? Yeah, because you know I'm right, don't you? Oh, and look, he's crying now… Tears of self-pity, from the poor, innocent victim! …You little chicken-shit!'

I pull the cover over my head.

The lights go out…

…

'Don't listen to her.'

It's Yuri! The lights have come on again, and I hear her voice. I throw back the blanket and there she is, sitting on the toilet. She's dressed like she was at the Q-club, her hair in twin-tails.

'Yuri…'

'Don't listen to what she says. She doesn't know you. Only I know you. You are my lover; my slave and my master, and our hearts beat as one.'

'Yuri…'

'But I'm still mad at you, right now. I'm mad at you because you didn't call me. This terrible thing has happened to you today and you didn't even call me to tell me about it. You're entitled to one phone-call, right? You could have called me. Why didn't you call me?'

'Oh, Yuri… I… thought about it… But… I was… I was embarrassed… I didn't want you to know where I was… and what they're saying I've done…'

'That's so stupid. There should be no embarrassment between us. I am your lover; the most important person in your life; I am closer to you than anyone else can ever be, so you should always come first to me when you're in trouble.

You should come to me, just as I would come to you. Right?'

'Yes, you're right... I'm sorry...'

'Good. I accept your apology. Did you think that I would believe what they are saying about you? That you committed this offence? Did you think I could believe that? Never! I will always be here for you, Chad I am yours, my darling; now and forever...'

'Yuri...'

The lights go out...

'Yuri...?'

...

Chapter Seventeen

'You went to Herschell House?'

'That's right. I lied when I said we just went to Grantchester for a walk; we went out there for a specific reason; and that reason was to check out Herschell House. We thought we might find our friends Mel and Muriel there. They've gone missing, you see.'

'They've gone missing? They've been reported as missing persons?'

'No, it hasn't been reported; although I suppose I'm reporting it now, really. Mel and Muriel were taken away by these people called the removal men. They work for a man we call the Sallow Man, and they make people disappear. Have you heard of them?'

'No, Mr Fenton, I haven't.'

'Well, they're out there. My friend Martin rang me up one morning and said these removal men were coming to get him. That was how I first found out about it. Martin told me he had evidence about their activities hidden in his bathroom. He said they knew he was onto them, and that was why they were coming to get him. And then we got cut off. I didn't believe him at first, thought it was a put-on; but then

I went round to his place just to check; and he'd gone. The front door was wide open when I got there. In the place where he told me to look, I found a roll of camera film. Then the removal men came into the flat and I got out through the window. A big furniture van had just arrived and they were emptying his apartment, taking everything away. They always do that; when they make someone disappear, they take away everything that belongs to them.

'I went and got the film developed and found there were pictures of the removal men and their boss, the Sallow Man. There were pictures of these people outside the houses of other people who have been Disappeared… And there was a picture of a warehouse that looked like their main depot. The first person I told all this to was Esther—that's how she got involved.

'The next thing that happened was I saw the Sallow Man in town; and I followed him to a building in a courtyard down a side street. He went inside. A day or two later I went back to the place with Esther and we went in and we found it was a small apartment. It looked like the Sallow Man lived there. We found a notebook there that had the names and addresses of all the people who had been Disappeared. There were ten of them on the list; all of them were people we knew. We were still in the building when the Sallow Man turned up in a van with one of his men. We managed to get out of the building while they were inside, and we hid in the back of their van. When they came out again, they drove us back to their main warehouse; the one in the photograph. The warehouse is on an industrial estate in Cherry Hinton, and inside we found all the furniture and belongings of the missing people, all stacked up. But we must have been seen leaving the place, because when we came back later the place had been cleared out; the removal men had gone and there was just a printing factory there.

'And then, on Monday, our friends Mel and Muriel were taken away. The only possible lead we had was the name of

Herschell House, which was mentioned in the Sallow Man's notebook. We had an idea that all the Disappearers were being kept prisoner in that house; we knew it was a long shot, but it was our only lead. But the lead turned out to be a false one, cuz when we got there, there was nothing there except the family who lived there, and they didn't know anything about the Sallow Man or the Disappearers. The people we saw were a woman called Letty—short for Letitia I suppose—and her daughter, Constance. If you ask them, they can confirm we were both there that day and also the explanation we gave them for our being there. All you've got to do is ask them.

'So, that's pretty much it. It must be the Sallow Man who's taken Esther; they haven't taken her belongings, but it's still got to be him.'

'I see...'

'Good. I didn't tell you before because I know it's a hard story to swallow.'

'...I see that you're trying to get off with a diminished responsibility plea. Wouldn't that be right, sir? You don't even expect me to believe this story of yours, do you? You just want to make me think you're a basket case...'

So now I'm waiting to hear the result. I've been pretty insistent that they inquire at Herschell House. The only trouble is, it doesn't alibi me completely. I could, theoretically, have murdered Esther on the way back from that place... But those two women will at least be able to say that I didn't look like someone who was planning to murder his friend...

But there's another problem: What if Letty and Constance deny that we ever came to their house? They might. I made a point of not mentioning their BDSM parties, but it's possible they might think it better for themselves and their privacy to deny they ever even saw us... But then, I know their names—how could I know their names if I've never been to the house?

I hear the cell door open and I emerge from my cocoon. It's Sergeant Wilde. He doesn't look happy.

'Alright, you can leave.'

I'm free! I jump up off the bed.

'I'm not being charged, then?'

'No, you're not being charged.'

'Because you checked with Herschell House?' I ask.

'We did check, yes, and they confirm that you and the girl were both there, telling them the same bullshit story you told me this morning. But that's not the main reason we're letting you go. We've been analysing CCTV footage from that afternoon, and we've managed to identify Esther Laurence, walking alone down Cherry Hinton Road; the time and place tallies with the time you said you parted company with her on Hill's Road.'

On principle, I've always been against the use of CCTV cameras; but right now, I'm very grateful for their existence. 'So you've got footage of her walking home? Have you turned up anything else? Have you worked out where it was she disappeared?'

'We're still examining the footage,' Wilde tells me. 'There's a lot of it to get through. And anyway, that's our business; all you need to know is you're being released. Come on.'

He leads me out of the holding cells and through to the back office. Just as I'm passing a half-glassed door leading to a smarter-looking part of the station, I catch sight of a man in black in conference with a uniformed officer at the far end of the corridor. I stop in my tracks. The man in black is the Sallow Man.

I have my hand on the door handle.

'Oi! Not that way!' It's Sergeant Wilde. He's come back and grabbed my arm.

'It's him!' I shout. I point through the glass—but now the corridor is empty. 'He was there! The Sallow Man!'

'Will you shut up about your "Sallow Man"?' says Wilde. 'Come on.'

'He was just down there!' I insist. 'He was talking to one of your bosses!'

I make another grab for the door, but Wilde catches hold of my arm again, drags me off, grating out: 'Will *you come on?*'

'But—'

'Look, you're not going down there. That part of the station's private. Now for the last time, come on.'

Reluctantly I'm led to the back reception office. The front reception desk is the nice one where they receive members of the public; round the back is the grubby reception desk for the receiving of drunks and detainees. The doors here open onto the station's rear carpark. Here, they give me back my fags, my lighter and my keys, preserved in plastic bags; then I scribble my name on some forms.

'Can I go now?' I ask.

'This way,' then says Sergeant Wilde, indicating an interior door.

'What now? I thought I was free to go.'

'You are,' says Wilde. 'But I'm taking you to the front desk. There's someone there to see you.'

So, I follow him through the building to the front desk, and there's Yuri sitting in one of the visitor's chairs. When she sees me, her face lights up, and she gets up from the chair. We run into each other's arms.

We get the bus back to my place, Yuri paying, because I don't have my wallet with me.

Turns out Yuri isn't pissed off at me for not using my one phone-call on her. She hasn't even mentioned it, so I'm thinking she isn't even aware that I had that option. Come to think of it, I've heard that police interrogation procedures can be pretty intense in Japan; so they probably don't even have that one phone-call option over there.

Seems that news of my being dragged in for questioning is all over the place—Yuri got the heads up from Howard. They're all talking about me online it seems—thanks to Patricia, who's apparently proud of having dropped me in it with the police. And I really, *really* hope that this act of malice on her part is going to come back and bite her on her doughy misshapen arse.

All I want to do now though is get home and stay there.

I don't think I've mentioned this before, but there's a stop for the regular city centre bus service practically outside my door. So, once we're off the bus, then it's just across a carpark and up the covered staircase to my flat. These apartment buildings are old, so you won't find a lift anywhere—a real pain in the arse when it comes to moving furniture, but not really a problem the rest of the time.

I open the door with my key and we walk inside. I look fondly around my familiar living room as though I've been away for ages; it seems like ages, although in real, linear time, it's actually been less than twenty-four hours. The comforting smell of home. I pull my shoes off, throw myself down in my usual place on the sofa and reach for my cigarettes.

Yuri positions herself in front of me and starts taking her clothes off. It's become a ritual for her, this; a solemn duty.

'You don't have to do that, Yuri,' I tell her, smiling wearily. 'Not today.'

Her reply is a very firm one. 'Yes, I do. I made a solemn vow to you that I would always disrobe when I was inside your house, and that I would do this every time I passed through your front door, without exception; *every* time—even when menstruating. I will not break the promise I made to you.'

I'm not going to argue the point so I let her take her clothes off. 'You don't need to move,' she says. 'For the rest of today, I will do everything for you. First, refreshment. Would you like a cup of tea or coffee?'

'I would dearly love a cup of coffee,' I say. 'But come here first.'

Yuri obeys; she climbs onto the sofa and straddles my lap. We fold our arms around each other and hug—a long, silent hug that eases my mind, soothes my soul, and fills me with tears of gratitude. We separate. She smiles at me, wipes away my tears. Her face is close to mine; I can see every beautiful detail; every eyelash, every eyebrow hair, every pore of her lovely skin.

'Thank you,' I say.

We exchange soft, brief kisses.

'Thank you,' I say again.

I feel a warmness flooding over me—and then I *do* feel a warmness flooding over me; in the region of my lower abdomen.

I laugh. 'Yuri...?' I say, looking into her fathomless eyes.

'Yes, my master?'

'...Why are you peeing all over me?'

She smiles with all her overbite.

'Because I'm so happy...'

Bless her.

Chapter Eighteen

Howard is the oldest person in Chad's immediate circle of friends. He has passed forty and his distinguishing features are those of being fat and bald. Obviously, a great many people pass the age of forty without becoming fat and bald, and for that matter many people *below* the age of forty can be bald and fat, but Howard himself perceives his baldness and fatness as two glaring indicators of his inexorably advancing age.

Howard keeps himself very busy. He edits and publishes a (once printed but now online) fanzine called *Hot Rock* which is devoted to the local, national and international alternative rock scene; in addition to this he organises gigs showcasing local, as well as touring, indie-rock bands. More recently he has extended *Hot Rock* into an indie record label, releasing compilation albums and records (some of them even on vinyl!) from local bands—and, as we've already seen, he also DJs at his nightclub *Club Hot Rock*.

If his tireless devotion to the rock music scene seems obsessive to you, that's because it is. Always keen on the local music scene, Howard threw himself into it with increased zeal after the collapse of a short and very unsatisfactory (on both sides) marriage. The problem was that Howard, as a married man, suffered from imposter syndrome; he was never able to shake the feeling that as a husband, he somehow was just not the real deal. And the perhaps inevitable result of this mental affliction was that, over time, his wife herself started to think that as a husband he wasn't the real deal either, and so she walked out on him.

And so now, he dedicates himself to championing the local and national alternative rock music scene, and has made himself a very important figure within that scene. But his tireless efforts are not always rewarded…

The Portland Arms, close to chucking-out time, and the fag-end of a very unsatisfactory evening for Howard. Tonight has been the night of another *Hot Rock* gig at the Portland—and not many people have turned up to it. It happens that way sometimes. Sometimes you could put on a gig and it would be packed, and there'd be a good vibe, and you would feel happy and satisfied with the whole thing, and reassured that the Cambridge rock music scene was still thriving and that there was lots of interest out there; but then sometimes you'd put on a gig, and there'd be about a dozen paying customers, most of them your friends, and you would feel depressed and dejected because it seemed like people just didn't care about music anymore… Tonight has been one of those latter nights. The entrance money he's made this evening is barely enough to pay the sound engineer. It's been a local bands showcase tonight, all new bands; and in his heart of hearts Howard feels that to a degree at least, the bands themselves have been responsible for the poor attendance. Yes, he'd done everything he could to promote the gig himself, but these up-and-coming bands ought to be pushing and promoting themselves as well; getting all their mates to come along and see them play. If Howard were the confrontational type, he might have been inclined to go up to some of the members of tonight's bands and tell them this to their faces; tell them to start pulling their fingers out—but tragically or otherwise, Howard is the reverse of the confrontational type, and so those words have gone unsaid.

He walks into the pub's saloon—which is emptying now, but has enjoyed a much better turn-out than the gig itself has—and joins some of his friends who are sitting in one of the booths (back of the room, near the fireplace.) Chad is there, along with his girlfriend Yuri. Hilary is there as well, and a couple of others (unnamed minor characters; non-speaking parts.)

Howard mops his perspiring face with the handkerchief he always keeps ready for the purpose. It's a warm evening, and even with the small audience it's been hot in the gig room.

Chad is completely shitfaced tonight, and he's sitting there, the centre of attention, holding forth in that deliberate, bellicose way in which the shitfaced generally do hold forth.

'...Iss the numbers, y'see,' he declares. 'Iss the numbers. If the numbers don't add up, then they gotta make some subtractions. But they can't jus' subtrac' any-old-one—NO!' thumping the table for emphasis. 'No! They've gotta be very p'ticular who they subtrac'. They gotta pick the people who are gunna varnish... vanish without leaving a ripple; the people who won't be mished... won't be missed... And, d'you know who that is?'

'Yes!' says Yuri who, like a dutiful girlfriend, has been

listening very attentively.

Chad looks at her owlishly for a moment. And then, turning to the others: 'Does anyone else know who that is?'

'People like us…?' ventures Hilary.

'Correct!' says Chad, giving the table another thump. 'People like ush; people like us… The square pegs. The misfits. Thas who they make disappear, and thas who they *are* makin' disappear...'

'You mean that these people took Esther?' asks Howard, wondering if there's any sense behind these drunken ramblings.

'Yes!' once again with table-bruising emphasis. 'Thas exactly what I'm sayin': they took Esther! An' not jus' Esther! She's only the ice of the titberg… Is that right…? Yeah, well, I dunno why, but they took her diff'rently and people noticed—but usually they make people disappear so that iss not noticed. Twelve people,' holding up his ten fingers to illustrate the figure. 'Twelve people. Yes, twelve people have been disappeared. And no-one's even noticed. 'Cept me and Esther—'

'And me,' says Yuri.

'And you,' concurs Chad.

'What twelve people?' asks Hilary. 'Do we know them?'

'You know 'em all. Or if you don't, you know someone who knows 'em.'

'Like who?'

'Like Muriel and Mel for a start.'

'But they just moved away didn't they?' says Howard. 'That's what I heard.'

'No,' is the sententious reply. 'They didn't move away. They were *re*moved away. By the removal men.'

'What removal men?'

'*The* removal men. The removal men who remove the people as well as their furniture. This is true. I'm dead serious here; so listen. They come first thing in the morning. Mostly. Maybe not always. And they park their panty…

panta... their big van outside your house and then they jus' walk right in. I dunno how they get in—they must have skellington keys or something. But once they're inside, thassit. You've had it. You're gone. Disappeared.'

Where did this all come from? wonders Howard. Has Chad come up with this entire story just as a theory to explain Esther's disappearance? It doesn't even fit. Nobody thinks that Esther's just moved house. All the evidence suggests that she's been abducted—grabbed off the street by someone. An opportunistic crime; that's what they're saying. The only other alternative is that Esther decided to voluntarily pull a disappearing act; and she's the last person to have done something like that...

Yes, she must have been abducted, and thank God Chad has been cleared of any involvement. And thank God Patricia hasn't turned up tonight, as well! She's one person Howard is glad didn't make it to this evening's gig. But then, she probably guessed that Chad would be here; and giving Chad a wide berth will be a very wise career move for her right now.

At least Chad's got Yuri to comfort him... He can't help envying Chad his girlfriend... Howard hasn't been in a romantic relationship with another human being since that day his wife walked out on him... He knows what people say about him: that he's not interested in that sort of thing any longer; that he's dedicated to his music and his fanzine and his promoting; that he's asexual, happily celibate...

Well, people are wrong about that one: he's *not* happily celibate. He just hasn't been able to do anything to rectify the situation...

Next morning, Howard wakes up with a splitting headache.

Three pints! That's all he drank last night: three lousy pints of beer. Ten years ago, three pints would never have given him a hangover like this. There's no justice in the world. Well, at least it's Sunday, so he doesn't have to go to work today.

It's getting older, that's what it is—your body starts to let you down. Things you used to take for granted, like a smoothly-functioning digestive system, start acting up. Old injuries can come back to haunt you. Tea and coffee go from being drinks you *like* to drink to drinks you *need* to drink. And you can't indulge in things like alcohol without paying the price for them more than you used to when you were younger…

Howard throws back the duvet and drags himself out of bed. (He's wearing pyjamas; you don't have to look away.) He plods through to the bathroom, opens the medicine cabinet, pops a couple of painkillers from a blister-pack, and swallows them down with a glass of tap water, and drinks a second glass of water for good measure… That's another thing about encroaching age, he remembers: your body becomes slower to let you know that it's dehydrated, which means you have to start anticipating these things…

Back in the bedroom, the sound of a heavy vehicle pulling up outside draws him to the window. A removal van… Someone must be moving out today… He wonders who it could be; he hadn't noticed any estate agent's signs… Removal men… It puts him in mind of all that stuff Chad was spouting at the pub last night… Funny coincidence, that…

Chapter Nineteen

They've started dragging the river looking for Esther's body. They won't find her. She hasn't been raped and murdered and had her body dumped somewhere; she's been Disappeared. And the cops damn well know it. I know I didn't just imagine seeing the Sallow Man talking in that corridor at Parkside Station; he was there—that means the cops are in on it. Maybe not all of them; maybe not the small-fry like Sergeant Wilde and Constable Boon; but the higher-ups; the executives; they're in on it—they know about the Disappearances. But Esther's disappearance was different; the way they did it, it's become a reported crime; people know about it. And because people know about it, they have to go through the motions; they have to go on with the search, and waste a lot of money looking for something that's not ever going to be found.

And another thing. It didn't occur to me before, but it should've: to have grabbed Esther the way they did that day, they had to have been following her. And that must mean they must have also had her house under surveillance. The police think (or *say* they think) that Esther's abduction had to have been an opportunistic crime; that some passing psycho who liked the look of Esther, grabbed her and bundled her into his car when no-one was looking—How can anyone seriously believe that? Esther was a big, strong girl; she wasn't some little kid. Little kids get grabbed like that because they're grabbable—but no one guy on his own could have overpowered Esther like that. It would need to have been more than one guy; in other words, a bunch of removal men in one of those vans of theirs. That's how Esther was spirited away.

And if I'm right about that, and they were watching and following Esther; does that mean they're watching and following *me* as well? Have they got their sights on me? I've started keeping my eyes open, but so far I haven't seen anything.

The only thing I've had is that dream where the Sallow Man's watching my flat; standing down in the carpark, looking up at the window. I've had that same dream several times now, always just before I wake up—but so far it's only been a dream; when I look out the window there's never anyone out there.

But I know that he's been in my flat. I know that he has, cuz those photographs have disappeared from under my bed.

I searched the rest of my place after I got out of the nick that day, but I didn't find them and I knew I wouldn't. I'd never put that wallet of photos anywhere other than under my mattress. The Sallow Man, or one of his minions broke into my flat and found them and took them. Maybe it wasn't so smart of me to hide them under the mattress; it seemed like a good place, but it must have been an obvious one to them since they found them so easily. And they did it without disturbing anything else in my flat, and with no signs of a break-in. The Sallow Man or his zombies just got into my flat the same way it seems they can get into any place they want to; they must have some universal key that can unlock every door in existence.

No Yuri this evening; and I won't be seeing her tomorrow, either. Busy with her coursework. So, tonight I'm just stretched out on my sofa, chilling out, thinking of her while I listen to J-rock girl bands on my stereo; the music she introduced me to. Everything makes me think of Yuri—I couldn't get her out of my head if I wanted to. She's engrained herself so deeply into my life that thoughts of her have attached themselves to almost everything around me.

I'm listening to The Go-Devils, this female garage band. Not exactly prolific, this band; they only produced a demo tape, a single and an EP over a period of fourteen years; not exactly living up to the stereotype of the workaholic Japanese (unless they were workaholic about their day jobs.) All their stuff's collected on one CD, and it's very good music, very polished. (Like the saying goes: Anything America can do, Japan can do better!) The main song's called 'Super Stuff' and the singer sings 'I can't get enough of his super stuff.' Obviously, the song's about her fucking her boyfriend, but it's not quite clear whether his 'super stuff' refers to the guy's sexual performance in general, or more specifically his cock or his sperm. We were talking about this, me and Yuri, and she thinks the super stuff is the sperm, and she might be right. The cover illustration of the band does feature a giant can of whipped cream, so that could be an indicator. This reminds me of the time Yuri got me to dip my cock into a can of Ambrosia Devon Custard so that she could lick it all off me… I don't think I'll ever be able to look at a can of that custard the same way again.

My phone starts buzzing; a surprise, because I don't actually get many direct phone calls these days. Most people prefer to send texts and emails; I'm one of those people myself.

I'm even more surprised when I see that my caller is Hilary. I know Hilary and I know he hates talking on the phone; so for him to be actually calling me, it must be something important. I pause the music I'm listening to and take the call.

'Hey,' I say. 'What's up, Hilary?'

'Hi…' says Hilary. 'Are you busy at the moment?'

He sounds nervous, uncertain.

'No,' I assure him. 'I'm not busy at the moment; just at home on my own. What's up?'

'Well, you remember what you said about those removal men…? And how they were taking people away…?'

Ah. He's referring to last Saturday night at the Portland, when I got myself completely shitfaced and let my mouth run away with me—so technically, no, I don't remember what I said; but Yuri filled me in on the broad details. So, I say: 'Yeah, I remember. What about it?'

'I think they've taken Howard away…'

'Howard? Why; what's happened? Has he disappeared?' Howard!

'Yeah… You're not on Facebook, so you wouldn't know. People are talking. He hasn't posted anything for days; and he usually posts a lot of stuff… And there were people saying how they couldn't get in touch with him anywhere; asking if anyone knew what was going on…'

'And has anyone actually been to his house? Is it empty?

Is his furniture gone?'

'Yeah, I did. I went round there yesterday, and his furniture *is* all gone; the place is empty and they've put up a "for sale" sign...'

'That's it, then,' I say. 'You're right; it must be that. Howard's been Disappeared.'

Howard. For some reason I'm surprised they'd take him. I mean yeah, he's one of our crowd, the people being targeted; but he's older. Everyone else they've taken away has been in their teens or twenties... I must have somehow thought that he might be safe because he was older; that maybe they only target young people... But now that I think about it, why should they only target young people? A statistic is a statistic; and if this is all about balancing the books, every statistic removed is still a statistic removed; so I suppose it doesn't really matter whether that statistic would've otherwise been around for sixty more years or for thirty...

'And there's something else...' says Hilary.

'What is it?'

'I think... I think they're after me, now...'

'After you? What do you mean, Hilary? Tell me what's happened. Have you seen them? Are they watching you?'

'Yeah... I think they are...'

'And what, are they outside your place right now?'

'I... I'm not sure... It's dark... I saw them earlier... I mean, I think it was them...'

'You mean you saw the removal men?'

'Yeah, the ones you were talking about...'

'Okay, tell me where and when you think you saw them; and what did they look like?'

'Well, they weren't in a removal van; it was just a small van... But they had those beige overalls and caps like you said, and the van was that colour, as well. And there was something about their faces... They were like stone or something; no expression at all... And they were staring at me and it... it really made my scared... I know it sounds stupid, but—'

'No, it doesn't sound stupid, Hilary. I've seen these people; I know exactly what you mean. But where was it you saw them? Were they outside your flat?'

'Not exactly outside... A bit further down the street. That's why I don't know if they're still there.... I was walking past them... just coming back from the shops... And it was like they were waiting for me; they just stood there staring at me...'

'And when was it? When did this happen?'

'This afternoon.'

'Did they start following you?'

'No, they just stood there...'

'And what about since then? Have you seen them again?'

'No, but I feel like they're still there... I haven't gone out to check.... I'm scared...'

'Okay, Hilary. You just stay where you are. I'm coming right over.'

'You are...?' I can hear the relief in his voice.

'Sure. Just hang tight; I'll be there in ten minutes.'

Hilary lives in Arbury, in that maze of backstreets off Carlton Way that's all apartment buildings and terrace houses. It's kebab van territory, same as Kings Hedges, where I live.

I pull my trainers on, grab my cigarettes and set off.

It's dark and there aren't many people about so I've got that usual edge of fear as I walk down Mere Way; which I guess is partly from the race memory inherited from our ancestors, who kept themselves safely tucked away in their caves after dark—and partly from my own personal knowledge that the streets at night can contain bad people... For a girl walking alone at night, it'll be the fear of being raped that's in the corner of her mind; but for us guys (even though we're not exactly immune to sexual assault), it's more the fear of getting our heads kicked in.

And yet society tells us that it's no big deal, one of those things, and just something we should shrug off. I even remember once seeing 'getting beaten up' as one of the items on a list of Things a Man Should Have Done Before He Reaches Thirty. Well, I've passed that milestone; I got beaten up once—can't say I found it that easy to just shrug off, though… The people who beat me up were laughing while they kicked me—and if nothing else, that was definitely a wake-up call for me. Before it happened, I don't think I'd really even been conscious that there were people like that around—so I suppose I ought to thank my attackers for setting me straight on that one, and giving me such a valuable life experience… I've always felt like I'm not entitled to anyone's sympathy on account of what happened; that because I'm a guy and I didn't get raped, I should just shrug the whole thing off as a minor incident. And then, when I can't do that, I start to feel guilty about it; like I'm just feeling sorry for myself, and need to man up and grow a pair.

(Just think, though. If someone came up with a list of Things a Woman Should Have Done Before She Reaches Thirty, that included 'getting raped,' people would be up in arms!)

However, I make it to the street where Hilary lives without getting a kicking or even being threatened with one. Hilary lives in one of those blocks of flats where the front doors all face the street and they've got those verandas for all the upstairs floors. Hilary lives in one of the more burglar-friendly ground floor flats. Walking along, I look at the cars parked along the kerb; this would be the way Hilary walked when he was coming back from the shops; when he said he saw the removal men and one of their vans. There's no sign of them now.

But then, they wouldn't come along and take Hilary away in the evening, would they? The removal men always come for you first thing in the morning… At least, I've always thought that's what they do; but I guess that's only because I know they came in the morning in the cases of Martin, and Mel and Muriel. But then, even if that is their general procedure, I know they've already deviated from that at least once with the way they took Esther.

When I get within sight of Hilary's place, there's no light showing in his front window. Shit! Could they have taken him? In the ten minutes, fifteen at the most, since I got off the phone with him—have they come and taken him away?

I run up to the door and ring the doorbell. After a pause, the door opens slowly; I hear the sound of the chain drawn taut. There's enough light from the streetlights for me to see Hilary's face peering at me through the gap; he looks terrified.

'Hey,' I say. 'It's me.'

'Are they still there?'

'The removal men? No, I didn't see their van. All's clear. So, are you going to let me in?'

He closes the door, releases the chain, and then opens it again to let me in. The front door opens into his living room and the room's in pitch darkness.

'Why've you got the lights out?' I ask. 'Were you in bed?'

'No, but I didn't want to turn the lights on while they were out there,' answers Hilary. 'I thought it might… that it might make them… do something…'

'They're not moths, Hilary. If they knew you were home, it wouldn't make any difference whether you had the lights on or off. And anyway, like I said, they're not even there anymore, so how about shedding some light on the subject?'

'Okay…' says Hilary.

He switches the light on. Hilary's living room is an absolute tip; books, magazines, CDs, DVDs all over the floor and hardly room to walk without stepping on something. Basically, Hilary's place looks like how people who don't know me any better expect my place to look. I sit myself down in an armchair and look around. I used to come to this place a lot a few years back, and nothing's really changed since those days.

Back then, after we first met at the therapy group, me and Hilary used to be much closer friends than we are now. We'd always be round each other's places, going out to the pub together... But then, somehow, and I don't exactly know what happened, but it just kind of cooled off between us... It's not like we had a major argument or falling out or anything, we just seemed to drift apart (pardon the cliché); I dunno; maybe we both realised that we weren't as fond of each other as we used to be... And now, well we're still part of the same set and we still see each other, but only in company; we don't hang out together like we used to... And whenever we *do* find ourselves alone together, like if we're the first people to arrive at the pub, there's this awkward feeling hanging in the air between us... Maybe we both feel guilty about not being as good friends as we used to be...

'Are they coming to take me away, then?' asks Hilary.

'What? Those people who aren't even out there anymore?'

'But they *were* there...'

'I know; I'm not saying I don't believe you; but just because you saw them doesn't mean—Look, have you just been sitting here in the dark fretting about this all evening?'

'Yes...'

'Then what you need is a drink!' I tell him. 'Have you got any booze in the house?'

'I've got some beer in the fridge...'

'Good! Then let's both have one! Right?'

'Okay...'

He mooches into the kitchen and returns with two cans of Fosters. I notice that he still got that round-shouldered walk of his. I remember telling him he needed to correct that; that if he walked straighter, he'd feel better... but here he is, still round-shouldered.

I crack open my can.

'Cheers!' I say.

He returns the salute in a lackadaisical way.

'What do they do with them when they take them away?' he asks.

'That I don't know,' I tell him. 'I mean I've thought about it; and I've got loads of theories—but theories are all they are. I just don't know.'

'Do you think they kill them, or do they take them somewhere?'

'I don't *know*. It could be either, Hilary.'

'Maybe the place they take them to is actually somewhere nice...' says Hilary. 'Maybe they pick people like us so they can take us to some special place; not like in *The Prisoner*; but somewhere that's nice...'

'I seriously doubt that, Hilary. I don't think these people have got our best interests at heart.'

'They *might* have, though. You don't know; you said so yourself...' He looks at me. I can see there's something he wants to say; something that's on his mind. I wait for him to measure his words. 'I went to the Doc Cotton Club a few weeks ago...'

'Oh, yeah?' I say. Hilary's not gay, but I'm not that surprised to hear that he went to the gay club. When you're lonely, you'll look for company wherever you can find it. 'And... did something happen when you were there?'

'Yeah... I don't remember most of it; I was drunk; I mean really drunk. I was already completely hammered when I arrived at the club; surprised they let me in... It's all a blur. There was one boy I remember talking to; he seemed really nice; I think we might have talked for a long time... I thought it was him I left the club with, but when I looked round it was someone else; it was a much older guy; I don't know how I ended up walking with him... I didn't even remember seeing him before...'

I'm not liking the sound of this. 'And then what happened? You didn't go home with this bloke, did you?'

'No... but we... we ended up in his car...'

'And what? You mean he fucked you?'

'Yeah...'

'And did he use a condom?' I demand. 'Can you remember that?'

'No... I don't think he did...'

'Jesus Christ, Hilary! You need to see your doctor! Have you done that? You need to get tested! He might've infected you!'

'I s'pose...'

Oh, Christ. I know Hilary. I know he'd rather not get tested and carry on just hoping that nothing's wrong; he'd rather do that than hear the worst. But if he's infected, he needs to know about it.

I watch him necking his beer. This must have been on his mind for weeks now.

'I tell you what,' I say; 'I'll stay round here tonight, okay? I'll crash on the sofa, like I used to. And then, tomorrow morning, we'll go over to the surgery together, and get you an appointment with your GP; so you can get tested.'

'My GP'll be booked up,' says Hilary.

'Then we'll just see the duty doctor,' I say. I don't want to alarm him by suggesting we make it an emergency appointment. 'But for now, how about making a night of it? Knock back some beers and watch some DVDs; it'll be like old times, won't it? How much more beer have you got in the fridge?'

'Six more cans...'

'Three each; that's plenty! What shall we watch?'

Hilary chooses *Red Dwarf*. Our four cans of lager see us through all of *Red Dwarf V* (arguably the best series.) We're both laughing out loud by the time we're on our last cans. ('To be diddled by a giant squid on the first date? Think how we'd feel in the morning!') It's past one o'clock by the time we turn in; Hilary goes to his bedroom and I curl up on the sofa under his spare duvet.

I wake up in broad daylight to find myself lying on a carpeted floor in an empty room.

For a minute my mind is all over the shop, madly scrambling around, rounding up scattered thoughts. I went to sleep on Hilary's sofa in Hilary's front room... How did I get here...? Wait! Have they got me? Have I been Disappeared?

Then I realise I'm still in Hilary's front room; it's his front room, but it's been stripped bare; every stick of furniture, all his belongings that were strewn around the place; everything's gone—even the smell of beer and tobacco that ought to be hanging in the air.

No. *I* haven't been taken away—*Hilary* has.

Chapter Twenty

Hilary was always an imitator; he was always parroting things he's heard other people say; it was like he didn't have any opinions of his own; he'd just soak up other people's. I'd hear him quoting things I'd said to him to other people, like it was his own original material. Sometimes he'd even quote my own material back to me; those times he must have forgotten that he got it from me in the first place. Yes, I'd always known that about him, even since our days together at the therapy group; I'd always known it, but for some reason it only started getting on my nerves much later. In the early days, I'd just let it slide... And now I'm thinking: is that why I let things start to cool off between us? Is that why I started seeing less of him, started spending less time with him? If it was, then it was a bloody silly, petty reason to have done that...

And yes, I know I'm only thinking this now because now he's gone and it's too late to do anything about it.

It's hot today—severe weather warning hot.

I've gone back to my apartment because that's all I can do, and I'm lying on my bed because that's all I feel like doing. I've got the window wide open and I can hear cars going past, kids on their way to school messing around; all the usual noises of the everyday world...

And I feel like that's not my world; I feel like my world has changed because dark forces have some along and are busy taking my world apart all around me, piece by piece. Martin, Esther, Mel and Muriel, Howard, and now Hilary; the people from my set who were closest to me have all been taken away. And the ones that are left... Well, they're more acquaintances than friends; acquaintances or friends of friends; outright enemies in one or two cases.

Why is this happening? I know that it's normal to think that everything that happens has to somehow relate to ourselves—at least, it's normal enough for someone like me... But that's really how it feels right now. I feel like the Sallow Man is doing all this to me; that I'm the real target; that everything that he's been orchestrating has been about me; about breaking up my world... Looking back, I can imagine that's what he wanted to let me know that night at the Q-club; that it's *me* he's got his eye on; that it's me who's his target; that he's watching me...

In my mind's eye, I keep seeing him standing down there in the carpark, leaning on his car, looking up at my bedroom window. I know it's only a dream I've been having, but the image is so real; I can picture it so vividly...

But it can't be that. I'm forgetting my own unimportance. And that's what this is all supposed to be about—getting rid of the unimportant ones; the ones who won't be missed.

I wish Yuri was here. I'm not supposed to be seeing her until tomorrow, but I want to see her now; I need her with me. She's the one thing I've got left—the one thing that's tangible and real and that can't be taken away from me. She's an outsider; she's not affected by all this; she's not involved;

she's a foreigner with a student visa, so she's not part of all this that's happening. Yuri exists on some other list of statistics back in her own country; she's not included on the list here that's currently under revision. I've got to try and get hold of her. I know she's got her own life and she's got work to do; that she can't be on-call for me, twenty-four-seven; but I need her now. I've got to try and get hold of her. Sometimes, when she's not around I can get by with just thinking about her; but not right now; right now, I need her in the flesh; I need her living presence here with me. I'll send her a text and hope she looks at her phone.

I'm walking into town, light as air.

I managed to get through to her! I managed to get through to Yuri by text—she replied! Said she was in college right now, but she could meet me in her room at her hall of residence at four! She says she'll cook dinner for me! I know she's super-busy (her expression) with coursework right now, but she's still making time for me. That's what she's like. She loves me and she'll do anything for me and I'm the luckiest guy in the world.

I passed some of the time I had to wait looking through those pictures of her; just lying on my bed, swiping through them on my smartphone screen. The pictures look raw and amateurish; but that's fine; that's how pictures like this *should* look; that's how they're meant to be. (In porn these days, they sometimes photoshop professional pictures to make them look more claustrophobic and amateurish; make them look like smartphone porn.) It's like an endless gallery of Yuri passing before my eyes; Yuri, Yuri, Yuri… Posing naked cuz it's fun and it's good to let go like that and be dirty and sexy… She's so beautiful I could cry… Her cute, crooked, smiling overbite, her long, long hair, her nipples like space capsules, the pink soles of her feet, the dark line of hair along her arse-crack… I was working the hand-pump while I scrolled through those pictures and I was supposed to be edging because I wanted to keep my tanks full for Yuri, but then I went and stopped too late and shot my load…

But that's okay—just thinking that I'm going to be seeing Yuri in a while should have my balls working overtime. My sperm count seems to have shot up since I've been fucking Yuri; I'd swear that production has gone into overdrive. It's like my balls want to shoot out as much of their 'super stuff' as possible, just to make Yuri happy… Actually, no; it'll be to make Yuri *pregnant*, more like—that's what those two want. It's all they ever think about, the one-track minded, species-perpetuation obsessed buggers.

If you ask me, everyone should choose their partner in life from another country. Travel broadens the mind, they say—so, just fall in love with a foreigner, and on top of all the other benefits of a happy relationship and lots of good sex, you get that mind-broadening factor thrown in as well. Yuri tells me a lot about life back home in Japan; you know, all those little everyday details; everything that's the same as it is here, everything that's different. There's so much to learn. Thinking about it, maybe that's why so many same-culture relationships go stale so easily: they just can't have much to talk to each other about, have they? Nothing to learn from each other. Idiots! That's what you get for being so insular.

Yuri's my religion. They tell us we all need something to believe in, right? Something to help us make sense of our lives, to be our guiding star. Well, I don't want any intangible deity whose backstory was written up centuries ago, and is full of out-of-date information and out-of-date attitudes; I've got Yuri, my tactile goddess; and she lives very much in the here and now. I know she's not omniscient, infallible or anything; I don't pretend that she is, and I don't have to. I know she's a flawed human being like the rest of us—but she's still my goddess, perfect even in her imperfections. She is what she is to me; and that's all that matters to me. Who or what she is to anyone else, I couldn't give a shit. For me, she's just Yuri: always cheerful, always optimistic, loyal, full of love, endlessly compassionate, amazingly talented in her art, and as a lover resolutely submissive, forthright in her yielding… I'm reflected in her eyes, and she's reflected in mine—our hearts beat as one, as she puts it herself.

There's a song by this J-rock band Seagull Screaming Kiss Her Kiss Her where the vocalist sings 'Kiss my pretty ass.' That's how you should worship your goddess. Yuri's arse is my shrine and my altar.

I've been to Yuri's Hall of Residence before, so I know where it is; but we usually prefer to meet round mine, because her room there's just a poky little bedsit with an even pokier built-in bathroom that's not even a bathroom cuz it doesn't have a bath. (Japanese people like to soak in the tub, so Yuri always likes to use my bath whenever she comes over.) And she doesn't have her own kitchen at all; she has to share one with everyone else on her floor of the building.

The Hall's not far from where Yuri's college is, so she will have gone straight back from there when she finished. I'm almost there now, and checking my watch, I see that I've got here almost half an hour early. I did (because I was impatient) set off sooner than I needed to, but my plan was to pace myself, to walk slowly so's not to get there too soon; but it looks like, with all these happy thoughts buzzing round my head, I've gone and done the opposite and speed-walked all the way. It's as hot as hell and I'm hardly even noticing it…

The Hall's just a big four-storeyed brick box, and I'm in sight of it when I see a grey-haired man in a black suit step out through the main entrance and head off down the street away from me.

I freeze in my tracks.

It's the Sallow Man.

The Sallow Man coming out of Yuri's Hall of Residence.

Oh, no. Dear Lord, no. Don't tell me he's—

I charge up to the building, barging into a couple of people in my haste, and then I'm up the steps and madly pressing Yuri's room number on the intercom next to the doors. There's no answer. I press the button again, and keep it pressed. She should be in; if she left college when she said she was going to, she should be home by now; she should be in.

Then there's a click and Yuri's voice saying: 'Hello?'
Thank Christ.
'It's Chad,' I say. 'Are you okay?'
'Oh, hi! Yes, I'm okay; I was just in the shower. I didn't expect you so soon! Come on up.'

Yuri presses a button at her end and the front doors unlock for me. I walk through into the hallway. She's alright. False alarm. I thought the Sallow Man might've got her, made her disappear or something, but she's okay; she was taking a shower and she's okay…

Wait a minute. I definitely saw the Sallow Man coming out of this place; there's no mistake about that. So, if it wasn't to see Yuri, what was he doing here…?

A thought hits me, and it stops me in my tracks. It's a thought so horrible, so monstrous, that when it crashes over me, it literally makes me stagger under its weight.

Yuri. The Sallow Man was here. What other reason could he have had for being in this building if it wasn't to see Yuri? This is a student Hall of Residence; you don't just walk into the place like it was an hotel; if you're not a resident here, you can only get in if a resident lets you in. Who would've let the Sallow Man into this place? Who's he likely to have known here? Who's the only person in this place who is in any way connected with the Sallow Man?

And I arrived early. I arrived early and the Sallow Man was just leaving. The Sallow Man was just leaving, and Yuri was in the shower…

And suddenly it all makes sense, and I've been the biggest fucking idiot in the universe. How could I actually have believed that someone could love me the way Yuri did? Couldn't I see it was all just too good to be true? And that's because it wasn't true—it was all an act. She's a spy. Yuri is the Sallow Man's spy. It all fits. She turned up in my life just around the time the Disappearances started, and then she worked her way into my affections, reading me like a book, knowing exactly what to say and what to do to become the perfect lover for an idiot like me; that's what she did because that's what she was ordered to do. She's the only one who could've taken those pictures from under my bed; and then there was the day I got released from Parkside: she was there waiting for me—and I'd just seen the Sallow Man there. They must've arrived together. Yuri's the Sallow Man's spy, and she's his whore as well because he was just up there fucking her and all the time she's been fucking me she's been fucking him as well the two-faced lying fucking bitch—

I storm up to the lift and stab the button. The lift takes too long, and I swear at the lift doors and then I take the stairs instead, going up them two steps at a time. Yuri's room is up on the second floor. I slam open the stairwell door and march up the corridor to her door.

I hammer on the door.

It opens. Yuri's wearing her black silk dressing gown, and she's in the middle of towelling her wet hair. She's not wearing her glasses.

'Hi! Come on in!'

She looks so innocent; like she's pleased to see me… But then, she's the consummate actress, isn't she? She has to be. It's her job. She's been fooling me all this time with her studied performance as the loyal and submissive Japanese woman.

I don't say anything; I just walk in. Like I said, it's a small room. The bed is made, the linen unrumpled. That doesn't prove anything. She's had time to straighten up the bed while I was on my way up.

I look at her, scrutinising her face, looking for something—something I must have missed until now; some index of her real character. I don't see anything, just confusion.

'What's up, Chad? Why are you looking at me like that?'

'I saw him leaving,' I tell her.

'Saw who leave where?'

'I saw *him* leave *here*,' I growl. 'The Sallow Man. I saw him just now, walk out through the front doors.'

She looks genuinely surprised. 'That guy? The Sallow Man? Are you sure it was him? What was he doing here?'

'Yes; what *was* he doing here? How about you tell me that? He was *here*, wasn't he? He was seeing you!'

Still that look of innocent confusion. 'No, he wasn't here… I was in the shower until you arrived…'

'Yes… and why were you taking a shower, anyway? Funny time of the day to be having a shower, isn't it?'

'No… I showered because it's super-hot today, and I wanted to be nice and clean for you, Chad… Why are you looking at me like that, Chad? You look so angry… What do you think I've done? Please tell me…'

'I *know* what you've done!' I snarl. 'You've been fucking him, haven't you? The Sallow Man: you've been spying on me for him and you've been fucking him!'

'That's crazy, Chad…' She's crying now; crying and smiling helplessly. 'I love you only… I'm not a spy… How could you think such a thing?'

'Because I saw him *leaving!* I got here just a bit soon, didn't I? Weren't expecting me, were you? If I'd arrived when I was supposed to have, it would've been alright, wouldn't it? The Sallow Man would've been and gone and I'd have been none the wiser. But because like a fucking idiot I was so eager to be with you, I got here early, and because of that I saw him leave! So don't try to deny it, you fucking bitch!'

She's shaking her head now, her damp uncombed hair flapping around. 'No, Chad… No, no, no… Not to see me; not to see me. He didn't come here to see me. You have to believe me, Chad…'

'Believe you?' I roar. I grab her by the front of her dressing gown and shake her. 'I *did* believe in you, you bitch! I always believed in you! I never doubted you for one second! And all along you were putting on an act; you were spying on me for *him*; and reporting back to him and fucking him you fucking whore!'

'No, Chad; no! You've got it wrong—!'

'SHUT UP!'

I shake her, I spin her around and I push her away. She falls back onto the bed. Her dressing gown falls open. She lies there, chest heaving, legs open. Breathing hard, cheeks wet with tears, she looks at me with an imploring look in her eyes.

I stand there. I stand there glaring at her, a million thoughts racing round in my head. I stand there and suddenly I'm disgusted and I turn and walk out of the room.

Chapter Twenty-One

laughing at me the whole time the buck-toothed bitch laughing behind my back and laughing in her thoughts laughing with *him* fucking her after me sticky seconds thirds fourths gullible fucking idiot believed her lies you are my master my world fucked her without a condom bet he fucked her without a condom probably infected my cock feels funny been clapped don't even know what clap is kiss my pretty ass kissed her pretty arse kissed her ring like it was the fucking Pope's pissed herself laughing pissed all over me because I'm so happy yeah right and I believed it because I trusted you delicate Japanese flower evil Japanese bitch sadist spying on me sallow man's a fucking pervert young enough to be his daughter laughing at me keeps messaging me not going to answer give her the chance to talk me into her lying world I love you only you want to be with you forever hearts beat as one bullshit who does she think I am traitor traitor selling me out selling me lies selling her body thought she loved me stupid fucking idiot believe anything now she's knocking at the door Chad Chad let me in won't let her in won't let her listen to her words lying words take me in take me for a ride won't listen won't listen go away

Appetite's gone. Haven't eaten anything for days. Haven't done anything.

I just stay in my bed all day. Shut out the world, keep the curtains closed. I think I've been delirious… Today… Well, today I don't feel any better, just not quite as bad… The anger's gone… at least for now… Right now, I'm all jittery, all keyed-up…

She won't leave me alone. She's persecuting me. She keeps coming to my door, calling me through the letterbox. She just won't give up. But I'm not going to listen to her, because I know that if I listen to her, she'll take me in all over again. She'll know what to say to make me believe her; she'll know exactly what to say…

It's been quiet today… Maybe she's given up. Maybe she's finally given up…

There are people who say that animals and little kids trust instinctively and they never get it wrong—but that's bullshit because animals and little kids trust impulsively and they often get it wrong. And that's pretty much what I did with Yuri. I trusted her because I wanted to. She knew me; she knew me inside and out and she knew exactly what to say and what to do to be exactly the kind of person she knew I wanted her to be—in other words, she flattered my vanity, and I completely fell for it; hook, line and sinker.

And now, now I despise myself for believing in her; I despise myself for my gullibility, my stupid vanity… But it's the betrayal that hurts the most; that's what's killing me—it's this unbearable feeling of betrayal—loss, disillusionment, frustration... I can't take it... I mean, technically she didn't betray me: she was my enemy all along, so it was deceit rather than betrayal... But it still feels like betrayal; and that's what I can't cope with... I've never felt this bad in my life...

I've started rocking myself; rocking myself in bed. I used to do it back when I was a kid; lying on my side, I'd rock myself, just my upper body really, moving my hips and my shoulders, back and forth. In my teens I made the effort to stop doing it; I thought it was just something kids did, and it was time I stopped doing it—and I *did* stop doing it, but it was only later I found out that rocking in bed *wasn't* something that little kids do; not the normal ones, anyway. It's actually something that only babies are supposed to do; they rock themselves like that to go to sleep; basically doing what a cradle would do for them if they were in a cradle...

But I carried on doing it until I was about twelve, and now I've started doing it again. I rock and I rock and I rock myself on my mattress for hours on end because it feels better than trying to keep still and my thoughts keep whirling round and round and round...

Someone coming up the stairs. Even from in here in my bedroom I can hear it whenever anyone walks up and down those stairs, and every time I hear it, my heart starts beating fast; I feel panicky... Is it her...? No.... No, maybe not. Too heavy; too noisy; sounds like more than one person; the people from number thirteen or number fourteen maybe...

Someone knocks on my door.

'Chad?'

Oh *no*. It *is* Yuri.

'Chad?'

I don't move. I'm frozen. Heart racing like mad.

Another knock and my name called out again.

Why can't she go away? Does she think she can still talk

her way out of this? That she can talk me into believing in her?

'Please, Chad. Let me in.'

Tears are streaming down my face—go away go away go away go away go away

I hear something pushed through the letterbox.

No more knocking.

Has she gone?

And then: 'Chad? Are you there?'

go away go away go away go away go away

And then I hear the noise of footsteps going down the stairs—and something else; something being dragged along and bumped down the steps. Has she got wheelie luggage with her?

I wait, and then when I don't hear anything, I get up and go to the bedroom door. I open it and look into the living room, and look at the front door like I want to see through it or something. Has she really gone? Or is it a trick? Might have been somebody else going downstairs. What did she put through the letterbox? I take a cautious step into the living room. Have to be careful. Some of the floorboards creak. If she's still there she might hear me. I hunker down and crawl over to the sofa, keeping it between me and the door. When I'm behind it, I peep over the top of it. I can see a coloured envelope, pale violet, lying on the doormat. A letter. She wants me to read it. Is it a trap? Is she still there, ready to open the letterbox and catch me out in the open?

Stealth is the best option. I get down flat on the floor, and I slither my way across the room. Now, I'm right under the door—if she looks through the letterbox now, she won't be able to see me; I'll be below her field of vision. I look at the envelope. It's from Yuri's Hello Kitty stationery set and it's got my name written on it in her elegant handwriting: Chad. I listen. I'm right beside the door and if she's squatting down out there, there's only this piece of wood between me and her. Can't hear anything.

I don't want to take any chances, so I pick up the envelope, and holding it between my teeth, I slither back across the room, all the way to my bedroom door. And then I'm up and I'm through the door and I've closed it and I'm safe.

Back under my mattress I look at the envelope; it's bulky; there's a lot of folded paper inside it. Just how long a letter has she written? I think about it for a while, and I imagine all the things she might say to me in a long letter and how she'd say them all... The only way to know for sure is to open it and read it; but part of me doesn't want to read it... Slowly, I pull up the flap of the envelope (self-adhesive, or did she lick it with her tongue?) and I manage to get it open without tearing it. Then I pull out the letter and I see that it's actually two letters; one of them is a government document on official headed stationery and the other is a letter in Yuri's handwriting on Hello Kitty notepaper the same colour as the envelope.

Wondering what it could be about, I look at the official letter first. It's not for me, it's addressed to Yuri. It says:

> We regret to inform you that a problem has arisen with regards to your residency and authorisation to study in the United Kingdom. We have come to the decision that it is not possible for you to remain in this country at the present time. As you are no doubt aware, the number of Japanese females permitted to study, produce, and/or exhibit visual/pictorial/photographic Art within the bounds of the United Kingdom at any given time is strictly regulated (as per the Yoko Ono act of 1969—ref 7188), and it has been discovered that, in the present instance, and due to an unfortunate administrative oversight, this number has been exceeded by one, and that your student visa was in fact granted in error. This unfortunately means that your studies are hereby

terminated, your student visa revoked, and you will be obliged to return to your country of origin. This mandate is effective immediately. While we sympathise with any distress this sudden announcement may cause you, we are sure you will understand that the rules must be strictly adhered to, and any attempt to make an exception to or infringe these rules can only lead to widespread anarchy, looting and the disenfranchisement of the British Royal Family. To facilitate your departure, we have enclosed a ticket for your flight from Heathrow to Japan; you will see that the ticket is dated for tomorrow. If you are not onboard the flight indicated, you will be immediately taken into police custody, pending deportation procedures. These procedures can take up to five years, and during that time you will not be eligible for bail. This decision is final and cannot be appealed against.

We apologise for the inconvenience.

I throw the letter aside and I snatch up Yuri's letter. It goes:

Dear Chad,

My darling lover, my one true master, please let me see you one last time! I have to go away. I have no choice. I will enclose the letter that tells me that I have to leave. It is so sudden. I believe that evil man is behind this; the one you call the Sallow Man. He wishes to drive us apart, my darling. He wants to destroy our love. He is an evil man. It was he who planted those seeds of suspicion in your head, and made you believe that I had betrayed your trust; and now he is sending me away to prevent the bond he has severed from being repaired.

Oh Chad, how could you have ever believed my love for you was a deception? My darling, I have never known true happiness until the first time you put your penis inside me and made love to me. You are my all. I think about you every minute of the day. I have dedicated my art to you; your approbation inspires me to succeed, to do my very best. I have made so many happy memories of our time together. It has made me so happy to make you happy, to see my own love reflected in your eyes. Oh my darling, don't let your love for me turn to bitterness because of what that man has done. I forgive you for your suspicions of me, for doubting my love for you—you were tricked by that evil man. Him I will never forgive.

That day when it happened—why did you leave me like that, my darling? Why did you turn away? When you threw me on the bed, I wanted you to rape me; I would have folded you in my arms and taken all those bad feelings away from you and given you my love in return. But you didn't do this; you ignored my silent entreaty, and you looked at me as though I disgusted you—and it hurt me so much; more than I have ever been hurt before. You are my lover, my one and only, my prince, my lord—I do not want that image of you to be my last memory of you. It would destroy me. Please see me. If you are reading this, then there is still time. I am out here waiting for you. But the minutes are precious; they are ticking away; so, please, please speak to me one last time before I have to leave you.

with all my love, forever and always, Yuri

NO!

Frantically, I scramble around for some clothes; a pair of jeans; a t-shirt... I run through to the living room and pull on a pair of trainers.

And then I'm out of the flat and hurtling down the stairs. I'm running across the carpark. A bus is just pulling away from the stop across the road. I stop in my tracks.

She's on that bus. I know she is. It's the city centre bus and it also goes to the train station. The bus is turning onto Arbury Road and I'm looking at all the windows and I can't see her but I know she's on that bus. She's on that bus and she's going to the train station and to Heathrow airport and she's getting on that flight back to Japan, and if I'd just read her letter as soon as she put it through the door instead of waiting I'd have been in time to see her and speak to her and I know now that I got it completely wrong about her and she wasn't a spy and a traitor and she loved me all the time—

I collapse onto the concrete surface of the carpark and I howl like some wounded animal.

Chapter Twenty-Two

One miserable rainy day back when I was twenty, I walked up to Elizabeth Way bridge with a view to jumping off it and into the river. It was a miserable, depressing day, and the grey sky and drizzle seemed like a reflection of my state of mind at the time. When I got to the bridge I stood there for a while, looking down into the murky water—but in the end I didn't jump. I didn't jump, but it wasn't the thought that maybe things weren't so bad after all that stopped me from jumping; nope, instead, while I was looking down into the water, wondering what drowning would feel like, this idea came up out of nowhere and rooted itself in my head; the idea that if I died I wouldn't find the blessed oblivion I was looking for—but that instead my consciousness would survive, and I'd find myself bodiless but still aware in this black limbo, this big black nothingness, and all the things that were preying on my mind would still be there, and I would be stuck with them for all eternity, stuck with those thoughts going round and round my head and with absolutely no possibility of any physical distractions, never a moment of relief from these intolerable thoughts. That's what stopped me from jumping; the certainty that had seized hold of me that this is what I would have to look forward to if I killed myself. It stopped me from jumping, alright—but it didn't make me feel any better. I know now that it was a survival mechanism at work; my mind coming up with something to stop me from destroying my body—I just wish my mind could have come up with some better way of doing it.

Since that time, I've come to the decision that if things get so bad that I want to kill myself, it will have to be something quick and painless, like jumping in front of a train. I don't want something that's too painful, and I definitely don't want something that gives you time to change your mind about killing yourself when it's too late. I used to think that asphyxiation would be a nice way to go; just tying a plastic bag round your head and lying on your bed waiting for the air to run out. I even tried it out once or twice; just putting the bag over my head for a few minutes—a sort of dry run. It was Esther who told me about the major drawback to that one: how that when you're running out of air your body will become numb, from the lack of oxygen to your brain or something, so if you did change your mind at the last minute and decide you didn't want to die, you would find you wouldn't be able to move your arms to take the bag off your head. Makes you wonder how many people who chose that method of suicide did have those second thoughts when it was too late to do anything about it…

Yes, it'll have to be a train…

I was wrong. Betrayal isn't the worst feeling there is to be overwhelmed by. It's regret. That's the worst one.

I mean real regret. Any regret that can be put that right is just a minor regret. But the kind of regret when you know that the opportunity you missed is gone forever, that the moment has passed irrevocably, and that it needn't have turned out that way at all if only you'd done something differently—that's the kind that crushes you. You know you have to live with that regret for the rest of your life; and you know that kind of an existence will be insupportable.

This is how it is for me. This is what's killing me. My last chance to see Yuri before she had to go away, to repair all that damage I'd made with my stupid suspicions... If only I hadn't ignored Yuri all those times she was knocking at my door... If only I'd picked up and read her letter sooner...

If only... The most miserable words in the world...

And now she's gone—Yuri's gone. I had the best thing I'd ever had in my life; something precious; a perfect connection with another human being—and I let it slip away.

And now I've gone from hating myself for believing in Yuri to hating myself for having doubted her. I'd never doubted or suspected her for one minute before that thrice-accursed day, but all it took was to see the Sallow Man coming out of her building and I went Casimir Fleetwood on her. I ought to have remembered that book and taken a lesson from it: because it was a set-up from the start; the Sallow Man, he arranged the whole thing. He knew I was on my way to see Yuri, and he made damn sure I'd see him coming out of that building. He'd probably planned it way in advance; when I saw him that day at the cop shop just before Yuri showed up, it wasn't an accident; that was the first link in the chain. And taking those photos from under my bed: that was him as well, sowing the seeds.

And now Yuri's gone; after making me suffer for long enough he's had deported, taken her away from me, so that I can realise my suspicions were all wrong and I can suffer even more. Oh God, Yuri... She's back in Japan now, and I can't even contact her. I can't talk to her. I've been cut off from her. The Sallow Man's been inside my phone and he's deleted her number from my phonebook. I know he's been in there, lurking and listening in—he knew I was going to Yuri's Hall of Residence that day, and that was something we'd arranged via text messages. And now he's deleted her mobile number which of course I never memorised—nobody bothers memorising phone numbers these days.

And all those beautiful porny photographs of her—they've gone as well. I'd never got round to transferring them to my laptop; when she wasn't with me, I always used to lie on my bed and look at them on my phone; it was more convenient that way... After that day I lost Yuri, I thought I didn't want to look at those pictures ever again; I thought that seeing them would only torment me... But now I feel like I've lost my last connection with Yuri... I don't trust my memory; I'm worried I'll start to forget her face; that beautiful face with those intense epicanthic eyes, that fanged joyful smile of hers...

I hate this feeling. I can't live with this; it hurts too much. I keep crying all the time. I haven't cried since I was a kid and now I can't stop.

Oh Christ, Yuri...

I dream about that building every night now. That bare white building standing there in the middle of the flat countryside, that used to fill me with a sense of unease whenever I saw it from the car window as a kid... It was sinister and elusive, that building; always out of reach...

Maybe that's why I keep dreaming that I need to get to that building... Maybe my mind thinks I can settle my childhood fears of the place by seeing it up close... Like it's some too-long unresolved issue... That's what Yuri said when I told her about the dream...

I dream about that building every night and I think about it every day; it twists itself up with all my tortured thoughts about Yuri, and it gets so confused it starts to feel like somehow they're connected; Yuri and that building...

I had to get outside.

I've been summoned by my keyworker Susan for another appointment. I got the letter in the post and I was all ready to ignore the appointment, but today, being shut inside my bedroom has suddenly gone from being imperative to being unbearable, and so I have to go outside, and if I'm going to go outside, I might as well go to that appointment.

I'm not sure why she wants to see me again so soon—last time we met we'd pretty much reached an impasse in terms of working out what I wanted to do. Whatever bright idea she's come up with, I'm going to turn it down; in fact, I'm going to ask to be taken off their books. I'm fed up with that place; I'm fed up with everything…

I turn off Cherry Hinton Road and onto the industrial estate and make my way to the foundation office. Alice, the granny receptionist, is at her usual place behind the front desk.

'Take a seat,' she says, without looking away from her typing.

I'm surprised; she's usually more friendly. But today, not a word of greeting; she just sits there typing. No talk about the weather. No comments about the newspaper headlines. Nothing. On my way here, I'd been thinking about that missing airliner story, thinking she'd probably start talking about the latest revelations. They still haven't found the plane, but there's a new theory explaining the disappearance that's been released, and this time a lot of people seem to think that it's the right one—a murder-slash-suicide with the plane's pilot as the culprit; that's the theory. They reckon he flew the plane off course out into the middle of the ocean, put on an oxygen mask, depressurised the cabins to knock everyone out, and then just flew the plane into the ocean. Apparently, they've been investigating the background of this pilot, and they've found out that the guy was a total screw-up, and just the type who would do something like this. It's a selfish way to go, taking all those other people with you—but, somehow, a story like this coming out right now, kind of fits with my mood.

Alice is still typing away. I wonder if I should broach the subject myself. I decide to test the water first.

'Hot, isn't it?' I say.

'Yes,' is the curt reply, still typing.

I decide not to pursue the matter. Finally, Susan comes along.

'Come with me,' she says.

That's it. No smile. No greeting. I follow her through to her office.

She sits down on her chair and gets out my folder, all business-like. I sit in the chair facing her. She looks at me, and I see a look in her face like there are barriers up—like she wants to keep me at a distance.

'I'll come straight to the point,' she says, coming straight to the point. 'I've discussed your case with my colleagues, and we've decided to take you off our books. We don't think this foundation can help you anymore.'

Now this is exactly what I was going to ask them to do—but having the decision snatched out of my hands like this does not feel good. It feels like a rejection; it feels like being arbitrarily given the sack when you were all set to hand in your resignation...

'This is a bit sudden...' I say. 'What am I supposed to do next?'

'You should go and see your GP,' she tells me. 'I've written to him, and I've suggested that you be referred to the mental health team for a complete psychological evaluation.'

'Do what?'

'A psychological assessment. To find out what's wrong with you.'

'But I know what's wrong with me,' I say. 'I've got depression.'

She looks at me. 'Yes, but that's always been just your own diagnosis, hasn't it?' she says. 'The real problem might be something more serious.'

'Like what?' I squawk, alarmed.

'That's what the assessment will determine, won't it?'

'Yeah, but you can't just suddenly throw this at me! I mean, what—?'

'There's no point discussing this any further,' says Susan, busying herself with her notes. 'You need to go and see your GP. Goodbye.'

I remember last time I was here, and how I suddenly wondered if Susan didn't actually like me—I guess I was right. There's nothing else I can do, so I shrug my shoulders and I get up and leave.

I walk down the corridor, through the reception office where I am ignored by Alice, and I step out through the door and depart from the precincts of the charitable institution for the last time. Another door closed in my face.

What was all that about? Why this sudden dismissal? And "Something more serious"? Like what? Are they saying they think I'm insane? But 'insane' isn't even an accepted medical definition, is it? So, what is it? What do they mean? What the hell do they think I've got wrong with me...?

Can't remember if I mentioned this before, but this industrial estate is set quite a way back from the main road, so there's a long access road with just brick walls on either side running between the two. When I turn onto this road, I see a stationary van ahead of me, with two people standing beside it. They're not removal men, and it's not one of their vans. They're a man and a woman; they're both wearing jackets and jeans. I get closer and I see that the woman is blonde, and she's got a tip-tilted nose and looks like the horror film actress Ingrid Pitt. She's maybe in her early thirties. The guy is dark haired, a bit older, and there's also something Eastern European about the way he looks... They're both smoking cigarettes and not paying any attention to me. I wonder what they're doing parked here...

I'm walking past them when they pounce on me, twisting

my arms back and dragging me to the rear of the van. The doors are opened by someone waiting inside. I struggle like mad; I swear at them to let me go, but then the person inside the van clamps a reeking wet handkerchief over my nose and mouth and as everything starts to fade out I wonder to myself if this is how they got Esther...

Chapter Twenty-Three

The room smells musty and damp.

I'm lying on a bed. There's daylight outside, but the room is dim. I'm lying here fully dressed apart from my trainers, and I feel lousy; my mouth is dry, my head is killing me, and my arms and legs ache.

It's an old iron bedstead with grubby sheets. Facing me are six squares of blue sky discoloured by dirty glass. The floor of the room is bare, the walls covered with faded wallpaper. At the opposite side of the room is a bricked-up fireplace. On the mantel shelf above it, a row of battered-looking paperback books bracketed by two brass candlesticks. Apart from the bed, the only other furniture is a bedside cabinet and a straight-backed wooden chair. My wallet, keys and cigarettes I notice are sitting on the cabinet.

Is this it? I wonder, as I look around. Have I been Disappeared? Is this my prison? Is this my 'Room with No View'? (Except that it does have a view.)

But then I think back to my abduction, and I'm thinking that it wasn't the removal men who took me—and I don't think they were removal men in mufti, either. That man and woman standing beside the van; from what I saw of them, they didn't have that look, that granite-faced look of the removal men. When they put that wet handkerchief over my mouth (chloroform? I don't know what chloroform's supposed to smell like, but in books it's usually chloroform), that was my last thought—that they must have got Esther like this; that she must have been jumped on in some quiet street, and chloroformed and bundled into the back of a van, just like I was…

But they weren't removal men, and if I haven't been taken by the removal men, then who have I been taken by? And where have I been taken to?

I swing my legs over the side of the bed. My trainers are on the floor. Happening to rub my chin, my hand encounters unexpected stubble. About three days' growth! Now, I only shave about once a week (I have sensitive skin, and the longer I leave it between shaves, the less I cut myself), so stubble is the norm with me—but I remember shaving this morning; or rather, the morning of the day I was abducted; I remember cuz it had been longer than usual since I'd last shaved and the bristles were getting thick… Yet here I am with three days' growth of beard! That means I must have been kept unconscious for at least two days! That's what the stubble on my chin is telling me, anyway. How long have I been out? What day is it now? Stupidly, I look at my watch, but my watch only tells me that it's ten past two.

Where the hell am I, then? How far from Cambridge have I been taken?

The window beckons to me. When I look through it, I can see that I'm in an upstairs room; below me is an overgrown front yard, with a brick wall in front of it, and a dirt track heading off in both directions. There's a blue van parked in the yard; it looks like the same one from before. On the other side of the dirt track, there's just arable farmland everywhere you look; no other buildings in sight; no sign of a road… I *could* still be in Cambridgeshire; it's flat farmland, and the horizon is clear; no hills or mountains in the distance… But that doesn't necessarily mean I'm still in East Anglia—there are plenty of other places with flatlands in Europe… Europe? Yeah, I might not even still be in England! If I've been kept under for days, it might mean that I've been travelling for days; that it took days for them to take me to where I am now...

But then, there's the van down there... As far as I can tell, it's the same one—the one that was parked on the access road to the industrial estate off Cherry Hinton Road in Cambridge... So we must have driven to wherever we are now... But that doesn't mean I'm still on the UK mainland, though; not necessarily; we could have crossed onto the Continent by ferry, or via the Channel Tunnel... And my kidnappers; the two of them I saw; I thought from the start that they both looked Eastern European... The woman looked like Ingrid Pitt...

I leave the window and go to the room's door. Locked of course. I thump on the door, just to let whoever's in the house know that I'm up and about now. How big is this house? Is Esther here? I wonder... If she *was* taken by the same people, maybe she's locked up in another room here...

There's no response to the noise I make, but the van's parked outside so there must be someone here. The paperbacks on the mantel shelf catch my eye. I'm one of those people who are always drawn to books; if I'm round someone's house and I see bookshelves, I'll always start nosing at them... From their spines, the books here look like commercial fiction; thrillers and whatnot... And they're not in English! I open one of the books, start leafing through it. The language uses the Latin alphabet, but a lot of the letters have squiggles on them; accents and umlauts and whatnot... It looks Eastern European... My abductors looked Eastern European... Is that where I am than? Have I been dragged across the continent? I have no idea of distances, so I don't even know if you can drive from one end of Europe to the other in two or three days...

I hear the sound of footsteps coming up a staircase. The footsteps stop outside the door. A key turns in the lock and the door opens. A gun appears in the opening, followed cautiously by a thin-faced man. He sees me standing by the fireplace and points the gun at me. A second man enters carrying a steaming mug and a sandwich on a plate. I recognise him as one of my kidnappers, the man who was with the woman next to the blue van. The first man keeps him covered while he puts the mug and plate down on the cabinet beside the bed.

'What's going on?' I ask, when it seems that neither of them is about to start the conversation. 'Where is this place?'

The second man ignores me, starts moving back towards the door. I move to grab him, but the man with the gun puts himself in my way and points the gun at my face. I back off.

'Spletzoski! Inrich spletzoski!'

'I don't understand!' I say. 'Speak English!'

The man backs towards the door.

'Spletzoski!'

He backs out through the door. The door shuts and the key turns in the lock again.

What language was that? I wonder. The same language as the paperbacks, I assume. I sit down on the bed and pick up the mug. Tea with milk. Do they usually drink milk tea in Eastern Europe? Or have they just done this for my benefit? I take a sip; no, they haven't gone and put sugar in it. The sandwich is just cheese. Thick slices of cheese between slices of white bread. I take an experimental bite. The bread tastes like it's got additives; the cheese tastes like cheddar—but is it really cheddar, or just some local cheese that tastes the same as cheddar? I drink the tea but I don't eat much of the sandwich—appetite's still gone. And I could really have done with some painkillers for my head.

What's going on? Have I really become a Disappearer? But then, why was I grabbed by these people and not the removal men? Where is the Sallow Man? And is this where all the Disappearers have ended up? Locked in rooms in some grotty old farmhouse? Is this place even big enough to hold everyone who's been taken? I go to the window. It won't open. I press my head to the glass, trying to see as much as I can. From the extent of the front yard, it doesn't look like that big a place...

Maybe this is some halfway house... Yeah, maybe this is only the first stage of my journey, before being taken on to... where? The only destination my mind can come up with is some secret village on an island (or in Wales) like the one in *The Prisoner*...

I'd always assumed, in spite of the Sallow Man's uncanny resemblance to a certain actor of Polish origin, that the conspiracy was a domestic one, something arranged by the powers that be in Great Britain. But now, if I'm really overseas, it looks like this might actually be some kind of international conspiracy... Global, even. Are these disappearances happening all over the world?

I'm lying on the bed smoking a cigarette when I hear the footsteps again. It's late afternoon according to my watch. It's the same thin-faced man with the gun, but this time it's the woman from before who's with him; my female abductor, the Ingrid Pitt lookalike.

Ingrid Pitt. She was a Pole, as well. Am I in Poland...?

I sit up on the bed. The woman looks angry. She walks straight up to me and slaps me round the face, backhand and fronthand.

'Dastoya! Erignu dastoya!'

'What did you do that for?' I demand.

She treats me to what sounds like a volley of abuse.

'No understand!' I keep saying. 'No speakee Polski!'

'Walpictur jit segnu! Spletzoski du fintokwnu!'

'What is wrong with you people? You know I'm English—why do you expect me to understand your stupid language?'

'Wnesdsyu flact segnu! Spletzoski!'

She reaches into her jeans pocket and pulls out a folded-up newspaper clipping. She opens it up and thrusts it under my nose, pointing to a small photograph.

'Spletzoski jit dastoya!'

I look at the picture. It's a grainy black and white portrait, but clear enough for me to see that it's the Sallow Man. From the surrounding text I can see that the newspaper is a foreign one. Funny thing is, the cutting looks old as well—but the Sallow Man looks the same as he does now; he doesn't look any younger. It doesn't look like a posed picture; just a shot someone snapped of him.

I look into the woman's eyes. All I see is an angry, interrogative look. Is she asking me if I know the Sallow Man? She isn't working for him then? In that case, who the fuck is she? Who have I been kidnapped by? I nod my head enthusiastically to show that I know the man in the photograph, hoping this will get a positive response. Instead, it gets me another two stinging slaps around the chops. Then she leans in close and I can smell her cigarette breath.

'*Spletzoski du fintokwnu.*' She says it slowly and deliberately, eyes boring into mine; but I'm none the wiser for it.

She refolds the newspaper clipping, and, with a signal with her friend with the gun, they both leave the room. I'm left with the impression that Ingrid doesn't like the Sallow Man.

It's dark. The room has a light; an old-fashioned filament bulb hanging from the ceiling; but I haven't had it on at all; I prefer to lie here in the darkness. (And if I needed further proof that I'm not in England anymore, I've located a plug socket behind the bedside cabinet, and it's a socket for a two-pin plug.)

I'm thinking that I haven't been disappeared; at least, not like the others were. I know it's mostly guesswork on my part, but it seems like Ingrid Pitt and her crew belong to some other group, a group who are opposed to the Sallow Man. And just who is the Sallow Man? Like I say, I always assumed he was some shadowy figure working for our lot; so why is there a snapshot of him in some foreign newspaper?

My abductors have obviously found some connection between yours truly and the Sallow Man, but, unless I'm misinterpreting those slaps round the face, they for some reason think I'm in league with him.

But then, why the hell have they kidnapped me, drugged me, and dragged me half way across Europe, apparently for interrogation, when not one of them speaks my language? This whole situation is ridiculous. They brought me some dinner earlier (which I couldn't have eaten even if I was hungry, cuz it had meat in it) and I tried to find out if they were holding Esther in this place as well. I've still got this idea they may have grabbed her the same way they grabbed me. If they have, then they'll have had the same lack of success questioning her, because she doesn't speak Polish either. But even if they couldn't speak to her, I assumed they would at least know her name, so I started saying 'Esther! Esther! Is she here?' over and over to Ingrid.

All I got for my pains was another couple of slaps.

Now, it sounds like everyone's turned in for the night. I don't even know how many of them there are; I've seen three of them, but there might be more. My thoughts turn towards getting out of this place. How I'm going to do this I don't know. The window won't open and the door is locked. It does seem like they always leave the key in the door on the other side, so I think about that old dodge where you push the key out from your side using a screwdriver or something, let it land on a piece of paper you've pushed under the door and then you drag the key back to you. Unfortunately, there's not enough of a gap under this particular door for that ploy to work. I've also examined the bricked-up fireplace, thinking that maybe the chimney shaft also connects with a ground-floor fireplace, but the brickwork is solid; none of those conveniently loose bricks that help in these situations.

What would I do if I got out anyway? It looks like I'm in the middle of nowhere; I can't drive which means pinching their van isn't an option; so I'd have to set off on foot, and I'm alone without a passport in a foreign country… I keep thinking I'm in Poland, but it's just an assumption; I don't know it for sure…

I can't get the idea out of my head that Esther might be in this place, locked up in another room. Maybe it's wishful thinking—like I just *want* her to be here, because then I wouldn't be alone, and we could escape together…

Even as I'm thinking this, I hear movement through the wall close to my bed; the sound of someone walking across creaking floorboards. I put my ear to the wall…

In spite of everything I managed to fall asleep, and now it's morning. Headache's gone. I can hear that people are up and about, so I'm expecting my breakfast anytime now. What do they eat for breakfast in Poland? I could also do with another trip to the bathroom to relieve myself…

Last night I really thought it might have been Esther walking about in the room next to mine. I started tapping on the wall. The movement stopped, so I started tapping more loudly and calling out her name. I was still tapping and calling when that Ingrid woman burst into my room, marched straight up to me, slapped me twice around the face, and then walked straight out again. Seems that the bedroom next to mine is hers…

I get up, stretch and, putting my trainers on, move over to the window. What's going to happen today? More pointless attempts at questioning? Or maybe they're going to take me to someone who can actually speak English…

The blue van is still parked below my window in the same dusty yard. The same depressing landscape of farmland. I'm just turning away when I hear the sound of a vehicle approaching. I turn back and wait for it appear—and when it heaves into view, it's one of the removal men's beige vans.

A hole opens up in the ground and all my theories disappear into it. So, I have been Disappeared after all!

These people aren't some opposing faction: they're in league with the removal men! Then what was all that face-slapping about?

The van pulls up and two removal men, dressed in the usual caps and overalls get out of the cab. They march towards the house and out of my field of vision.

I step back from the window. My heart's beating fast. Is this it, then? Are they coming to take me away to my final destination? To wherever it is that all the rest of the Disappeared have been taken?

But then all hell breaks loose.

The sound of a door being forced violently open.

Shouts and exclamations.

Gunshots.

Screams.

And then everything goes quiet. I'm rooted to the spot, ears straining for a sound. One thing is obvious: the removal men weren't expected—they were intruders. There's been a fight down there—but who's won? I heard gunshots; I know that Ingrid and her friends have at least one gun between them, and the removal men didn't look like they were armed at all... And there's the numbers; only two removal men and Ingrid's crew numbers at least three, maybe more... The odds were on their side... So why aren't I hearing anything?

And then I *do* hear something: slow, heavy footsteps coming up the stairs. It isn't Ingrid or any of her friends. I've heard them going up and down those stairs lots of times now; and they move quickly and lightly, like people do when they're using a staircase they're familiar with because they use it all the time. These are the footsteps of an intruder— one of the removal men. The footsteps are up on the landing now. My instinct is to hide and I quickly crawl under the bed. No-one's cleaned under here since forever; the dust is about an inch deep.

The footsteps come nearer. The key turns in the lock, the door opens. I see a pair of beige trouser-legs enter the room.

They pause, just inside the door.

Come on, you bastard; you either know I'm in this room or you don't—and if you know I'm in the room then you know that I'm hiding under the bed, because it's the only possible hiding-place.

Is he doing this on purpose? Making me sweat before he squats down on the floor and drags me out from under the bed?

The legs turn and walk out of the room.

I let out the breath I'd been holding in.

I hear footsteps descending the stairs.

Now what?

I can't hear a sound now. What are they doing?

I wait. I stay where I am and I wait, and then I hear the sound from outside: vehicle doors being opened and closed. The sound of an engine ignition. They're leaving! I crawl out from under the bed and scuttle over to the window. I raise my head cautiously over the sill, until I can see down into the yard. I'm rewarded with the sight of the beige van reversing out of the yard. It turns and heads back down the dirt track the same way it came.

Silence.

The removal man who came in left the door open, and I step out of my prison and onto the landing. The staircase beckons to me. It takes me down into a hallway. The bannisters at the foot of the stairs are broken, like something really heavy smashed into them. I can tell from the splinters that these breaks are new; not some old damage that's never been repaired. There's an overturned hatstand and a broken table in the hallway, an old-fashioned Bakelite telephone lying beside it. The front door is wide open, with splinters in the framework from where it was forced open…

So, the removal men broke in, and Ingrid and her friends shot at them… And then what? How did they lose when they were the only ones with guns? They must have been really lousy shots to have missed their targets in this narrow hallway... And where are they? There's nobody here...!

I check out the rest of the ground floor of the house. Aside from the kitchen at the back, most of the rooms look unused. I go back upstairs and check the rooms there. Apart from mine, there are three other bedrooms that look like they were being used; the beds are still unmade. No sign that there were any other captives apart from me.

I go back down to the hall and pick up the telephone—it's dead; the cord has been snapped.

The only explanation I can think of is that Ingrid and her friends were no match for the removal men because bullets can't stop them. I can believe that, the way they look. So, the removal men won the fight and Ingrid and her friends (or their corpses) have been taken away.

I step outside. It's muggy and close and completely silent. I look around the horizon and can't see a single moving thing. I step out onto the track and look back at the house. It's just a ramshackle old farmhouse; I don't know if it looks like a Polish farmhouse because I don't know what a Polish farmhouse is supposed to look like. Behind the farmhouse it's more of the same: flat countryside as far as you can see.

I don't know where I am or how far I am from civilisation, but as I can't drive the van, I'll just have to hoof it until I find someone or find a town or village where I can throw myself on the mercy of the local authorities. Hopefully from there I'll be handed over to the British consulate and sent back home.

Lighting a ciggie, I set off along the dirt track, heading in the same direction the van went. My eye catches a movement off to the left; something crawling along the horizon... Yes, it's a car! I keep my eyes locked on it; it's too far off to even tell what colour it is, never mind the make. Is it coming this way...?

Yes, it's definitely getting closer... But now it's receding again, heading off to the right. It must be on a main road—this track I'm on must join up with a main road up ahead, and that car was going along the road…

So I start walking again, and I walk for about ten minutes and I come to the main road. I haven't seen another car since that first one. I turn onto the road, heading off to the right, because that was the way the car was going.

I'm soon wishing I'd turned left instead, when my aching calves start to tell me that the ground ahead is rising steadily. Still no traffic. I must be miles from anywhere. Another twenty minutes and trees appear over the horizon ahead; it looks like the beginning of a forest…

And then I'm in the forest; the road cuts straight through it. The trees are tall, but I don't know what kind they are—trees are just trees to me, and even if I could tell what kind they are, I still wouldn't know whether they have them in Poland or not…

The ground is still rising; I can see it now; I'm walking up a visible slope. I'm hoping I'll be able to see something when I get to the top. There's got to be some sign of life soon; this silent wilderness can't go on forever.

I make it to the top of the hill; the forest suddenly ends and the road turns off to the right and in front of me, at the top of the rise, is a layby and a crash barrier. I walk up to the crash barrier, and beyond it, the ground drops steeply and below me is a city. Suddenly there's noise: cars are passing up and down the road behind me; an airliner is flying overhead… The big building with the chimneys in the foreground is Addenbrooke's hospital, and the city I'm looking at is Cambridge.

Chapter Twenty-Four

'It's all about respect, isn't it? Everyone saying you've got "respect" everyone else—that you can't say anything that might upset or offend anyone!'

'So, what's wrong with that?'

'Everything! What about freedom of speech? What about my right to say what I want to say? What about not being allowed to even say what I really think about anything, just because it might "upset" someone; it might "offend" them? So fucking what? I'm entitled to my opinions, aren't I? And I'm entitled to say them out loud if I want to! That's freedom of speech! If you have to keep watching your words all the time, not saying what you really want to say, just cuz you might "offend" someone—then I'm being denied my freedom of speech! I might as well be in one of those countries where you get taken away by the police if you say the wrong thing; only difference is, here in the "free world" it's internet backlash you've got to worry about—that or being stabbed in the street by some nut-job. People need to get over themselves! If you don't like what someone's said, if they've said something that "offends" you, then that's your fucking problem! You have to deal with those emotions internally, and when you've done that, you get on with something else—you can't just demand someone's head on a platter, or go out and kill them yourself, just because they said something you didn't like! No, I stand by my right to be as disrespectful to other people as I want to be; as long my lack of respect isn't violating anybody's basic human rights. So, if I think somebody else's belief system or whatever is stupid, then I've got a right to say that I think it's stupid!'

'Yes, but—'

'And another thing! It's not just freedom of speech, it's freedom of expression in people's art that's under attack! Take a look at comedy—people are coming down on comedy all the time these days! Any gallows humour, any irony, any politically incorrect joke that someone doesn't like: it has to go! The way things are going, the only comedy we're going to have left will be fucking *Portlandia*!'

I think it was then that I first really noticed Yuri; I saw her looking at me. We'd 'gone on' to Howard's place after one of his gigs at the Portland, and she'd just tagged along. I think it was like everyone saw she was with us, and they just assumed that somebody else knew her—when actually none of us knew her. So there was me holding forth in Howard's front room, setting the world to rights like I sometimes do when I've had a few, and I noticed her cuz she was looking at me very intently, like she was really interested in what I was saying. (I don't think she actually was that interested—it was more that she was staring at me because she'd decided she liked the look of me.) So I went up to her, and we started talking...

Now that I think about it, I think that party might have been the last time I saw Martin. Yes... I remember going upstairs for a piss, and Martin was there on the landing, waiting for the bathroom to become unoccupied. He was looking glum, like he had something on his mind. What was it he asked me...? Oh, yeah:

'Do you think Patrick McGoohan was right to turn down James Bond?'

The story goes that McGoohan was offered the part of Bond before anyone had even heard of Sean Connery, but he point-blank refused; wouldn't even sit down to talk with them about it.

'Well, he didn't like the character, did he? He said James Bond was "a rat." He was Catholic and he had moral objections to the character; didn't like the way he slept around.'

'Yeah, but was he right to put his ethics before his career? If he'd taken on that role, think how different his career would've been. He'd have been a much bigger star than he was, right? Would've been in a lot more films; a lot more starring role, right?'

'Well... I think if he'd played Bond, he'd have been a lot closer to the James Bond in Fleming's novels than Sean Connery or any of the others have been... But then, if he'd become James Bond, he might never have made *The Prisoner*...'

'So, you think he was right to put his ethics first, and turn down 007?'

'Well, I'd say yes; but then, I like *The Prisoner*, so I'm prejudiced there... so, what's up, Martin? Have you been offered a corporate office job or something, and you're trying to decide whether you should stick to your code of ethics or just take the money and run?'

'Something like that...'

I didn't really think about what he was saying; not at the time—all I could think about was the fact that I was bursting for a piss and whoever was in the bathroom was taking a bloody long time.

'Is someone having a dump in there?'

'No, Zoe and Debra are in there. I think they're having a girlie talk.'

'What? And you're just standing here, meekly waiting? They can have their fucking girlie talk somewhere else!'

I put my ear to the bathroom door, and sure enough, I could hear the sound of stage-whispered conversation. I hammered on the door. 'Look, can you two ladies have your little talk somewhere else? There's people waiting out here about to piss their pants!'

And the two girls came out, shooting me dirty looks like I was the one in the wrong.

They've got Errol. I'm outside his flat right now. It's empty and there's a 'To Let' sign up on the wall. (Some wiseacre's already graffitied a letter 'I' between the two words.) So, even that annoying little geek has been taken; I'm the only one they haven't bothered with.

I'm on my way home. Home is all I've got left, now—apart from that I haven't got a life at all. My life has been taken away from me, bit by bit.

I make it back, climb up the staircase, unlock the door, open it—and walk into somebody else's living room. The furniture is different, a vicious-looking status dog is barking its head off at me and an equally vicious-looking young couple straight from a BNP pamphlet are sitting on the sofa in front of the television—they were watching the teatime soap operas, but now they're looking at me, and looking completely gobsmacked; the kind of gobsmacked look that you'd have if a complete stranger had just strolled into your house like they owned the place.

The man finds his voice first. 'What the fuck?'

'What are you doing in my flat?' I demand.

'This is *our* fucking flat!' retorts the woman.

'If this is number fifteen Abbot Flats, then it's mine.'

The man gets up, crosses the room and being taller than me, glares down at me. 'This *is* number fifteen, and it's fucking ours! I don't know how you got our fucking key, but you can fucking well give it back!'

And he snatches the key from my hand.

'And now you can fuck off!'

He shoves me out through the still open door and slams it shut.

I stare at the closed door. *My* door. At least it was my door when I walked out through it yesterday. (It's only been a day, in spite of the stubble.) My home for the last seven years has been taken away from me.

I was wrong. I *have* been disappeared; like all the others, I've been disappeared—except that in my case they haven't even bothered to come along and take away my sorry carcass.

Chapter Twenty-Five

'Chad?'

'What the hell do you want, Martin? It's five o'clock in the morning!'

'I know what time it is, dude. I'm in trouble. They're coming to get me! The removal men!'

'Again?'

'Yes, again! You've got to save me, dude.'

'How can I save you? By the time I got to your place, you'd already been Disappeared.'

'That's cuz you didn't come straight away! You sat around thinking about it for a about an hour, didn't you? So you only set off when it was too late. Don't you see? This time you can make it in time!'

'Make it in time for what? I can't stop the removal men.'

'Just get here, man! Grow a spine and get here!'

So I grow a spine and set off for Martin's house in the silent early morning. I know I'm not going to bump into Errol this time; it's too early for him to be heading into work.

I arrive at the block of flats. There's no sign of the removal men, no pantechnicon, no beige vans. Nothing. Am I already too late? Or is Martin pulling my leg?

I cross the carpark and just like last time the front door is ajar. And just like last time I walk in to find the place deserted.

I go through to the bathroom and feel around behind the sink... Wait a minute! Martin didn't say anything about anything being hidden there, did he? Not this time. Maybe this time there is no roll of film...

No... No, there is a roll of film... I put it in my pocket...

I hear someone come into the next room. That will be the removal men returning. Just to make sure, I peek through the gap in the bathroom door. Yes, it's them; ransacking the apartment like they did last time.

I go to the window, open it, and squeeze through the gap. I crawl out onto the projecting roof, shin down a drainpipe, then it's across another projecting roof, down another drainpipe, through a window, down a hidden staircase, and then I'm out on the street and on my way to get the film developed!

I arrive at Boots and go upstairs to the photo developing section. The young woman at the counter smiles at me as I approach. I reach into my pocket for the film. Panic! I can't find it!

'Hello, Mr Fenton. Your prints are ready for collection,' says the woman at the counter. With a wink and a knowing smile, she hands over a wallet of photographs.

Of course! I handed the film in yesterday! Today, I'm collecting it. What's wrong with me? Mind like a sieve!

I go down the escalator. Now should be the moment I bump into Mel and Muriel at the Petty Cury exit. And yes, there they are!

'What you got there? What you got there?' says Mel, bouncing around me like a pogo-stick.

'Just my lunch,' I say. And then I realise I haven't bought any lunch this time! All I've got in my hands are the photographs in the laminated card wallet. But the girls seem satisfied with my answer and let me pass. They must just assume I've got my lunch inside the wallet.

Now I go to Christ's Piece and sit down under a tree to examine the photographs. Let me see... Yes, the first pictures, I recall, will be those totally pointless shots of Limekiln Close nature reserve... Why did Martin take those pictures? They haven't come into the story at all; they have absolutely nothing to do with the removal men and the disappearances...

Expecting to see trees and shrubs, I'm surprised instead to see a close-up shot of a pair of yellow buttocks mooning at the camera, with a purple-lipped vagina and a crap-ton of pubic hair.

'Kiss my pretty ass...'

It's Yuri, of course. I'd recognise her anywhere. I flick through the photographs—it's the pictures I took of her! Of course, it is; what else would they be? No wonder the shop assistant gave me that sly look! Yeah, I bet they got a kick out of developing—hang on a minute! Half a millisecond!

I'd swear I took those pictures on my smartphone... I didn't take them with a regular camera, because I don't have a regular camera... Did I borrow Martin's camera? That would explain why he had the film, but still, I could've sworn they were on my phone...

I know; I'll just go and ask Yuri. She'll remember. I go round to the College of Visual and Performing Arts on King's Street. Should I ring her up...? No need; we arranged to meet for lunch, didn't we? She should be out any second.

A second later, Yuri appears, smiling happily.

'Let's go to McDonald's!' says Yuri.

'Sure!' I say.

We set off. I'll ask Yuri about the photographs—wait a minute; where are they? I haven't got them anymore! Did I put them down somewhere...?

And then I see Vladek Sheybal walking through the crowd. Last time he appeared after we had eaten at McDonald's, this time it's before.

'I can't tell you why, but we have to follow that man,' I say to Yuri. 'You stay here.'

'Sure!' says Yuri, coming with me.

We follow him through the lunchtime crowd and into those gothic-looking streets and through the archway into the courtyard. Vladek goes up the rickety fire-stairs and through the door at the top.

We follow him up the stairs, Yuri leading the way.

We walk through the door and find ourselves in a huge dark warehouse. There are stacks of furniture and stacks of cardboard boxes.

'Ah, so,' says Yuri, adjusting her glasses with an index finger. 'This is without a doubt the removal men's main warehouse. Note the stacks of furniture; these can only be the furniture of the people who have been Disappeared. This clearly indicates that the Disappearers have been taken to some place where they will not need furniture, or one in which the furniture is already supplied. Perhaps a ready-furnished desert island…'

I look at Yuri. She's dressed like Sherlock Holmes. I don't remember her being a detective. Or does she just play bass for Thee Headcoatees…?

'So where do you think they've all been taken?' I ask.

'I wouldn't care to speculate at this juncture,' replies Yuri.

'This warehouse shouldn't be in this room,' says I. 'It wasn't here last time…'

I turn, return to the door and walk out, followed by Yuri.

We are in an industrial estate.

'Yes, this is where it should be. We're back in the right place…'

We walk out onto Coldham's Lane.

'At least we've got this,' says Esther, waving Vladek Sheybal's notebook. She flicks through the book. 'Hmm. It says we've got to go to Herschell House.'

'Does it say when?'

'Yes! Right away!'

'Then let's go!'

We set off for Herschell House. I know what we are going to find there: just a mother and daughter who organise BDSM parties. Should I tell Esther this? No, best not to; no spoilers…

We walk up the drive to the house.

'Let's try around the back,' says Esther.

'No need,' I tell her. No, there's no need to go through all that being captured and locked up rigmarole—might as well go straight to the front door!

Brimming over with self-confidence, I do just that. I knock on the door with a jaunty air.

'Are you sure this is alright?' says Esther.

'Trust me.'

The butler comes to the door.

'Ah, my good man, could you take us to see… take us to see…' My confidence evaporates. I've forgotten their names! That woman and her daughter: what were their names, dammit?

'Take you to see…?' prompts the butler.

'Whoever's in charge,' speaks up Esther.

'Very good.'

We are led through to the living room. There's the mother, sitting there in her kinky SS outfit. Standing beside her the daughter, in bondage queen gear. And what are their bloody names?

The daughter walks up to me and pushes me down onto a chair. She peels off her PVC knickers, revealing a familiar beige bush. I look up and the bondage queen is somehow now Esther.

Smiling at me, she unzips me and extracts my penis which springs gratifyingly erect. She lowers herself onto me and starts riding me. Vaguely, I wonder if I'm being unfaithful to Yuri. I can't remember if we've actually started going out yet… Which means I can't have taken the porny pictures of her yet, either. No wonder I couldn't find them!

Esther's got a tight grip down there and she soon makes me come, and I flood her with several pints of semen.

'Time for you whippersnappers to leave, I think,' says the mother. (What was her name?)

We're walking home now. With a thrill, I remember that this is where Esther disappeared… Well, not this time! I'm not going to part company with her until I see her safely to her front door!

We reach Hill's Road.

'See you, then,' says Esther.

'Ta-ta,' says I, and we walk off in opposite directions.

I'm halfway down East Road before I remember that I'd made a solemn vow to myself not to lose sight of Esther.

No worries—I can cut her off at the pass!

Straight down Mill Road to Romsey Town, and I'm knocking on the door of her house.

Patricia answers the door.

'What have you done with Esther?' she demands.

'Is Esther home yet?'

'No; she isn't home and she never will be! What have you done with her?'

'I haven't done anything!'

'Arrest that man!'

Patricia points imperiously, and police officers appear and grab me and drag me into a police van. We drive to Parkside Station and to the interview room from *The Bill*. Sitting across the table from me are Sergeant Wilde and for some reason, Patricia.

'What have you done with Esther Laurence?' asks Wilde.

'I haven't done anything with her.'

'Did you have sexual intercourse with her?'

'No…' This is a fib, but sometimes it pays to be discreet.

'No? No, he says? Well, that's very interesting, sir. Because we DNA tested your penis and found that you *have* had sexual relations with her.'

'You raped and murdered her!' spits Patricia. 'Admit it!'

'I did not!' I retort. 'Okay, I did rape her, but it was entirely consensual. There were witnesses; you can ask them!'

'And who are these witnesses?' asks Wilde.

'Well, I can't remember their names…' I admit.

'Very convenient. People watched you having sex with Miss Laurence and you can't remember who they are?'

'I can remember who they are! Just not their names! They're the mother and daughter who run the BDSM club at Herschell House. Go'n ask them!'

'He's guilty!' screams Patricia. 'Lock him up and throw away the key!'

'You shouldn't even be here!' I rage, standing up. 'I'm not staying here to be insulted by this bitch! I'm leaving, and don't try to stop me!'

I cross the room and walk out the door. Out of the interview room, I weave my way through the corridors of the police station and find my way out through the front door.

Nobody tries to stop me. And quite right! I'm completely innocent.

Yuri's Hall of Residence is just round the corner. I decide to go and see her. She is someone who can always be relied on to tell me how wonderful I am.

As I near the building it occurs to me that I'm approaching from the wrong direction; I should be walking away from Parkside, but somehow I'm walking towards it.

And then I see why. Vladek Sheybal emerges from the apartment building and heads off in the other direction. Oh, so it's this again! That's his game, is it?

I march straight into the building and hammer on Yuri's door.

Same as last time, she answers wearing her dressing gown, her glasses askew and her hair dripping wet.

'You were having sex with Vladek Sheybal, weren't you?' I demand, ignoring her friendly greeting.

'No! It's not true!' she cries, posing theatrically.

'Liar!'

'No! It's true!'

'Well, is it true, or *not* true? You just said it was both!'

'It's true!'

'So, it's true!'

'Yes! It's true that I said it was both!'

'You're a liar!' I say. 'And there's the proof!'

I point to her legs. Semen is streaming down her thighs.

Yuri starts to cry, tears streaming from her eyes and nostrils. 'How can you doubt me? I love only you, my love!'

'Liar!'

I push her down on the bed and then walk out.

Outside, Ingrid Pitt and her friend are standing beside their van. What are they doing here now, the idiots? I'm not due to be kidnapped yet!

I go up to Ingrid to tell her her mistake, but someone slaps a wet rag over my face and everything fades to black.

And now I'm lying on the bed in that Polish farmhouse

again. Except that this time I'm tied to the iron bedstead with ropes.

Ingrid Pitt walks into the room, and, standing over the bed, she starts to undress. Clearly she intends to consensually rape me while I'm helpless. This is curious, because I always thought that Ingrid didn't really like me, what with all that face-slapping…

Having stripped herself naked, Ingrid unzips me and extracts my penis which is soon pointing at the ceiling. She straddles me, and as she lowers herself onto me I'm slightly surprised to note that Ingrid has suddenly become Yuri.

'You see!' she says as she starts riding him. 'You're the only man for me!'

She pounds away at me, screaming and swearing in Japanese. I discharge a few gallons of semen.

Yuri climbs off me and points triumphantly at the semen streaming down her legs. 'You see! It was yours all along! Yours and only yours! I just can't get enough of your super stuff!'

'I can't get enough of his super stuff…'

Of course! I went to Yuri's flat *after* this! So it was *my* sperm that was running down her legs! Not Vladek Sheybal's.

Exultantly, I rise from the bed and walk onto the stage where my old form teacher is waiting to give me award for reading all sixteen of Dostoevsky's novels.

***

I wake up and then I wish I hadn't.

I see daylight and wooden rafters. I can smell straw. I can feel that I'm lying on the stuff. I'm cold and my body aches. My head is killing me. I feel nauseous. The inside of my mouth is like the Sahara. My ears are ringing like I've been to a gig and forgot to put in earplugs.

And I'm paralysed with fear. 'Nameless fear' they call it. Fear without a cause. Just this overwhelming sense of terror with nothing external to fix it to. Fear. And along with the fear is its pal self-loathing. Mix those two together and you get despair.

But then my memories start to come back and realise that I do have plenty to feel terrified and hopeless about after all. I'm a pariah. I'm a complete outcast. I have nothing and no-one to call my own. I used to think of myself as an outcast and be pleased about it—but now I really am one and I don't like it at all.

I detect some irony here. This is all part of the joke the Sallow Man has been playing on me. I've been the one he's had in his sights since day one.

I piece together the previous evening—what I can remember of it, anyway. After I found out I was officially homeless, stranded and with nowhere to go and nobody to turn to, I reacted to my new situation in the time-honoured way: I went out and got plastered. I bought myself a couple of four-packs from an off-license and I sat down by myself in the park and set about drinking myself silly. I remember something else: I'd tried to pay for the beer with my debit card, but the card reader in the shop wouldn't accept it. So, after I left the shop, I went to a cash-point to try and find out what was wrong; and the machine kept saying my pin was incorrect, which was bullshit. I knew I was keying in the right number. So I kept keying in what I knew was the right number over and over again, and after however many attempts, the fucking machine decided to confiscate my card.

So now I'm homeless and penniless.

I can't remember much about what happened after the eight beers. Just this one brief vision: walking by myself down a country road at night, veering back and forth across the road, laughing and singing 'Super Stuff'…

And now here I am, lying on some straw in a barn and

feeling like hell.

I want to move but the fear won't let me. I want to drink about a gallon of water. I want to take something for this splitting headache.

The skin on my face itches, but I can't even make the effort to move my hand to scratch it; my arms feel glued to my sides. My body is completely rigid, tensed up. I've probably slept the whole night with my body like this, snoring my head off.

I've pissed myself as well. The crotch of my jeans feels tight and damp. Eight cans of beer wouldn't normally make me do that, but this time it has.

I've got to get up. The only way I can relieve this fear, stop these tormenting thoughts that are spinning round in my head is to just get up and do something.

I know this, but even so, it's always hard to make that first move; so I just think about it, I picture myself sitting up and then standing up, and I imagine the sensations that will accompany the actions...

I sit up. Pain lances through my head. My stomach churns.

In front of me is the open doorway of the barn. I see hazy sky and flat countryside.

I stand up, and the dizziness and nausea nearly floor me again. Awkwardly and painfully, I walk out of the barn. Fields. Just fields. Not a building in sight. Just a few trees here and there.

I wonder how far I am from Cambridge.

I can't hear a damn thing. Apart from the singing in my ears, not a damn thing. No sound of distant traffic. Not even a bird.

That's not right. There should be birds.

I feel inside my pockets, vaguely hoping I might have had the foresight to buy some painkillers last night. Nope. I've got my wallet. Two tenners. A couple of quid in loose change. All the money I have left in the world. I find my fags in another pocket; the box looks crumpled and sorry for itself. I pull out a cigarette, straighten it, light it. After a couple of drags, I throw it down and grind it beneath my shoe. It's gross. It's fucking gross. Great. So now I can't even smoke.

I need water. Christ, I need water.

Which way back to Cambridge?

Does it matter? I just need to find somewhere, anywhere; anywhere I can get some water. There's a footpath alongside the barn, a kind of raised causeway between the fields of crops. Unless I walked right across the fields I must have got to this place via this path. But which direction did I come from?

I have this feeling that taking the path to the left will take me back to Cambridge, and so, deciding to distrust my feelings, I set off along the path to the right.

Fields. All around me fields. And the neutral hazy sky. Lots of sky. Always more sky in flat landscapes. The temperature is neutral as well. I don't feel hot or cold. All I feel is the pain in my body. My head screams out with every step I take. The stabbing pain even lances down the back of my neck. It's agony. I don't think I've ever had a headache as bad as this... But then, you don't really remember headaches—you just experience them...

I walk and I walk. I can't see any movement at all. Usually, you'd expect to see a car somewhere; just one lone car passing along the horizon to show that there is a road out there; but I don't see anything. It's like I'm alone in the world.

Fuck, I *am* alone. I don't exist anymore. Least, that's how it seems. My home is someone else's. All my worldly possessions have gone. My bank card eaten up by a machine that refused to recognise my pin number. My whole world has been stripped away from me. First everyone I knew; and now, my own identity...

Why me...? Why did the Sallow Man pick me out of

every loser in this world? Did they just pick my name out? I'm nobody... Did my number come up on some Losers' Lottery...?

Yuri... Oh Yuri, why aren't you with me? You're still out there. They didn't take you away. But you're back in Japan... I want to go to her. I want to get on the next flight to Tokyo and join her... Except I've got no money and no passport... You have to exist to be able to apply for a passport...

I haven't got anyone... Well, there's my family... None of them live locally anymore, but they're still out there... Haven't spoken to any of them for ages; not really family-oriented... I think I can even remember my parents' phone number... Yeah, don't need my mobile for that. Find a phone box, I could ring them up... But I'm a Disappearer—will they even know me? Maybe it will be: 'We never had a son named Charles; stop crank-calling us,' like that *Twilight Zone* episode; the one with Rod Taylor where they get deleted from history by some alien entity...

Thinking about my family makes me think back on the time I still lived with them; and I remember what a selfish and demanding little so-and-so I was back then, and I despise myself for it... Makes me think of an incident from back then, when I was still living in Mepal... I dunno how old I was, six or seven maybe; it was in the village play area one evening (and I seem to recall that in spite of being fenny oiks we always called it by the posh name 'recreation area.') This entertainment complex consisted of a set of swings, a rope tied to a tree branch, and a concrete sewer pipe that you could amuse yourself by crawling through. There were some of the big kids who went to Witchford secondary school sitting at the swings, and I can't remember how I ended up being there with them and with none of my friends around, but one of those big kids flopped his penis out and dared me to touch it. I remember I thought it was a trap, that once I was in range of his willy he'd start peeing on me—cuz that's what willies are for when you're a little kid; they're for peeing with. But this boy (I can't even remember his name) promised me he wouldn't do that, so I accepted the challenge and I went up to him and touched his flaccid penis with my hand. That was it. Over in a second. At least, that *would* have been it, except that when I got home, and in all innocence, I mentioned what I'd done to my mum. And then it hit the fan. I think my sister, who was at school with this boy, charged out of the house and went looking for him. I'm not sure what finally came of it all; no-one told me; but I'm pretty sure the police weren't brought into it, maybe not even his school... I remember that the boy gave me a Curly Wurly when my next birthday came around; a sort of apology present.

Still nothing and no-one in sight.

My legs are starting to hurt. I want to stop and rest, but I feel like I have to keep walking, that now is not the time to stop. It's not just rehydration and painkillers I need, it's energy; I haven't had my morning caffeine-fix. I'm running on empty.

And I need to shit. My bowels are telling me this and it's adding to how uncomfortable I feel—but I have a feeling of repulsion at the idea of stopping to perform this simple bodily function; it just disgusts me that I even have to do this, and out in the open with dock leaves for bog roll... Whose stupid idea was it that we have to shit? 7.8 billion people inhabit this terrestrial globe of ours, and every one of them shits; people are shitting all the time, millions and millions of them, every second of every day. If we didn't flush it all out into the oceans, we'd be up to our necks in shit, wading through it all the time...

I feel like I'm wading through shit right now...

A stand of trees up ahead. Might be the windbreak for a farmhouse or something...

The footpath I've been following comes to an end when I come to these trees. I walk through them and I'm in an overground field with a lone building standing in the middle of it. It's not a house; it's a circular building with a conical roof, a grain silo or a dovecote. It looks old and abandoned... And it's familiar; I've seen this place before... I make my brain hurt some more and then it comes to me: It's that dream I'm always having where I'm walking across the countryside... Sometimes in those dreams I pass this place...

And what comes next...? Yes, in the next field I should come to a bridge over a sluice-gate, and after that there's a field with a rusting heap of a car on the edge of it; that's how it goes in the dream...

And that's what happens. In the next field I come to a humpbacked bridge with a sluice-gate. After this, I'm in a stubble field, and there on its margin, the remains of an ancient car, the patches of paintwork still clinging to the body bleached by the sun from red to an unhealthy-looking pink...

How am I even here? I remember these landmarks from a dream, and they say the stuff of dreams comes from memories, but I don't remember ever being here before apart from in my dreams... Am I dreaming now...? I don't think that I'm dreaming, but I know that I've had dreams like this before; dreams in which I was convinced I wasn't dreaming...

No... No, I can't be dreaming. I'm in agony. You don't feel physical pain like this in dreams. Dreams are all emotion, not sensation...

And in my dreams, this path I'm travelling is always on the way to that white building... Is that what I'm going to find now? Is this what's going to happen? Am I really that close to the white building...? If I am then it means I've been walking away from Cambridge instead of towards it, and I've walked a very long way... But then, I don't even know how far from Cambridge I was already when I set off from that barn...

After the field with the car comes a jungle of brushwood. I wade through it and then I'm out in the open again...

There it is. I *am* here... There, way across the fields, very small and far away, that white flat-roofed building.

How many years has it been? How many years since I last saw that place outside of my dreams? I haven't been back to this neck of the woods since I moved to Cambridge, when I was eleven.

Why has it been haunting me? I'm sure I'd completely forgotten about that building until recently, when it started showing up in my dreams. And those dreams became more and more persistent, and now the dreams have become reality because I'm here. I've found my way here when I didn't even mean to... I could say that destiny has brought me here, but dreams don't foretell the future; that's just superstition...

I shamble forward.

I come to the road. This is it; this is the main road running from Sutton to Ely, the road my family and always along on those Saturday shopping trips to Ely, and I'd be sitting the back seat of the car, and I'd see that distant building and wonder about it and think that there was something sinister and mysterious about it...

I look up and down the road. No traffic; not a car in sight.

I cross the road, and I start walking across the fields. My body feels like it's made of lead; the pain in my head's so bad I'm starting to see splinters of light before my eyes... I force myself onwards.

In my dreams I would always wake up around now. I'd be trying to get to the building, but even though I kept on walking towards it, the building wouldn't get any closer... And then I'd wake up...

But this time I'm not dreaming because the building *is* getting closer... Yes, I'm closing in on it. The front of the building becomes clearer: a white-washed wall and a strip of windows across the upper floor; nothing on the ground floor; no doors or windows or anything... The windows are just blank; you can't see anything inside...

I'm staggering now; it's becoming more and more of an effort to put one foot in front of the other, but I keep on going, plodding across the fallow fields. I have to get to this building. Even if I drop down dead the moment I reach it, I have to get there…

In my mind this place is all mixed up with what's been happening—the Disappearers, the removal men, the Sallow Man. This building from the landscape of my childhood has woven itself into the present time… I told Yuri about this place… She told me I should go it… Said I wouldn't stop dreaming about it until I'd gone to it…

Well, I'm doing that and now I'm here. The building stands before me; it's here, it's no longer something only seen from a distance. I look at it and the featureless white surfaces seem to convey a concealed menace, like painted-over warning signs. I stagger up to the nearest wall, and fall against it, pressing my palms to its surface, smooth, dry, and chill to the touch. It has been calling out to me, this building; invading my dreams; its summons has been an imperative one; but now that I'm here, it greets me coldly…

But I'm here; I'm finally here…

I push myself away from the wall, backing away and looking up at that row of windows, the building's sightless eyes. Staring at those panes of glass all I can see are angles of light and shadow… But no, there's something… One of those shapes… I squeeze my eyes shut, open them again… Yes: there… It looks like the silhouette of a man… Half hidden; just one arm and shoulder, the curve of the head… But it's completely still. If it moved, if it disappeared from sight, I'd know for sure… But it's completely motionless… An accident of light shadow…? Or is there someone up there…? Are they looking down at me…?

I stagger round to the side of the building. This wall is a complete void; featureless… The opposite side wall is the same… These are the three walls that are visible from the road; I know what these walls look like… It is only the rear wall of the building that has always been an enigma to me...

I can see now that there's a gravel access road running parallel to the building round the back. I turn the corner. Here, there is a concrete yard, and facing it is the building's entrance—a pair of doors; unglazed, the single feature on this side of the building.

And parked in the yard is a removal van—a beige coloured pantechnicon; just the same as the one I saw outside Martin's apartment building the day this all began...

Somehow, I'm not surprised.

I walk up to the doors, take the handles and open them.

They're waiting for me inside: two of the removal men; silent sentinels in an empty foyer. They pinion my arms and drag me across the room to the stairs. They don't say a word; their faces are like stone. The way they grip my arms it feels like they could snap them with ease if they wanted to.

They march me up the stairs, and at the top of the stairs is a landing and another pair of doors.

I'm escorted through the doors and suddenly it's all brightness and I'm in the room on the other side of those windows. It's a big room; banks of electronic equipment and computer workstations all along the walls; everything bright and antiseptic under the LED strip lights—except for the monstrosity in the middle of the room.

It's a huge round tank, filling the room from the floor to the ceiling. The surface of the ribbed metal, studded with huge rivets, sickly glistens with streaks of grease or slime or something. And, inset into this cylinder, is a riveted steel door with a wheel lock mechanism, painted bright red.

It just looks obscene, standing there, this tank. Grotesquely out of place, like a tumour on a wedding dress.

Standing facing me is the Sallow Man. He's dressed like he's always dressed; black suit, rollneck sweater. He doesn't say anything; he just stands there, legs apart, hands behind his back, and stares at me with those bird of prey eyes; there's intensity in those eyes, but otherwise the face is expressionless.

There are three other people in the room. Two more removal men standing at the instrument banks, holding clipboards; they've stopped whatever they were doing and are looking at me. The fourth person is seated at one of the computer terminals under the windows; a stocky man wearing a white lab coat over a business suit. He swivels round in his chair, turns his head, and his eyes briefly meet mine—then guiltily slide away, the head bowing.

It's Martin.

And then my eyes are back on the Sallow Man because he's putting a respirator over his face. And now Martin is doing the same. The removal men with the clipboards haven't moved at all.

What's going on…?

The Sallow Man nods his head, and the two removal men holding me start to drag me over to that evil-looking tank in the middle of the room. One of the technician removal men steps forward, goes up to the red door and turns the wheel mechanism. There's a loud click and then he pulls open the door.

The stench of decay hits me like a wall; a stench of blood and shit and putrescence. It's like nothing I've ever known. It assails me, making my stomach heave, my eyes water. And then my stomach revolts and I'm spewing up brown liquid vomit; it burns my throat and splatters noisily onto the immaculate tiled floor.

I'm still throwing up when removal men start dragging me towards the open door. They're going to put me in there; in there with whatever's raising that unholy stench. I try to struggle, stop them from pulling me forward—but it's no good; my body's too weak, I'm gagging on my own vomit, and my captor's arms are gripping me like vices. My legs give way and they just drag me bodily the rest of the way. Through the doorway there's a light on the opposite wall; just a feeble orange light protected by a grill. Everything else is blackness. I'm dragged all the way up to this door, and then propelled through it.

And I'm falling into pitch blackness, like I've been tossed into a pit.

I hit water and I go straight under. It's icy cold and it's not water, it's liquid putrescence; it stings my eyes and I have to clamp them shut. And there are things in this cesspool; moving things! They're all around me, throwing themselves against me! What kind of horrific creatures could live in a place like this? I lash out, flailing wildly, expecting teeth to sink into me, tails to sting me, tentacles to grab me... Now I'm grappling with one of them, and it's icy cold and smooth to the touch. I break the surface. I open my eyes and take a gasping breath, but all my lungs take in are noxious fumes. The charnel house stench is all around me now, the stench of rot and decay, blood and liquid excrement.

Now there's light enough for me to see what it is I've been grappling with—a human corpse. Its head lolls, eyes turned up showing only the whites, jaw hanging open. It's pale and it's bloated, but I recognise the face.

Hilary! Jesus Christ, it's Hilary!

I push him away, struggling frantically in the stinking cesspool; they're all around me; floating corpses all around me. Another one seems to throw itself at me.

Esther.

Oh my God! Oh Jesus Christ!

Now I see Muriel. Now Howard.

They're all here! All of them!

And I'm drowning! Drowning in the corpses of all my friends!

Jesus Christ! Jesus fucking Christ!

I can't stay afloat. My strength has completely gone, the foul air is making me nauseous. The orange light is way above me; the rest is darkness; they must have closed the hatch as soon as they'd thrown me in here...

There's no escape... No way out...

Help me! Help me someone!

I scream, and the foul liquid fills my mouth. Choking, gagging, I flail around and now thick tendrils grab hold of me and start to twine themselves around me. What is it? Seaweed? Tentacles? I grab hold of the stuff, and it gets caught up in my hands, clinging like spiderweb, coiling itself around my fingers. It's hair! It's long, human hair! And at the centre of all this hair I see an eye; an epicanthic eye; and a row of teeth, sharp canines…

It's Yuri.

NO! Not her! She wasn't part of this…! They didn't have to take her…!

I can't breathe…

Yuri comes towards me, throwing her cold, leaden arms around me, forcing me under the surface; the liquid putrescence closes over our heads and we're sinking in a final embrace…

Samurai West

disappearer007@gmail.com

Printed in Dunstable, United Kingdom